ChangelingPress.com

Cinder/Cowboy Duet

Harley Wylde

Cinder/Cowboy Duet

Harley Wylde

ISBN: 9798634570631

Publisher:
Changeling Press LLC
315 N. Centre St.
Martinsburg, WV 25404
ChangelingPress.com

Printed in the U.S.A.

Editor: Crystal Esau
Cover Artist: Bryan Keller

The individual stories in this anthology have been previously released in E-Book format.

Table of Contents

Cinder (Devil's Boneyard MC 5)

Harley Wylde

Meg -- For ten years I suffered at the hands of a monster, bought at auction and forced to be a slave, at the whim of a Colombian drug lord who also ran underground fights. Then the Devil's Boneyard came to rescue one of their own and I was free. I don't know who I am anymore, or what my purpose is. I only know one thing. Cinder, the President of Devil's Boneyard, makes me feel safe and that's something I haven't felt in forever. But one kiss and I'm seeing him in a new light, and I know that one kiss will never be enough.

Cinder -- Meg's a sweet girl, a little angel who tends to sing and distract me as she cleans my house. I never said she had to pay for her keep around here, but she insists. She's easily thirty years my junior, which makes me feel like a sick fuck every time I get hard around her, especially after all she's suffered. Then I royally fucked up and kissed her.

Now that I've had a taste, I want more, even though I know we're doomed. A threat to my club, and to Meg, has her under my roof 24/7, and I have no idea how I'll keep myself from giving in to temptation. Whoever leaked her information to The Inferno is going to pay in blood. Even if I haven't claimed her, Meg is mine, and I always protect what's mine.

Chapter One

Cinder

That damn woman was singing again. How the fuck was I supposed to concentrate on club business when she was sashaying all over the damn house belting out whatever song she'd last heard on the radio? All the women from Colombia were re-homed and off living their lives. Then there was Meg. Damn woman refused to leave the compound unless I sent two men with her. She was constantly jumping at shadows, and doing things like organizing my fucking closet by item type and color. Who the fuck did that shit?

When she started the song over, I growled and threw my pen across the room, watching it bounce off the wall and clatter to the floor. No matter how damn annoying I found it, I couldn't very well go down there and growl at her. I'd tried it once and she'd promptly burst into tears before running from my house. Then I'd felt like an asshole for scaring her. I didn't know what to do with her. The men gave her a wide berth most of the time, unless she needed something. They were all there in an instant if they thought Meg was having trouble, or needed protection.

She was always cooking for someone or other, cleaning my fucking house, doing my laundry. Hell, she even bought my groceries. I should be thrilled I didn't have to handle any of that crap anymore, and I might have been, if the woman didn't make me hard all the damn time. Even now, with her singing the same thing over and over, I was hard as a fucking steel post. I was staring sixty in the eye and Meg couldn't be more than twenty-five or twenty-six. Young enough to be my daughter, damn near young enough to be my granddaughter. Made me feel like a sick fuck, even though the age difference didn't seem to bother my VP. He was more than twenty years older than his wife, Clarity, and I'd never seen two people so in love. Except maybe Havoc and that psycho woman of his.

When I'd reached forty and hadn't found a woman, I'd decided that family shit just wasn't for me. I hadn't even touched the club sluts, not in a long-ass time. It had gotten too fucking complicated when I discovered some of them were trying to get pregnant on purpose to trap me and the others in my club. After that, I went on dates here and there with older women in surrounding towns. I hadn't scratched that itch in probably six months, which might explain why Meg was getting a rise out of my dick all the damn time. Or maybe it was just how sweetly she was curved. I had no doubt she'd be a nice handful if I had her in my bed.

My eye twitched when Meg started her damn song yet again. It wasn't that the song was annoying so much as it pissed me off that my dick seemed to like her voice a little too much. I unfastened my pants, knowing there was only one way to fix this shit, at least for an hour or two. I pulled open the desk drawer and grabbed the bottle of lube and dragged the box of tissue closer. After squirting a liberal amount of the liquid on my palm, I wrapped my hand around my shaft and started stroking. My eyes slammed shut as her voice carried through the closed door, and I imagined the sounds she'd make as I pounded into her. It only took a few strokes after that for my cum to cover my hand and hit the desk. I groaned as my dick twitched but didn't completely deflate.

After cleaning myself and the desk up, I tossed the tissues into the trash and shoved my chair back. I rose to my feet, fastened my pants, and decided enough was enough. The way she was affecting me today, I knew I'd be hard again within an hour, and I had too much shit to do to keep jerking off. I went through the house to the kitchen, where she'd dumped the laundry all over the table and seemed to be matching socks. Her hips swayed back and forth as she belted out the lyrics to whatever pop song was stuck in her head this time.

"Is all that fucking racket really necessary?" I asked, my tone a bit harsher than I'd intended.

She gasped, her hand at her throat as she spun to face me. Her wide, frightened eyes made me feel like a complete shit, but I could only handle so much. I needed her gone. Not just from my house, but from the compound. I just hadn't figured out how to make that happen yet. I couldn't exactly toss her out without anywhere to go or a way to take care of herself. I wasn't that big a monster, but she was too fucking tempting.

"I can't work with you singing at the top of your lungs," I said. "I need to get the week's numbers to Shade by end of the day so he can pay everyone, and it requires concentration."

"I'm s-sorry, Cinder. I didn't mean to keep you from working." She glanced at the table full of laundry. "I can come back and finish this later. I was going to make lasagna for dinner with garlic bread, and I can always fold this stuff while it's cooking."

I ran a hand down my face, not sure how to make this clear to her without making her cry. "Meg, I appreciate you helping around here, and that you seem hell-bent on fattening me up, but I'm a grown-ass man and can take care of myself."

"Right," she said softly, her hands wringing in front of her. "I'll just go, then. Sorry about the mess."

She couldn't quite hide the flash of pain in her eyes before she hurried out of the kitchen. A moment later, I heard the front door shut. I stared at the pile of laundry and wondered how asking for some quiet in my own fucking house could make me feel like such a bad man. It wasn't like she was my fucking wife. I'd given her a place to stay, but it seemed she was always under my damn feet.

I went over to the table and swept the laundry back into the basket, then carried it to my room and dropped it on the bed. I'd fold the shit later and put it away. I couldn't help but notice she'd made the damn bed already, with military precision at that. She'd been a quick study of how I liked to keep things, and made sure everything was perfect. Too perfect, if my closet was anything to go by. I had to wonder if she wasn't a bit OCD.

Now that there was peace in the house, I could focus on the fucking reports and make sure my men were all paid. We'd sold a truck full of guns and ammo to some ex-military men I knew who had become vigilantes. Since they didn't harm innocents, I didn't mind doing business with them. Even the drugs we sold never made it into the hands of kids. I made damn sure of that. Anyone who bought from us knew better than to pull that shit, or they'd end up with a bullet between their eyes. These days we only dealt in pot, but I didn't want to hear about some fifteen-year-old getting high off the stuff we grew and killing themselves or someone else.

I'd scaled back quite a bit on our illegal dealings, for the most part. We still had the chop shop and had opened a second one outside of town. The marijuana pulled in a small profit, and the guns were a nice bonus. When Scratch had discovered his daughter was alive, and he was going to be a grandpa, I'd pulled back from the heavier stuff. Didn't want any of that blowing back on my VP's family. Shade had said he could invest some of the club funds and double our profits, so I'd given him a few hundred grand to play with. Now he was investing over half a million on a monthly basis thanks to the nest egg those initial profits had brought in.

We'd never be completely legit, and I was fine with that, but I also didn't want the law breathing down our necks and chance any of the men with families getting locked up. It was my job to protect everyone in the Devil's Boneyard, down to the smallest kid. If that meant fewer illegal dealings, then so be it. I still took the odd job from the government as well, but the older I got, the less they called on me. Couldn't blame them. I was still sharp, still had perfect vision, but I was getting old compared to the eighteen-year-olds they were recruiting.

I'd just finished the week's numbers and stuffed everything in a folder for Shade when my doorbell rang. I rubbed my eyes and hoped like hell Meg wasn't on my doorstep. I needed to get laid, and soon, if I was going to keep having her underfoot. I shoved my chair back and went to see who the fuck was bothering me. When I jerked open the door I saw Jordan with her two-year-old daughter, Lanie.

"Jordan, everything okay?" I asked.

She glared at me, her lips a thin line of displeasure and her eyes snapping with fire. I didn't know who had pissed her off, but I had a feeling my afternoon just became incredibly busy. She was perfect for Havoc, but a general pain in my ass.

"Meg is crying and packing her shit," Jordan said.

My heart stuttered in my chest. "What do you mean she's packing? To go where?"

"She doesn't know and apparently doesn't care. You. Made. Her. Cry."

Fuck. I hadn't meant to drive Meg away completely, just out of my fucking house. Life was so much easier when I only had to deal with club sluts at the clubhouse. Adding women to the family just complicated shit and added drama I didn't need.

"I never told her she had to leave the compound," I said.

"No, just your damn house." I heard Jordan's jaw crack she was so damn angry. "If you don't fix this shit, I'm going to leave Lanie with you. For an entire week."

The demon spawn in her arms gave me a grin that I wasn't about to admit scared the shit out of me. I didn't do kids, especially not *this* kid. Loved Havoc, and Jordan for the most part, but their kid was damn frightening. Anyone else who spoke to me like this would have met my fist, but Jordan was a woman and I wouldn't lay a hand on her. Not to mention, if I upset her, then she'd make it hell on Havoc, and the last thing I needed was my Sergeant at Arms being pissed at the world because his wife was being a bitch, even though that seemed to be Jordan's default setting.

"I'll go talk to Meg," I said.

My phone started ringing in my pocket and I pulled it out, noting CJ's name on the screen. Jordan's brother was a pain just like his damn sister, and I had serious doubts he'd ever be allowed to patch in, even if he hadn't been fucking up as much lately.

"What?" I demanded as I answered.

"Uh, Pres, Meg is at the gate wanting to leave. Alone. With a bag in her hand. On foot."

I closed my eyes and counted to twenty. "Keep her there. Don't open that fucking gate for anything."

I slammed my door and pulled my keys from my pocket, then stared at my bike. I wasn't sure I could get Meg to climb onto the back of it, and I couldn't trust her to walk her butt back to her place. I grumbled as I started walking down the road that led past the clubhouse and to the front gate. Meg was standing there, pale and shaking, as she pleaded with CJ.

"You have to let me out," she said. "I need to leave."

"No can do, Meg. Cinder's orders," CJ said.

"I don't stay where I'm not wanted," she said quietly, but I fucking heard her.

"Goddammit, woman. I never said you had to leave the compound, just my fucking house," I said as I got closer.

She flinched at my tone and wouldn't turn to face me.

"Meg, look at me."

I saw her form tremble and I cursed under my breath before I moved in closer and set my hands on her shoulders. I turned her around, then tipped her chin up. Tears streaked her cheeks, and I felt like the biggest asshole on the planet to make this sweet girl cry. I wiped the moisture off her cheeks, then took her bag from her.

"Come on. I think we need to have a talk," I said, leading her back toward my house.

She didn't utter a word of protest and followed meekly along. There were times I wished that she'd yell back at me, tell me to fuck off, or just take up for herself in some small way, but I worried her time in Colombia had broken her. She'd been there the longest of the women we'd brought home, and had suffered the most abuse. I'd offered to send her home to her family, but she'd refused, saying it was better if they believed she were dead. I hadn't understood, and still didn't, but I wouldn't force her to go home to her parents.

I opened my front door and dragged her into the house behind me. The door slammed shut and I twisted the lock, not wanting any interruptions during this particular conversation. It seemed to be long overdue. I led her into the living room, then pointed to the couch.

"Sit."

She slowly sank onto the cushion and placed her hands in her lap, but I noticed they shook. In fact, she looked even paler than she had before. Her dark, glossy hair fell so that it hid her face as she dipped her chin. We'd never discussed her life prior to Colombia, but I was willing to bet she had a bit of Asian in her, possibly a few different races. Her eyes were a soft gray and a pretty almond shape. Her long dark hair always made me want to reach out and touch it, and her soft skin usually held a tanned glow. At the moment, she didn't have a drop of color in her cheeks.

"Meg, when I said I wanted you to leave earlier, I only meant my house. I appreciate everything you've done here, but I need..." I needed some peace and quiet, and alone time, but I didn't want to hurt her again.

"I'm in the way," she said. "It's okay. I get it. A man like you needs some space. I didn't realize... if I'd known the reason you weren't bringing women around was because of me, I'd have left you alone. I didn't think about them feeling awkward with me around."

I blinked and stared. Where the fuck had she come up with that? I couldn't remember a time I'd ever brought up women, especially around her. I didn't even discuss my few encounters with the men in my club, not even with Scratch.

"Meg, what the hell are you talking about?"

Her cheeks flushed. "I noticed that you were..." She gestured at my pants and I winced as I realized I hadn't been able to hide my reaction to her as well as I'd thought.

"Darlin', I don't bring women here. Ever. It was sweet of you to cook for me, to do my laundry and keep the house clean, but you don't have to do all that stuff. You have your own home here, and I'm not making you work for your keep."

"I like feeling useful," she said. "You haven't made me sleep with any of your men, and it seemed the least I could do."

Jesus fucking Christ. She was killing me. I knelt in front of her and reached for her hands, which were now knotted in her lap. She trembled as I wrapped my hand around both of hers. She was so fucking small compared to me. One hard squeeze, and I'd probably break her hands.

"Meg, I would never force you to be with anyone. You know that, right? You're free, darlin'. You don't have to stay at the compound. You can go out and find a job in town, or move anywhere you want.

I'd make sure you had some money to get you started, just like I did with the others."

"I want to stay," she said. "I feel safe here. You make me feel safe."

When her gaze found mine, the breath in my lungs froze for a moment. The vulnerability in her eyes was nearly my undoing. She was such a sweetheart, and I wished she'd find a way to be happy. I'd give her whatever she needed to make that happen, but she never asked for anything. I'd had to get Clarity to take her shopping because the woman refused to buy more than two outfits and one pair of shoes.

"Meg, I've never pried into your past, and I don't want to do that now, but exactly how long were you in Colombia with that man?" I asked. "You aren't moving on like the others did, and I'm concerned."

She looked away, but not before I saw the shame in her eyes.

"I was fifteen when I was stolen off the streets and sold. They drugged me, made me dance naked as men bid on me. Silva bought me and forced me to be a whore for the fighters he kept."

"You were there for ten years?" I asked.

She nodded.

My gut clenched when I thought about a frightened fifteen-year-old girl going through that. Losing her home, her family, and likely her virginity. She'd have been scared even before she was brutalized by who knew how many men. I could understand a bit better why she flinched when the men got too close or someone spoke too loudly. The fact she was letting me touch her right now was a damn miracle.

"I'm sorry, sweetheart. You should have never had to suffer like that. No woman deserves that, but especially not a kid."

If she wanted to stay at the compound forever, I wouldn't utter a word of complaint. I was glad that she felt safe here, or as safe as she seemed capable of feeling after those years in Colombia. If she'd been fifteen and stayed with Silva for ten years, then I was pretty accurate on guessing her age. Which still made her way too damn young for me to get hard every time I was near her, or heard her fucking singing some stupid-ass bubble gum song off the radio.

"I liked helping take care of your house and making meals for you," she said. "It was my way of giving back to you, to say thank you for saving me. You didn't have to bring me here, or give me a place to stay. Your club could have left all of us in Colombia, or brought us back to the US, then left us to fend for ourselves. But you didn't."

"I didn't mean to make you cry," I said. "It wasn't my intention to hurt you. I never want to be the cause of your pain, Meg. You're a sweet girl and you deserve the world, not some grouchy old cuss like me hurting your feelings."

"You're not old, and I know you didn't mean to make me cry," she nearly whispered. "Jordan says I need to be stronger, more confident. I'm more outgoing at their house because..."

She stopped and seemed anxious, her leg bouncing a bit as she looked away.

"Because Havoc is clearly taken and Jordan would geld him if he ever strayed," I said. "When you're there, you have no fear that you'll end up on your back."

She nodded.

"None of my men would force themselves on you, Meg. And neither would I. Even if I get hard when you're in the room, it doesn't mean I'm going to act on it. We don't force women in this club, and neither do the men we associate with."

Her eyes widened and her lips parted. "I did that? I'd thought maybe you were thinking of a woman you were seeing."

I chuckled a little and rubbed my free hand across the back of my neck. "No, I'm not seeing anyone. I've gone on some dates here and there, and there are some older women in the area that I've slept with on occasion. At my age, sex isn't as important as it once was."

She bit her lip and looked around the room a moment before locking her gaze with mine again. "I'd like to stay, if that's all right."

"You can stay at the Devil's Boneyard as long as you want. And if you really insist on keeping my house clean, then I won't throw you out of here, but I need you to keep the singing to a minimum, or at least at a lower volume." Or learn some different fucking songs. Ones that didn't make me want to stick a knife in my ear, or pull my dick out in the middle of my office.

I got a hesitant smile from her that warmed my heart.

"I can do that," she said.

"Why don't you take your bag back to your place? Take the day to do whatever you want."

"I'd prefer to stay busy today," she said.

It was the way she said it that intrigued me. What was it about today that was so different from the others? It wasn't a holiday.

"Meg, what's today?" I asked.

"My birthday," she said. "When Silva found out when my birthday was, he decided I would have a party every year. Except I was the entertainment."

I growled and wished that Silva were still alive so I could rip the asshole apart with my bare hands. The way he'd made this sweet girl suffer was beyond monstrous. I stood abruptly, then pulled Meg to her feet. She swayed a moment and I placed my hand at her waist to steady her. I felt her indrawn breath and watched a bit of color rise to her cheeks. Interesting. She didn't flinch, or look scared. The look in her eyes said that she was intrigued, and that was a very, very bad thing.

"Take your things home, Meg. Take a nice hot shower or bath, then put on something pretty. Be at the clubhouse in two hours, and not a moment sooner. And don't come back here before then either. Understand?" I asked.

"Yes, Cinder."

"Good girl. Now, go."

She picked up her bag and scurried out of the living room and out of house. The second I knew she wasn't coming back, I pulled my phone from my pocket and called my VP's wife. We had a party to plan and precious little time to do it.

"Clarity, I need your help," I said when she answered.

"Whatever it is, you know you can count on me," she said.

"I need a birthday party put together in less than two hours at the clubhouse."

"Birthday party?' she asked.

"It's Meg. She hasn't had a good experience on her birthday since that asshole Silva bought her. She was just a kid, Clarity. Just a scared little kid and he made her suffer horribly. We need to help her make new, happy memories to associate with her birthday. Pull out all the stops, but do it fast."

"I'm on it," she said, then disconnected the call.

I stared at my phone and tried not to think too hard on why I'd just done that. By all rights, I should pass Meg off to someone else, let them worry about whether or not she was happy, but for some reason I wanted to be the reason she smiled today.

Fuck me. I was so screwed.

Havoc, and Irish had each claimed a woman so far, and each had at least one kid. Then there was Jackal and Josie, and Scratch and Clarity. It was my hope, that one day we'd be like the Dixie Reapers and have a lot of families inside the gates. Right now, only Havoc and Irish lived at the compound with their families, and that was fine, but it was time for things to change.

We no longer had an ax hanging over our heads, unless you counted The Inferno. I still wasn't entirely sure what those dickheads were up to, or how to stop them, but I knew we weren't going up against them alone. We'd handled the idiots who had attacked Janessa, but I didn't kid myself. The Inferno would likely send more, and when they did, we'd send them packing. No way I was letting those assholes get a foothold in my territory, and I knew Torch felt the same, and so did Grizzly and Spider. I hadn't dealt much with Reckless Kings, but they weren't the type to roll over and let someone walk all over them.

But that was an issue for another day. Right now, I had to make sure that sweet girl who'd just left my house had a reason to smile on her birthday from this day forward. Whatever it took, I'd erase at least some of those bad memories.

Chapter Two

Meg

I didn't understand why I had to dress up, or what was happening at the clubhouse, but Cinder seemed to think it was important that I be there. I usually didn't bother with worrying over my appearance, but I'd taken extra care this time. After my shower, I'd blown my hair dry, then used the curling iron Janessa had given me a month ago. She'd tried to tell me it was something she just didn't use, but I'd noticed the box was still sealed. All of the Devil's Boneyard ladies had done something nice like that for me.

I didn't own makeup and had never worn any. I had a tinted lip balm and used that, but I'd never felt the need for all that other stuff. I didn't dislike makeup, but I didn't see the point. Women who wore makeup wanted to feel beautiful, and all I wanted to do was hide. The last thing I wanted to do was attract a man's attention.

The dress I'd put on hugged my curves a bit and flared out from my hips, falling softly around my knees. It was modest with a scooped neckline that didn't show even a hint of cleavage, and yet I felt practically naked. Since coming back to America, I'd been wearing jeans and T-shirts or sweaters, depending on the weather. Having my legs on display felt strange. At least the shoes didn't have much of a heel and were comfortable.

As I made my way to the front of the compound, I heard raised voices and my steps faltered a moment.

Angry men still frightened me, and I often flinched if someone moved too quickly. When I recognized Cinder's voice, I picked up my pace, and came in view of the gate just in time to see a big brute of a man take a swing at Cinder. I gasped and rushed forward, not even stopping to think. The man drew his fist back again and I lunged in front of Cinder. The blow was a direct hit to my stomach and knocked the wind out of me. I felt my eyes tear as I gasped and tried to suck down air, only panicking when I couldn't breathe at all.

"Jesus!" Cinder wrapped his arms around me and sank to the ground, cradling me close. "Calm down, Meg. Try to take slow, shallow breaths. Come on, sweetheart. Breathe for me. You're turning blue."

"I-I didn't mean to hit her," the huge man stammered. Before he could escape, Killian grabbed him by the back of his shirt and pushed him to the ground.

I focused my gaze on Cinder and listened to his calm voice and reassuring words. Slowly, I took another breath and found that I was able to suck in a little oxygen. After a moment, I was breathing, shallow choppy breaths, but it was better than nothing.

"You scared the shit out of me," Cinder said. "Don't ever get in the middle of a fight again. You hear me?"

I nodded, unsure I would be able to speak just yet.

"I swear I wouldn't have hurt her!" the other man was screaming. "It was an accident!"

"Wh-what…" I gasped again, not quite breathing regularly and couldn't form all the words I wanted to say.

"I slept with his wife, except I didn't realize she was married," Cinder said. "And like I told him, it was a one-night stand half a year ago. She wasn't wearing a ring and never mentioned having a husband or fiancé."

I reached up and ran my fingers over his beard. Cinder looked slightly amused, and my cheeks warmed, realizing what I'd just done. I struggled to sit up, but he held me tight.

"What do you want me to do this guy, Pres?" Killian asked.

"Let him go. He says he wouldn't have hit Meg and I believe him. She stepped in the way and it was just an accident. But his ass better never come here again. Next time, I might put a bullet in him," Cinder said. "I only allowed him inside so he could get justice for what he felt was a slight to both himself and his woman."

Killian nodded, then shoved the other man outside of the gate before closing it. The Prospect stood with his arms folded and stared the guy down, making sure he left. My gaze turned back to Cinder and I realized I was breathing easier now. He stood, pulling me up with him, and I only wobbled a moment before I could stay upright on my own.

"Why did you get in the way?" Cinder asked.

"I didn't want him to hurt you," I said, realizing it was the truth. At first, I'd just reacted, but now that I'd had time to process what happened, I knew that I'd seen Cinder in trouble and wanted to help in some way. He'd been so good to me, all of them had, and instinct had said I should protect him the way he protected me.

Cinder rolled his eyes skyward and shook his head, muttering about damn fool women. I glanced at

Killian to find him grinning like an idiot, and I didn't know what to make of the situation. Was Cinder mad at me? And what did Killian find so amusing?

"You look nice, Meg," Killian said.

"Thank you." I wrapped my arms around my waist, suddenly feeling self-conscious of what I was wearing. My stomach still hurt from the punch and I wondered if I'd have a bruise. The area was tender, but not too bad just yet. Experience told me the pain would be much worse tomorrow.

Cinder moved in closer and tipped my chin up. "Thank you for worrying about me, but I can handle a guy like that. I let him get a hit in because I'd slept with his wife, even if I hadn't realized it at the time. It was still wrong. What I don't want is for you to put yourself in danger."

"I didn't stop to think," I admitted. "I just saw him hurting you and reacted."

Killian snickered, then coughed to cover it up when Cinder glared at him.

"Sorry, Pres. Just find it cute that itty-bitty Meg wanted to protect you. At least you know she's loyal." Killian grinned.

I swallowed the knot in my throat, feeling incredibly stupid and silly. Of course, a man like Cinder didn't need me to protect him. I should have stayed out of the way, gone to the clubhouse like he'd told me to do. What if his club thought he was weak because of what I'd done? I'd never forgive myself.

Cinder pulled me against his chest and hugged me, his hand tangling in my hair.

"It was sweet of her," Cinder said, "even if it was foolish. She could have been seriously hurt. Promise me, Meg. Promise you won't do something like that again."

"I can't," I said. I wanted to promise the way he wanted me to, but I couldn't. If I saw someone trying to hurt him, I'd probably react again. It had been a compulsion I hadn't been able to stop. "I'm sorry."

"Don't be sorry, sweet girl," he said. "I'm flattered you wanted to help an old goat like me, but I don't want anything to happen to you."

"Are we having this party or what?" Jordan yelled from the steps of the clubhouse.

Cinder narrowed his gaze in her direction before herding me toward the clubhouse. I didn't know what party she meant, and I'd avoided most of the gatherings so far. For whatever reason, Cinder had wanted me here for this one. When we stepped inside the dimly lit clubhouse, I gasped at the balloons, streamers, and stacks of pizza boxes. There was also a large cake on a table at the back with a stack of wrapped presents.

"What's going on?" I asked, turning my gaze up at Cinder.

"It's your birthday and you deserve to have a happy memory to associate with today. I know it won't undo everything you've suffered, but it's a step in the right direction," he said. "Happy birthday, Meg."

Tears blurred my vision before I blinked them back. Jordan, Janessa, Clarity, and Josie all came toward me, and led me over to a table with flowers in the center. They pushed me down onto a chair and then handed me a plate filled with pizza and set a cold can of soda on the table. Cinder took the chair next to mine and I couldn't help but stare at him. He'd always been on the gruff side, and I'd seen how tough he was on his men, but this was the sweetest thing anyone had ever done for me.

"Thank you," I said.

"Who knew the Pres had a soft side?" Jordan joked, then winked at Cinder.

He flipped her off, which just made her cackle before she went off to join her husband and daughter. I knew that plenty of people feared Cinder. I'd witnessed it firsthand on the one and only occasion he'd gone into town with me, but the women who called the Devil's Boneyard home didn't seem all that scared of him. Maybe Jordan was right and he did have a soft side, even if he didn't show it often.

I nibbled on my pizza and tried to follow the flow of conversation around me. Each of the men from the club came by to wish me happy birthday, and Janessa insisted on taking pictures. There was a glint in her eyes and a mischievous smile on her lips as she nodded at Cinder.

"Come on, Pres. You set this up. I think you need a picture with the birthday girl," she said.

Cinder pushed his chair back a little and I stood to scoot mine closer, except being my usual graceful self, I tripped on the chair leg and fell onto his lap. He caught me easily and I saw the bright camera flash out of the corner of my eye. When I turned to look at Janessa, she was grinning.

"Both of you smile," she said, then took another one.

I was going to get up and move back to my chair, when Irish shoved a present into my hands.

"It's from us," he said.

Cinder placed his hand on my hip and adjusted so that I was more comfortable, and he tapped the present, clearly waiting on me to open it. I took my time, not having received a gift since before I was abducted, and pulled the paper off to reveal a small box with the picture of a camera on the top.

"It's nothing fancy," Irish said. "But it's digital so you don't have to worry about film. We thought you might like to take some pictures as you make new memories."

"Thank you," I said softly, running my fingers over the box. It was a really thoughtful gift, and one I would cherish. The cost didn't matter to me, it was the sentiment behind it. I was truly touched by their present.

Another box was set on the table in front of me and I picked it up. It was from Havoc and Jordan. This time, I opened the package a little faster, but I was still careful not to just rip the paper off in seconds. There was a stack of picture frames inside, each one different. Metal frames, wooden ones, even a frame that looked like mosaic tile.

Each club member handed me a gift until I had a mountain of them. Clarity had started stacking them on a nearby table after the fourth package. I'd gotten a little of everything. A manicure set with four different nail polish colors, quite a few gift cards to my favorite stores in the nearest mall, no fewer than three gift bags of paperback books and bookmarks, even a small bookshelf so I could keep them nice. Clarity and Scratch gave me one of the outfits I'd tried on and put back during my last shopping trip, simply because I'd thought it cost too much. Jackal and Josie gave me some scrapbooks and supplies, which I assumed was to be paired with the camera. The last three boxes ranged from the biggest I'd seen today to the tiniest. Clarity brought them over and set them down on the table.

"These are from me," Cinder said. He picked up the smallest and set it aside, then handed the middle one to me.

I opened it and discovered it was a photo printer, but I wasn't sure if I could just plug the camera straight into it, or how it would work since I didn't have a computer. I gave him a cautious smile, but before I could thank him, he lifted the biggest box, which I discovered was quite heavy as he set it across my lap. I couldn't contain my gasp as I opened the paper and saw it was a laptop.

"Cinder, I can't accept this. It's too much," I protested.

"You'll need it to go with the printer. And if you don't use it and the printer, then how will you use half of your other gifts?" he asked. "Don't worry about the cost, sweetheart. It's the first birthday you've celebrated in a long while. We wanted to make it special."

I looked at him. "You planned this."

"Not exactly. Irish told me what Janessa was picking up, and I decided to get you something to go with it. You can also access the wi-fi on the laptop. If you ever decide to look for your family, I wanted to make sure you had a way to do it without having to ask for help," he said. "But just so you know, Shade would gladly do some digging if you ever asked."

Cinder picked up the smallest and last box. He rolled it between his fingers before handing it to me. Clarity removed the laptop from my lap and shifted it over to the table of opened gifts. I stared at the tiny box and realized it looked like something jewelry would come in, but I dismissed the thought as ridiculous. It was probably just some small thing that went with the laptop or camera.

I opened the paper and stared down at the box that most definitely contained jewelry. My hands trembled a little as I opened the lid, and I gasped as I stared at the beautiful necklace inside. A hummingbird hung from a delicate gold chain. The body was an emerald and the wings were made of amethyst.

"It's beautiful," I said.

"You deserve something pretty and shiny," he said. "The hummingbird reminded me of you. Delicate but determined to survive."

My eyes teared up again as I looked at him. "Cinder, I… thank you. It's the best gift I've ever received."

He took the box from my hands and removed the necklace, then fastened it around my neck. On impulse, I moved in closer, my breasts pressed against his chest, and brushed my lips against his cheek. My heart felt like it was beating out of control, and I'd have sworn the room was spinning. Our gazes met and held. The noise of the party faded and it felt like it was just us in the room. He reached up and caressed my cheek and I leaned into his touch. This was the closest I'd been to a man since being rescued, and it felt incredibly right. I'd thought being touched like this would freak me out, but I found that I never wanted this moment to end.

"Happy birthday, Meg," he said, his voice deep and gruff.

"It's the best birthday ever," I said softly.

"Cake!" Jordan yelled.

I jolted and looked around, noticing that most of the club was trying not to look our way, but a few were smirking in our direction. I felt my cheeks warm and I wondered if I should get up. Cinder seemed to make the decision for me when he tightened his hold and shifted us a little so that I could blow out the candles on the cake when Havoc carried it over.

"We didn't know what kind you'd like so we just got a plain white cake with whipped frosting," Josie said.

It said *Happy Birthday Meg* in purple frosting, and there were confetti sprinkles on the corners. Janessa took a picture of the cake with the candles blazing, one of me blowing them out, and another as Clarity was slicing and distributing the birthday cake. I got the first piece, one that was much too big. Cinder waved off the piece offered to him, but I couldn't let him go without at least a little taste.

I cut off a bite and offered it to him. He watched me intently a moment before accepting the cake. I gave him a slight smile before cutting off a bite for myself. I offered him a few more, and it had to be the sweetest moment I'd ever shared with someone. I'd thought I would hate my birthday for the rest of my life, but I knew this day would be one of the best memories I ever had. I saw a flash go off when I fed Cinder another bite and glanced at Janessa right as she winked and moved off to take pictures of everyone else.

The party seemed to go on for hours, but people started heading off to do their own thing. Eventually, it was just me and Cinder with empty pizza boxes, birthday cake crumbs, and my stack of presents. I'd let the kids take the balloons with them, loving the joy on their faces over something so simple.

"I'll have Killian or Dixon deliver your presents to your place. They can load them into one of the SUVs and drive them over," Cinder said.

I swallowed hard and looked down at my lap. I knew the day would come to an end, that we'd part ways, but I wasn't ready. I didn't want to be alone today, not even for a second, but I also wasn't brave enough to ask to stay with him longer. Was I?

"Do you have plans tonight?" I asked.

"What did you have in mind?" he asked, drawing my gaze back to his.

"Could we watch a movie together? Or maybe play a game or something?"

He rubbed my hip and warmth spread through my body as tingles raced down my spine. I felt my nipples harden and I hoped he didn't notice. I didn't understand why my body was reacting the way it was. I'd never desired anyone, not really. I'd had a crush on a boy in high school, but that seemed like forever ago, and it hardly compared to how I felt right now.

"Scared to be alone?" he asked.

"Something like that. My place is too quiet and I don't want to ruin today with bad memories."

He studied me and I tried not to squirm. After a moment, he came to a decision, but it wasn't what I'd expected. I'd thought he'd offer to watch one movie, then send me on my way.

"Why don't you stay tonight at my place?" he asked. "You can have your own room, so don't feel like I'm trying to take advantage of you. I won't even touch your hand unless you say it's okay."

Stay with Cinder? Overnight? My heart started racing again. I didn't know what it was about him that made me feel so safe. He'd been there the day I was saved, even though he hadn't seemed all that thrilled with bringing me and the others home when they'd left Colombia. I knew Jordan had instigated it, and I would be forever grateful. As the other women had moved on, I'd worried that the day would come when Cinder would tell me it was time to leave.

I'd thought at first that it was the compound that made me feel secure, the gates and fence that would keep bad men away. Then I'd started cleaning Cinder's house, doing his laundry, making meals for him… and I'd quickly realized that it was him who made me feel safe. Even though he grumbled a lot, barked orders at people, and didn't seem to care for my singing, I'd known that with him around, no one was going to hurt me ever again. Despite what some of the people in town said, I knew he was honorable. I'd caught him without his shirt one day and I'd noticed the tattoo on his bicep, one I'd seen before. I didn't know when or how he'd served, but Cinder had been a Marine. Or as my friend's dad had once told me, once a Marine, always a Marine.

If I couldn't trust a Devil Dog, then who could I trust? Just because he might not walk on the right side of the law these days didn't mean it had always been that way. I was sure he had a reason for doing things the way he did. Maybe seeing war had soured him on life at some point. I might never know, but what I knew without a doubt was that the man currently holding me as if I were fine china would never hurt me. Not intentionally.

"If you're sure I won't be imposing, then I'd love to stay with you tonight," I said.

"Wouldn't have offered if you'd be in the way," he said. "Your place unlocked?"

I nodded. I'd been assured that I didn't have to worry while I was here, that I would always be kept safe. Even when those men had taken Janessa, I'd still not been afraid as long as I remained behind the gate. I was protected here, and I wasn't ready to leave anytime soon.

"I'll ask someone to drop your presents off and leave them inside your door," he said.

I got off his lap and waited while he made arrangements for my presents, then I walked alongside him as we went to his place. Cinder's house felt more like a home to me than mine did. Maybe because I hadn't really made the place mine. Even though his space was bare as far as pictures or knickknacks, it still seemed cozy and comfortable. I liked that it was all one floor and not a two-story like some of the other houses at the compound.

What I liked most about the place was that it belonged to Cinder, the one man I trusted with my very life. I didn't know what to expect of tonight, but I knew that being here with him, being close to him, felt right on so many levels. I also knew that he wasn't the type to settle down. If he hadn't been married yet, then it was doubtful he ever would, especially not with someone like me. Even if we only had this one night, I would cherish the memories always.

Chapter Three

Cinder

I was going to hell, assuming this wasn't it already. Having Meg in my lap earlier had felt a little too damn good, and now she was cuddled against my side like she belonged there. The scent of her, the feel of her soft skin and hair, was driving me crazy. I was a grown-ass man and knew how to keep myself in check, but fuck if I hadn't been hard since she'd tumbled onto my lap at the clubhouse. Being the idiot I am, I'd kept her there. I'd caught the looks from the others, but they were wrong. Just because I had a soft spot for Meg didn't mean that I was going to marry her and settle down.

I just needed to get laid. Trouble was that I didn't find anyone appealing these days. I'd had offers, and turned them all down after that last one-night stand roughly six months ago, and that sin had come knocking on my door today by way of an angry husband. Just proved that you couldn't trust a woman, or at least the ones I seemed to attract. When I'd been younger, I'd been chased by women who wanted a ring on their finger and a military man on their arm. I hadn't fallen into their traps, and I didn't plan on landing in any now.

Meg laughed at something happening on TV but I hadn't even been paying attention. She'd asked to watch a comedy, something lighthearted. It hadn't mattered to me what was on as long as she was happy. That was another thing that bothered me. I didn't give a shit if a woman was happy, not usually. I wanted my men's wives and old ladies to be happy because they were family, but Meg was just a stray who wouldn't go away. She'd had nowhere to go when Jordan had said the women were coming with us, and even though the others were long gone, she remained.

I didn't like the way my body responded to her, didn't like the way she was on my mind more often than she should be, or that I gave a shit at all what happened to her. Instead, I found my heart aching for all she'd suffered and wanting to see her smile. I hadn't even hesitated to set up a party for her when she'd told me about the last ten years of birthdays, knowing that I needed to give her some good memories. It hadn't escaped my attention that Irish and Janessa were matchmaking. I'd have to speak with them later and tell them to back the hell off. I didn't want Meg getting the wrong idea. I already cared too damn much about the woman as it was, but there wasn't a future for us.

My VP was nearly as damn old I was, but he had kids, and there were plenty of youngsters in the club for someone to take over when I decided to step down. Not that I planned to do that anytime soon. I might be nearing sixty, but I had a lot of life left in me. This club was all that mattered to me, and even when I took a step back, I'd still be a part of it. And like it or not, Meg was quickly becoming part of the Devil's Boneyard, which meant she mattered to me. That's all it was, her tie to the club.

I nearly snorted, not even believing it when I said the words to myself. No, whether I liked it or not, Meg mattered to me not because of the club but because of who she was. I'd never met a sweeter woman, except possibly Clarity. Even Clarity had more fire in her than Meg did, but Meg had shown me a side I'd never seen before tonight. She was also a protector. I hadn't needed her help, and it pissed me off that she'd gotten in the way of that hothead, but it also made me feel all warm and funny that she'd cared enough to try to help me.

She kept fidgeting with the hem of her dress and I wondered if she was uncomfortable. I hadn't exactly given her a chance to go back to her place for a change of clothes. I patted her as I stood up, and she blinked up at me, looking insecure and uncertain for a moment. I wanted to kick the shit out of every man responsible for that look. She was like an abused puppy, waiting to see if her new master was going to hurt her too. Oh hell. I closed my eyes and nearly groaned at that thought. Meg on her knees, hands in her lap, and staring up at me with those wide eyes, waiting on her next order.

Fucking. Hell. Yeah, good ol' Lucifer was definitely holding a place for me, likely at his right-hand side. Move over, princes of hell, because I was going to give them a run for their money at this rate.

"Something wrong?" she asked. "Should I go home?"

"You're fine staying here, but you're uncomfortable. None of my pants will fit you, but I have a shirt that will be long enough to cover everything important. The material should be more comfortable than what you have on right now."

She slowly stood and smoothed her dress down, the dress that was giving me impure thoughts no matter how demure it might be. I'd never seen her in one before, and now that I'd gotten a good look at those tempting legs, I was having a hard time not picturing them around my waist. Hell, maybe I wasn't going to be sitting at Lucifer's side. Maybe I was going to dethrone him and just take over.

"Y-you want to lend me a shirt?" she asked. "One of yours?"

I nodded and waited to see what she'd make of that. I had no idea what went through her mind most days. She'd either take it as a genuine offer for her comfort, or see the depraved thoughts going through my mind and run like hell. I wouldn't blame her for taking option two.

"I'd like that," she said.

She followed me to the back of the house, and we stepped into my bedroom. She'd been in here before, but never with me. I went over to the dresser and pulled open the second drawer, then picked a shirt I knew was soft and on the long side. I handed it to her, then started past her, giving her privacy to change, but she placed a hand on my arm and stopped me.

"Thank you," she said. "For everything. The party was wonderful, and I've enjoyed spending time here with you tonight. I know I'm a needy mess and you're probably looking forward to the day I leave, but I appreciate everything you've done for me."

"Not kicking you out," I said, my voice gruff as I fought down my emotions.

"That's because you're a good man. And don't try to shrug me off and say you aren't because I know different. I've seen evil, Cinder, looked it in the face every day for a decade. Just because you may not do things in a one hundred percent legal way doesn't make you a bad man."

"Don't make me into some sort of saint, Meg. I'm not. I'm just a man with faults and desires like everyone else."

She nodded and let me go, taking a step back and clutching the shirt to her chest. I turned to go and pulled the bedroom door behind me. At the last second, I looked over my shoulder and couldn't contain the growl that rose in my throat. She'd already pulled off her dress and had a large bruise on her abdomen from the jackass who had hit her earlier. Not caring if I scared her, I slammed the door back open and stormed inside. Her eyes went wide and she whimpered as I got closer.

"When were you going to tell me?" I asked.

She stared, her heart beating so hard I could see it thumping inside her chest and in the pulse point in her neck.

"The bruise, Meg," I said, waving at her stomach. "When were you going to tell me you were in pain?"

She glanced down as if just realizing it was there. "It's not the first one I've received. It will hurt for a while, and then it will fade."

I pinched the bridge of my nose and closed my eyes to contain my anger so I wouldn't lash out at her. After counting to twenty, then doing it again backward, I opened my eyes and looked down at her. She didn't seem all that bothered by the fact she was nearly naked in front of me, and I wasn't sure if I liked the fact she trusted me that much, or felt insulted that she didn't think I'd ever make a move on her. She was right, though. I wasn't. Or rather, I didn't plan to make one. Having her so close was fucking with my head, though, and I was wanting things I shouldn't.

"You need to ice it and take something for the pain," I said. "Get changed and I'll have an ice pack ready when you get back to the living room."

She pulled the T-shirt over her head, then reached behind her. I watched in fascination as she pulled her bra off through the sleeves of the shirt and let it fall to the floor. I'd heard of women who could do that, but I'd never seen it happen firsthand. Impressive.

And oddly, a big turn-on. Or maybe it was the fact I knew she only had on a pair of panties under my shirt.

Meg moved closer and reached out, sliding her hand into mine. It gave me a jolt, not having expected her to do such a thing. The kiss on my cheek earlier had shocked the hell out of me, and now she was holding onto me as if it were the most natural thing in the world. For a woman who never wanted anyone to touch her, she was making a lot of bold moves tonight. Someone else might have acted on that show of trust, but I knew I couldn't offer her what she needed.

I led her into the kitchen and had her sit at the table while I prepped an ice pack. When I was finished, I knelt at her feet and motioned for her to lift the shirt. She did without hesitation, holding it only high enough for me to see the mark on her skin, and I placed the pack against the bruise. She hissed in a breath as the cold material touched her skin and I couldn't help but notice her nipples hardened.

"Thank you," she said softly. "No one's ever cared before."

"You said it wasn't your first time being bruised. Silva and his men hit you?" I asked.

"Sometimes. Usually, they were content making me service them like a good little whore, but there were some who got off on hitting a woman or choking her."

A red haze settled over my vision as I thought about those men abusing her. She had such a sweet, gentle soul. I didn't know how she'd survived with her mind intact, but she'd managed. No matter what it took, I'd make sure she had the kind of life she deserved. If that meant she lived here at the compound for the rest of her life, then so be it. I'd find a way to deal with my attraction to her.

"Never again, Meg. You don't have to do any of that ever again. The next time you're with a man, it will be because you want it to happen. Any fucker who lays a hand on you without your permission will answer to me."

"And the ones who do have my permission?" she asked, staring at me intently.

"I can't exactly kick their ass if you invited them into your bed."

"What if there's only one man I might want in my bed?" She licked her lips and her gaze dropped to my mouth. "Did you know I've never really kissed anyone before? I didn't date in high school, and Silva and his men didn't kiss."

"Is that what the birthday girl wants? A birthday kiss?" I asked.

She nodded. "But only if it's from one particular man."

"And who might that be?" I asked, knowing I was playing with fucking fire.

"You. Would you kiss me, Cinder?"

"On one condition," I said. I'd lost my damn mind. It was the only reason I could think to do what I did next. "Call me Vincent. When it's just us anyway. In front of the club I'm still Cinder."

She smiled softly and her eyes lit up. It was like I'd just given her the best gift ever. I knew I was going to regret this, but I didn't want to deny her the one thing she truly seemed to want. It was a small request in the scheme of things.

"Then kiss me… Vincent."

I wrapped her hair around my hand and pulled her closer, my lips brushing against hers. It was akin to being struck by lightning, and that one small taste was nowhere near enough. I licked at her bottom lip until she opened, and then I deepened the kiss… and knew that I'd been right all along. I was going to hell. Not because I'd made a move on Meg, but because I was kissing an angel and was nowhere near worthy of her.

She melted against me and I held her tight, wanting to savor this moment because I had no doubt it would be a one-time thing. No way she'd want more from me. Even if she did, it would be a brief fling and nothing more. I couldn't give her the fairy-tale ending she needed, the one she deserved. I hadn't had a steady woman in my life in over thirty years.

I pulled back, needing to put some space between us, and I stood slowly. Her eyes were still closed, her lips parted, and there was a rosy hue to her cheeks. She was enchanting, and easily the most beautiful woman I'd ever seen. I rubbed the back of my neck and took a step back, then another, until I was far enough away that I couldn't feel her body heat.

"I never knew it could be like that," she said, her eyes opening. There was a smile curving the corners of her lips and a dreamy expression on her face. That's when I knew I was fucked.

"We should finish that movie while you ice your bruise," I said. "Let me get some Tylenol for you."

I reached into the cabinet next to the sink and took down the bottle, then got her a glass of water. I set both on the table. Slowly, she reached out and shook two pills from the bottle and downed them, but her gaze locked on me again.

"Vincent." She stood and moved closer.

I tensed, bracing myself for her touch and knew I shouldn't follow my instincts, which were screaming at me to toss her over my shoulder and carry her to the bedroom. What I needed to do was the get the hell away from her as fast as possible before I broke her more than Silva and his men had. She was recovering nicely from her time in Colombia, but I knew a broken heart could last a lifetime.

"The kiss shouldn't have happened, Meg. I'm sorry."

She paled a little and visibly swallowed before giving me a slight nod. Without another word, she quietly went back to the living room, this time sitting on the far end of the couch. I reclaimed my seat and tried not to think about how wrong it felt for her to be so far away. When the movie ended, she stood and shifted from foot to foot.

"Could you please show me where I'm sleeping tonight? You mentioned the guest room, but I can stay on the couch. Or should I go back to my place?" she asked.

"You can stay." I wouldn't go back on my offer, even if the idea of her being just down the hall was more temptation than I thought I could withstand. I showed her to the guest room, and she went inside, then shut the door in my face. I stared at it a moment, then went about locking up the house for the night and shutting off the TV and lights. I typically left my front door unlocked in case someone needed me quickly, but with Meg staying here I wasn't taking any chances.

I left my bedroom door partially open in case Meg needed anything tonight. I'd slept naked every night since leaving the Marines, but with a woman under my roof, I decided to leave the boxers on. I slid into bed and shut off my bedside lamp. Folding my arms behind my head, I stared up at the ceiling and wondered if I'd made a huge mistake by kissing Meg. The look on her face wasn't one I would likely forget anytime soon. First that look of complete contentment and then the shuttered expression after I pushed her away. It was better to hurt her a little now than a lot more later.

Sleep wouldn't claim me, and I kept playing the kiss over and over in my head, and her wounded expression when I'd told her it shouldn't have happened. I felt like the biggest asshole ever, but I'd done it to protect her. Right? At this point, I wasn't sure I could even convince myself of that fact, much less anyone else.

I always kept my cell phone on the bedside table at night, and the screen lit with an incoming message before the chime sounded. I grabbed it and unlocked the phone before reading the text from Shade. At first I couldn't understand a word of it, and then it all clicked into place. I tossed the covers aside and called Shade as I paced the bedroom.

"Sorry to interrupt your night," Shade said. "Heard Meg was staying with you."

"She's asleep in the guest room. Her birthday doesn't have good memories and she didn't want to be alone at her place," I said, then wondered why the hell I was justifying my actions to anyone.

"Right, so I didn't think this could wait until tomorrow. The Inferno didn't disappear completely like we'd hoped. From the reports I'm seeing, there are more of them in the area," Shade said.

"Okay, so we'll deal with them." Might have to call in extra clubs again, but I knew they'd be willing to help. The Inferno wasn't just our problem. They were an issue for all our allies.

"Not that easy. It's not just random woman they're going after, Cinder. They know we were part of the crew that took down their initiates. They've put a price on all our heads, and..." Shade stopped and I heard his keyboard clicking. "They've gotten pictures of the women and kids. I can't find anything more than their photos and a mention of a reward if the women and kids are captured, except one."

"Who are they targeting?" I asked.

"It's Meg, Cinder. They've already put her up for auction even though she's obviously sleeping soundly at your place. But it means they're confident enough about their ability to get their hands on her, which is a big red flag for me. That woman never goes anywhere unprotected, but that doesn't seem to be a deterrent for them. The post is new, just went up tonight, which means they somehow know she's important to you."

The line was quiet and I knew Shade hadn't told me everything. Fury was building inside of me that anyone would think to go after the women and kids of the club, and I was especially pissed they were already trying to sell Meg. I ignored his little dig about her being important to me. I could deny it all I wanted, but actions spoke louder and all that shit.

"We have a rat," I said. "Dig as deep as you need to into every patched member, every officer, and every Prospect. Someone is selling information and has put everyone in danger. I want to know who the fuck it is, and I want to know now, dammit."

"On it. I'll pull everyone's financials and hack into any of their online accounts. Everything from social media to email, I'll know every detail of their lives by noon tomorrow."

"Make it sooner, Shade. I don't give a shit what you have to do to make that happen. Call Outlaw and Wire. I trust the both of them. I'll call Torch and Griz to tell them what's going on. If these fuckers are coming after us, there's no reason they won't try the same with everyone who helped rescue Janessa. I'll talk to Reckless Kings and Hades Abyss, as well."

"Cinder, I know you well enough to understand you're resistant to having Meg in your life, but you seriously need to consider keeping her with you until we handle this shit. If we do have a rat, then she's not safe at her place."

I grunted, knowing he was right about her safety, and not liking that he knew me that damn well. He'd been a kid when he'd patched in, but Shade had become invaluable to this club. As I thought about it, I knew I could exclude Jackal, Havoc, and Scratch from the list of suspects. No way they'd put their families in danger.

"You can exclude anyone with a woman and kids," I said. "In fact, let Havoc know what's going on. I'll send a message to Scratch. We may need to meet, but I need to find a way to not make it suspicious for the others."

Shade was still clicking on the other end, but he paused mid-keystroke. "The Reapers have a playground at their compound, right?"

"Yeah, and a picnic area, and who knows what else by now. It's like their community exploded and looks more like a small town than a biker compound these days."

"Well, we have kids here. Why not meet somewhere off the path but inside the gates. We could say we're discussing the logistics of adding a family friendly area," Shade said. "I could print some shit off and make it look like we're checking out blueprints."

"Not a bad idea. Of course, neither is actually adding that kind of shit. We could add a fenced area with play stuff for the kids and maybe a covered pavilion with picnic tables and some grills. Doesn't have be huge, but a place where Josie, Clarity, Jordan, and Janessa can take the kids to play and not worry about chasing after them."

"I know some of the guys like Stripes will never settle down, but there are plenty of us who wouldn't mind a steady woman in our lives and maybe some kids," Shade said. "I think it would be a good investment. And there's something else."

"What?" I asked.

"The duplexes. I think we need to make sure they're all furnished and stocked with essentials. If shit gets bad, Scratch and Jackal will need to bring their families inside the gates. Where would they stay right now?" Shade asked.

"Good point. When you speak to Havoc, tell him to handle that shit. I want everyone inside these gates no later than noon tomorrow. Fuck, I can't even ask the Prospects to go guard them until then. Who the hell knows if I can trust any of them at this point?"

"We'll handle it, Pres. Just like we always do."

I sighed and hung up the phone, then spent the next hour spreading the word about our problem, at least to those I trusted. Reckless Kings offered to send Copper and two others to help. Hades Abyss was sending Fox and Shooter to us, as well as few members over to the Reapers just in case they were targeted too. Devil's Fury was sending Wolf and Dingo. Torch offered help, but in case The Inferno was going to hit him too, I declined. If things got worse, then I'd reconsider and accept aid from him. Now it was a waiting game while I got all my chess pieces into place and hoped like hell The Inferno didn't strike before then.

Chapter Four

Meg

I could hear Cinder talking to someone, but I only heard his voice. Phone. He must have received a phone call, and judging by the darkness outside the bedroom window, it was still late. Either that or he was talking to himself, but he didn't seem like the type for that sort of thing. I'd learned that late night phone calls didn't mean good things, or at least it hadn't in a military home. Most of my free time had been spent with my best friend, including lots of sleepovers, and whenever her dad got a call in the middle of the night it meant something bad was happening.

I crept down the hall and stopped in Cinder's doorway. He'd left it partially open and I saw him pacing across his floor in nothing but his boxers. For an older man, he'd stayed incredibly fit. I let his body distract me for a moment, and had a jolt of surprise when I realized I didn't feel even the slightest bit apprehensive. Any other man, and I'd have been running back to my room and locking the door. I should have known when he'd kissed me and I'd only wanted more. Whatever it was about Cinder, he didn't scare me even the teensiest bit. I felt safe and protected when he was nearby.

"I want to know who the fuck it is," Cinder said, his tone hard and demanding. "I can't believe I have a fucking rat in my house."

I gasped and felt the blood drain from my face. In his *house*? Did he mean me? I was the only one here other than him. Cinder spun and faced me, his expression unreadable as he told the other person he had to go. He tossed the phone on the bed and approached me. My body trembled and I couldn't seem to make my feet move.

"You think I'd do something like that?" I asked when he stopped in front of me. "I would never!"

"Calm down, Meg. I didn't mean my house as in my residence. I meant there's a rat in the club," he said, reaching for me slowly. He closed his hands over my arms and pulled me against his chest, holding me. "I never in a million years would ever think that you would do anything to hurt me or this club."

"There's a traitor in the club?" I asked.

"Yeah, sweet girl, there is. And he's feeding information about the women and children to The Inferno."

I felt ice fill my veins as I thought about the club that had attacked Janessa. I considered Clarity, Janessa, Josie, and Jordan my friends, or the closest thing I'd had to friends in a really long time. I hated the thought of someone trying to hurt them.

"Meg, there's something we need to discuss," he said. "But I should probably get dressed first."

His words made me all too aware of him pressed against me, and that a certain part of him seemed particularly interested in our current position. My cheeks warmed as I glanced up at him. Cinder looked like he was waging a war inside his head, but I didn't want him to. If he wanted me, then I wanted him to say something, do something. I'd never wanted anyone before, but I knew that being with him would be amazing. Just his kiss alone had told me that much. But I wasn't bold enough to make a move, not when he'd already said that kissing me was a mistake. It still hurt, knowing that he felt that way.

I stepped back and wrapped my arms around my waist, looking everywhere but at Cinder. I heard the rustle of his clothes and jumped when he touched my arm. Glancing his way, I saw that he'd pulled on a T-shirt and jeans, and I let him herd me toward the kitchen. Cinder brewed some coffee and put the kettle on the stove. He poured himself a cup of coffee and made some hot tea for me, then set the mugs on the table. When he sat, he heaved a sigh that told me whatever he had to say was weighing on him.

"I can go," I said. "Back to my place. Or I could…"

I couldn't even finish that thought. No, I couldn't leave. I had no money or anything, no way to support myself, and the thought of being away from the club terrified me. It was the only thing keeping me safe from men like Silva. If I walked away, I could be taken, and I knew I wouldn't survive going through that all over again. If the men didn't kill me, I'd likely end up taking my own life.

"I need you to stay here," Cinder said. "Indefinitely."

I opened and shut my mouth a few times, unsure of what to say to that.

"You can keep the guest room," he said, running a hand through his hair. "It's not safe for you to be at your place, not while I have a snitch in the club."

"But you said he was targeting the women and kids."

He stared at me. Hard. My heart started to race a little.

"You mean he's targeted me too?" I asked softly. "But why? I'm no one!"

"The Inferno has decided that you mean something to me, which means they're coming hard for you. Meg, I want to shelter you and protect you, but I know that doing that would only put you in more danger. What I'm going to tell you is scary, but I need you to try to stay calm."

"Just tell me," I said.

"The Inferno seems to think you'll be easy enough to capture. So easy they've already listed you for sale," he said.

There was a loud *whooshing* sound in my ears and the room spun. For sale. I was going to be sold again, to someone like Silva and his men. Used like I was nothing, not even human. My vision dimmed and I felt my body sway. I heard Cinder curse, and then his chair scraped. I must have blacked out for a moment because the next time I opened my eyes, I was in his lap and he looked concerned.

"I'm not going to let them take you, Meg. It's why I want you stay here at my house. It's safer."

"And when you aren't here?" I asked.

"I'll get an alarm installed. Wouldn't be a bad idea. The women and kids could all come here when they're going to be left alone. You'd like the company, wouldn't you?" he asked.

"What does it matter what I want?" I asked. "I'm just a stray who won't go away. I'm not anyone to any of you, Cinder. You made it clear that kissing me was a mistake you don't want to repeat."

I didn't know where I'd found the courage to say that, but it felt freeing. He smiled faintly for a moment, probably just as surprised by my outburst. I was the type to follow along and not make waves, at least the Meg who survived Colombia was that person. I didn't think I remembered how to be my old self. Of course, I'd been a kid the last time I felt freedom, so I'd be different now anyway. But I'd lost my spark, my fire.

In the year and a half I'd been with the Devil's Boneyard, I'd mostly kept to myself. I did enjoy speaking with the other women, and they'd taken me shopping here and there, but I'd spent the majority of my time here at Cinder's house, or hiding in the place they'd provided for me.

"Meg, you're a sweetheart, you really are. You're also the forever type of woman, and I don't have forever to give anyone. I don't believe in happily ever after and all that fairy-tale shit, not when it comes to me. It seems to be working for some of the others, but a guy like me isn't the type to settle down."

"Because you're a Marine?" I asked.

He raised his eyebrows and stared at me.

"The Devil Dog on your arm. You were in the Marines at some point. My friend's dad always said once a Marine, always a Marine."

"You know what a Devil Dog is?" he asked. "Most people just generally refer to it as the Marine dog or mascot."

I shrugged. "I don't know all the details about being a Marine or anything, but I listened whenever my friend's dad talked about being a Marine. It seemed interesting to a teen girl, and he was a hero to me."

"I'm no one's hero, Meg, so don't even go there."

"You're mine," I said softly. "You could have thrown me out, or left me in Colombia, but you didn't. And don't tell me it's because of Jordan. I know she wanted to bring us here, but you didn't have to give in to her. Everyone else acts like she's a ticking time bomb or something, but I know you aren't afraid of her."

"No, I'm not. Her daughter is another matter. But Jordan is amusing and a general pain in my ass, and seeing her try to kick the shit out of men three times her size always gives me a good laugh. She's an evil little shit when it comes to protecting her family, though, and I'm glad she's on our side. I'd been toying with the man who knew Havoc's whereabouts, not wanting to kill him before I'd extracted what I could, but I wasn't moving fast enough for Jordan. I'd gleaned a little info, but I wanted more than just Havoc's location. I never conveyed that to Jordan, or anyone else, and she decided to take matters into her own hands, and while she found out exactly what happened to her man, I wasn't able to discover if we would have a bigger problem on our hands in the future."

"Ticking time bomb," I said. "I think it fits."

"So does demonic little shit," he said with a laugh.

"Have you narrowed down who might be snitching on the club?" I asked.

"No, but it's obviously not anyone with a woman and kids. And it's not Shade because he brought the matter to my attention. I'd hate to think any of the patched members were responsible for leaking pictures and details of our family to those sick sons of bitches, but I can't rule anything out right now."

"They're not taking me," I said, knowing that I wouldn't go with them willingly. I'd do whatever it took to avoid that fate again. Anything.

"I won't let them near you, Meg."

"That's not what I meant." I looked away, not wanting to confess that I'd kill myself before I went back to that type of life. It wasn't a life at all, just one day of horror and misery after another, and the likelihood I'd be rescued a second time was slim to none.

"Sweetheart, look at me."

I refused and turned my head farther away.

Cinder gripped my chin and forced me to meet his gaze. He just stared at me, and I didn't know what to think or say. Slowly, he leaned closer and pressed his lips to mine. Surprise was my first response, but then the feel of his lips on mine had me melting. He might be this big, gruff biker, the President of Devil's Boneyard and feared by most people, but he would always be the man who'd saved me, who protected me. I could admit a slight case of hero worship when it came to Cinder.

"I thought kissing me was a mistake," I murmured.

"I already walk on the wrong side of the law. If I'm going to hell, I might as well do something enjoyable to earn my place."

I blinked at him. "Kissing me is going to send you to hell?"

"No. The thoughts I have when I kiss you will send me there." He smiled faintly. "I'm no good for you, Meg. You deserve so much better than an old man like me, but now that I've had a taste, I can't seem to keep my distance. I'm trying to do the right thing, but I don't know that I can resist for long."

"Maybe I don't want you to," I said.

"What are you saying, Meg? And you'd better be really clear right now. I don't want to start something only to scare you and send you running. The safest place for you is under this roof, and if I need to keep away from you, then I will. It won't be easy, but I'll do it."

"I'm saying that I want you. When you kiss me, I feel all warm and tingly. I've never given myself to anyone willingly, Vincent, but I want to. I want you to be the one who shows me that what happens between a man and a woman isn't something to fear and doesn't always cause pain."

"That's a tall order," he said.

"I'm sure you're up for the challenge," I teased, then sobered. I didn't know who this new Meg was who was starting to emerge, and it scared me and felt liberating at the same time.

"Oh, I'm up all right," he said.

I snorted, then giggled. Giggled! I couldn't remember the last time I'd done something like that. Even after all my time at the compound, I'd never truly relaxed and enjoyed myself. Not until tonight. Not until the man holding me turned my world upside down with a kiss.

"Are you sure that's what you want, Meg?" he asked.

"I'm sure. No one's ever made me feel the way you do. I know you won't hurt me. I trust you, Vincent, more than I trust anyone."

"You get scared at any point or want to stop, you tell me. I don't care how far along we are, I'll back off the second you need me to," he said.

"Like I said. I know I can trust you." I cupped his cheek. "You're a good man, even though you try really hard to pretend otherwise."

"You deserve a nice dinner, candlelight, and romantic music. Something. Anything other than what I can offer you tonight," he said.

"No. All I want and need is you. I don't need any fancy extras to make this moment special."

He studied me a moment, then stood with me in his arms and started walking toward the back of the house. When he entered his bedroom, he kicked the door shut and carried me over to the bed. He eased me down, then took a step back. I didn't want him second-guessing this moment or trying to back out. I'd been naked in front of men plenty of times, but the only one who mattered was this one. Reaching for the hem of my shirt, I slowly eased it over my head and tossed it aside. His gaze locked on my breasts. I loved the hunger etched on his face, the raw need. I shimmied out of my panties and tried to fight the tremor that was making my hands shake. I did trust him, more than I'd trusted anyone in a long time, but I was still nervous.

A groan rumbled from deep in his chest and he fisted his hands, almost as if he was trying to keep from reaching out to me. I swallowed hard as he removed his clothes and I got to see him completely naked for the first time. He was already hard, his cock fully erect and pre-cum gathering on the tip. He wasn't big enough that I worried it would hurt, but he was far from small. There was no way I'd be able to wrap my hand all the way around him. Perfect, that was the best word to use. Cinder was perfect in every way.

"We can stop right here and now," he said, catching my attention. My gaze locked with his and I shook my head.

"Don't stop." If he backed off now, I might never get the courage to do this again. I certainly wouldn't ask him after being rejected twice, and I had a hard time picturing myself with anyone else. Being vulnerable in front of a man wasn't easy.

"There are things you should know," he said. "I can be a bit rough in the bedroom, and I prefer to tie my women up. I don't know if you can handle that Meg."

I swallowed hard, but the fear I'd thought would come stayed at bay. Deep down, I knew that he wouldn't hurt me, that if I let him tie me up that he would only give me pleasure. "I'm all right with that," I said.

He approached the bed and I slid back a little, then reclined on my elbows. Cinder ran his hands up my thighs and I noticed his heart was pounding as hard as mine was, the telling thumps noticeable in his broad chest. The look he gave me was reverent. His body covered mine as he leaned across the bed, bracing his weight on his hands on either side of me.

"I like seeing you sprawled across my bed, ready and willing. More than I should."

Cinder kissed me slowly, the heat and weight of his body pressing against me. I wrapped my hand around the back of his neck, wanting to hold him close a while longer. It felt like we kissed forever before he moved farther down my body. I felt the rasp of his beard along my neck, then between my breasts. I shivered as my body responded, my pussy getting wetter and my nipples harder. It was both frightening and exciting. His lips closed over my nipple, his teeth lightly grazing the hard peak. I couldn't contain my whimpers and cries as my body heated even more. It felt like little zaps of pleasure were going straight from my breasts to my clit as he teased one side, then the other.

He tightened his hand on my hip as his tongue slid across my nipple again. He bit down gently and I cried out, my body bucking underneath him. Everything felt so good, and I wanted more. I wished this moment could last forever.

He started to move farther down my body, but I placed a hand on his shoulder.

"Wait. We forgot something."

"What?" he asked, looking up at me.

"I don't think I can have children since I never conceived in Colombia, and the club doctor tested me and said I'm clean."

"Are you asking me to take you bare?" he asked. "Because I've never fucked a woman without a condom."

"If you want to use one, I understand," I said.

Cinder moved back up over me until we were eye to eye. "I haven't been with anyone in about six months, and I got tested after being with her. I'm clean."

"Then… no condoms?" I asked.

He hesitated and I squeezed his arm, understanding completely why he might not want to take the chance. I honestly didn't think I could get pregnant, but if a man like him ever had children, he wouldn't want it to be with someone like me. He might claim not to be the forever kind of guy, but I knew the truth. It was that he didn't want forever with me, and that was fine. I'd take all the happy memories I could make with him and I would cherish them always. I already knew I was probably too broken to have a normal life, be the other half of someone, a partner in all ways.

"We can use one," I said. "It's fine. I don't mind."

"Meg, it's not that I don't trust you."

"But you don't, and it's okay. A man in your position can't be too careful, right? You're smart to always use one."

He kissed me again, then I felt his hand wrap around my wrist. I gaped as a cuff was attached to me, then he did the same to the other side. I tugged at them and realized I couldn't break free. Staring up at him, I could tell he was waiting for me to freak out, but I wouldn't. I gave him a nod so he'd know I was okay.

"Why do you have these if you don't bring women here?" I asked, the question slipping past my lips before I could recall them.

"When I bought this bed, Scratch thought it would be damn funny to hang the cuffs off the headboard. He tossed the key, some condoms, and a bunch of other crap into the bedside table drawer, but I've never had a woman in my bed until now."

Cinder pinched my nipples again, twisting and tugging on them. I moaned and thrashed as much as my body could while shackled to his bed. He leaned down and bit, not hard enough to break the skin, but the sharp sting of pain did something I'd never expected. It was like an overload of pleasure, my clit pulsing, and then I was coming. My thighs trembled as he switched to the other breast. His beard scraped against my tender skin as he lapped at the hard peak. The moment he bit down again, he swiped across my clit with his fingers, and I screamed, I came so hard. Before I could even come down from my high, his body covered mine and he slowly pushed inside of me, completely bare. I gasped and my eyes went wide as I stared up at him. I got a slow, sexy smile out of him before he started moving.

"Some rules are made to be broken," he said. "If I was ever going to break that one, it would be with you, Meg."

My heart felt full to bursting in that moment. It meant the world to me, having this man's trust. I hoped that I never gave him cause to doubt me. I would die for Cinder, if it ever came to that. He'd given me a chance at a new life when he could have left me behind. I'd always be grateful, and some small part of me would always love him for all he'd done.

I gripped his hips with my thighs as he stroked in and out of me, slowly as if he were savoring the moment. It felt amazing, better than anything I'd experienced before. He shifted and every thrust had him brushing against my clit. Little sparks of pleasure shot through me and it didn't take long before I was coming. I bit my lip to keep from screaming out his name this time, and I felt a gush of moisture between my legs. My cheeks warmed as I felt my release soak the bed under me, but it just seemed to turn him on even more. His eyes flared with heat as he took me harder, faster. Every flex of his hips drove him into me. The bed shook underneath us as he powered into me, slamming his cock deep with every stroke. It was a thorough fucking, with no other way to describe it. The orgasm turned into another one, and as my body trembled from the force of one more release, I felt the hot splash of his cum inside of me.

Cinder thrust a few more times, then groaned as his body went taut and he stilled. I felt the pulse of his cock and wished we could stay like this a while longer. It was nice, feeling connected to him, even if only for a little bit.

"If I were younger, I'd say give me twenty minutes and I'll improve on that," he said as he uncuffed me, then rolled to the side.

I didn't know the protocol for what happened after. Before, I'd either been passed off to someone else or just kicked out into the hall. This was different, though. Was I supposed to go back to my room now? Did he want me to stay? Was once all he wanted from me? As if sensing my thoughts, he reached for me, pulling me tight against his side.

"You don't need to improve on anything," I said.

He chuckled, then groaned. "Christ, Meg. Just proves how innocent you are despite everything. Trust me, I owe you a do-over. I should have been gentle, not fucked you so damn hard."

"Oh." I was quiet a moment. "Does that mean we're going to do it again?"

I wasn't opposed to the idea. In fact, I was all for it.

He laughed again, the bed shaking from his mirth. "Yeah, sweetheart. We'll do it again, just not any time soon. I'm too damn old to get hard again that fast. Give me an hour or two."

I cuddled against him, content and happier than I'd been in forever. He might have thought what we'd just shared was lacking, but to me it was wonderful. I couldn't imagine it getting any better. Not just because he'd made me come multiple times, but because of who I'd shared the experience with.

"Sorry about your bed. I've never done that before," I said.

"That definitely isn't something to apologize for. Hell, I hope it happens again. Do you have any idea how fucking hot it is that I made you come that hard? Makes me want to beat my chest or some other caveman-type shit."

I smiled and pressed a kiss to his chest. "It's a rather impressive chest."

"You're good for an old man's ego, sweet girl."

"Not old," I said. Maybe if I said it often enough, he'd eventually believe me. I knew he was a lot older than me, and the oldest member of the club, but I didn't care. Men my age and younger had hurt me horribly, so age was just a number and didn't mean a damn thing when it came to what a man was made of. Cinder had always been kind. Even when he'd barked at me about leaving his house there hadn't been any real heat behind his words, and now I knew that he'd just sent me away because of how I affected him.

As I cuddled next to him, his arm around me, I knew without a doubt that I could easily fall in love with Cinder. I might already be a little in love with him. I knew we could never work, that he wouldn't love me in return, but for the first time in ten years, I wanted something other than my freedom. I wanted the man lying next to me to ask me to stay, to be his. It would never happen, and I was doomed to have a broken heart, but it didn't stop me from wishing it were possible.

Chapter Five

Cinder

What the hell had I done? Meg murmured something in her sleep as she pressed as tightly to me as she could. I'd promised myself I would keep my distance, not touch her, and I'd gone and fucked her. I knew it wasn't going anywhere, couldn't, but when she'd asked me I hadn't been able to say no. Meg had never asked for a damn thing as long as she'd been here. Clothes and essentials had practically been forced upon her because she didn't want to put anyone out. Of all the requests she could have made, this wasn't one I'd anticipated.

Her small body felt a little too perfect lying so close to me. Taking her without a condom was fucking stupid as hell, but she'd been so hot and wet, and felt so incredible. It was something I'd remember for the rest of my life. I couldn't regret what I'd done. I hoped she was right about not being able to have kids. Small humans weren't something I wanted running around my house right now, or ever. The time for me to have a family had come and gone. Just because Scratch made it look easy didn't mean it was. I knew Torch had started a family later in life too, but that kind of thing just wasn't in the cards for me.

Right now, I'd focus on keeping the women of the club safe, making sure The Inferno didn't get anywhere near Meg, and then I'd have to talk to her about the future. Hers, not ours. There would never be an *us*. Maybe I could convince her to go to Devil's Fury or Hades Abyss. Even the Dixie Reapers would be a good place for her. Anywhere other than here, where I'd have to see her every day.

I glanced at the clock by the bed. Only five in the morning. I had a little ways to go until I met with Havoc, Scratch, Jackal, and Shade. I hadn't come up with a single damn idea on how to handle this shit. Might have had something to do with the sexy woman in my bed. The first time hadn't been enough. I'd taken my time the second round, made sure she came at least four more times. I couldn't remember the last time I'd had a woman in my bed. I knew it hadn't happened in the last twenty years. I never brought women to the compound, and if I'd fucked a club slut, I'd done it at the clubhouse and never in one of the beds. That was just an invitation for them to stick around longer, and once I got off I was done with them. At least, when they weren't Meg.

Having Meg under my roof all day, every day was going to be different. Part of me wanted to keep her here in my bed, but I knew it would be better to send her back to the guest room. As amazing as it had been, we didn't need to repeat the last several hours. The little devil on my shoulder whispered that The Inferno already thought she was mine so I should enjoy the benefits. The voice of reason, on the other hand, said it was all kinds of wrong to give her ideas that this could become something permanent. I'd need to speak with her later about her plans for the future, but for now I'd just enjoy holding her against me.

Even after the sun was blazing through the window and I knew it was time to go, I wanted to linger a while longer. I'd never held a woman all night long, and it was fucking with my head. The fact it was Meg, and that she trusted me enough to fall asleep in my bed, made me feel all twisted up inside. I eased away from her, careful not to wake her, and I went to grab a quick shower. I had to admit I felt more relaxed than I had in a while, despite the trouble hanging over our heads, and I knew it was all due to the woman still sleeping soundly. I washed but didn't linger in the shower, then dried off and pulled on some clothes.

I gave her one last look before I walked out of the bedroom and went to meet the others. Whatever it took, I'd keep her safe. When she'd told me that she wasn't going back to that way of life, and I'd realized she meant to end her life before things could get that far, it had felt like someone was twisting a knife in my gut. I didn't like the thought of a world without Meg. Even if she wasn't here with me, knowing she was safe and happy somewhere was good enough.

Havoc, Scratch, Jackal, and Shade were already waiting when I got there, each of them eyeing me with some concern.

"You're never late," Havoc said.

"It's by five minutes," I said. "I'm an old man and like my sleep."

Scratch snorted and I knew he didn't buy my bullshit, but no one called me on it. Shade handed me a small stack of papers and I glanced down to see playground schematics on top. I flipped the page and read over the reports he'd managed to gather on each of our prospects and patched members, present company excluded. I didn't see any big payouts that didn't come from the club, but it didn't mean someone hadn't betrayed us. There was no way those pictures could have gotten into the hands of The Inferno any other way.

"What if it's not a Prospect or one of our brothers?" Scratch asked.

"Who the fuck else would be able to give them pictures and info on the women and kids?" I asked.

"Club sluts," Havoc said. "You know as well as I do, those women would turn on any of us for the right price, especially if they feel slighted in any way. With more of us settling down, they're seeing their chances slip through their fingers."

"What chance?" Jackal asked. "Like any of us want to be shackled permanently to club pussy."

Havoc shrugged.

"I can pull their records," Shade said. "I'd rather believe one of them capable of this shit than someone I call family."

"Me too," I agreed. "Havoc, I need an alarm installed on my house, state of the art. Whenever we aren't with the women, they can all hang out at my place, kids too. I'm sure Meg would like the company."

Scratch arched a brow. "Meg, huh? Thought she went home last night."

"Yeah, to his," Shade said, smirking a little.

"Enough. She's staying as a guest. I gave her the spare room. She didn't want to be alone on her birthday, and after what Shade told me, there was no way I was sending her back to her house. If I don't know who to trust inside my own damn gates, then I can't guarantee she's safe here."

That seemed to sober them.

"Scratch, you, Clarity, and the boys need to move inside the gates. Jackal, same goes for your family. I don't want anyone within easy reach of The Inferno until this shit is settled," I said. "And if I find the fucker that put a target on our women, I'm going to tear them apart."

"Get in line," Havoc said. "No one's coming after Jordan and my daughter. Then again, might be amusing to watch them try."

Jackal grinned. "If Jordan is taking on one of those bastards, I want ringside seats and popcorn. I bet she'd make him cry like a little bitch."

"That's because his woman is scary as fuck," Scratch said. "They're like a match made in hell."

"She's a sweetheart," Havoc said. "Just don't piss her off or she turns into a rabid Chihuahua."

Shade stared at him a moment before snickering. "I'm so telling your woman you compared her to a Chihuahua. She'll have your balls."

Havoc winced and shifted his stance, obviously picturing that very thing. I didn't envy him whenever Jordan went off on one of her rants, but I had to admit they were pretty damn perfect together. Anyone less ballsy would have been steamrolled by Havoc, but Jordan could stand up for herself and wasn't afraid to fight someone three times her size. Fuck if she didn't win most of the time too. Not that I would expect any less of a woman who was not only married to my Sergeant at Arms, but also related to two other bikers.

Speaking of that little shit… "Are we sure CJ isn't doing this? I hate to even ask, but as many problems as we've had from him regarding the women of the club…"

"It's a valid concern," Jackal said. "Sorry, Havoc. I know he's technically your family through Jordan, but the guy's an asshole."

"I'd have to agree," Havoc said. "Cinder, I know you've been giving him chances left and right because of his connection to Jordan, but I don't know if I can trust that guy to have my back."

"We can discuss CJ later, unless we find out he's behind this shit," I said. "Shade, see what you can find on the club pussy. If one of those bitches turned on us, I want to fucking know."

"If Jordan finds out a woman put her and our kid in danger, I don't know that I can rein her in. She's going to go nuclear on any woman not attached to someone. Meg excluded, of course. She loves Meg," Havoc said.

"Where's Meg right now?" Shade asked.

"Asleep," I said.

"But if everyone you trust is right here..." Shade let the thought trail off and I cursed before taking off. I heard my brothers on my heels and I hoped that I was panicking for nothing, that Meg was still safe and sound right where I'd left her. I knew that someone was after her, yet I'd left her unprotected. Just proved that fucking her had been a mistake. It was making me sloppy, and if I screwed up, then people could die.

"Where are the others?" I asked.

"I left Jordan and Lanie at home, but my woman is armed to the teeth. No one's coming through that door and getting out alive," Havoc said.

"I had a panic room installed after that shit with Janessa," Jackal said. "I left Josie and the kids tucked in there. They have snacks, drinks, and a half-bath in case they need to be in there a while."

"Clarity and the boys are at home, but I had cameras installed around the outside of the house, as well as motion sensors and a state-of-the-art alarm system. No one's getting to them without the police being notified, as well as me," Scratch said.

Right. So, everyone had protected their families except me. Even if Meg wasn't really mine, she was still my responsibility, and I'd been so worried about her reading too much into us having sex that I'd left her vulnerable. Made me the biggest asshole ever.

When I reached the house, I saw the front door was ajar. My heart pounded as I raced inside and started searching for Meg. Havoc was by my side, his gun drawn as we cleared each room. I found her in the guest room, putting some clothes into the dresser. She turned and gave me a hesitant smile when she noticed me in the doorway. I was glad that she was safe, but I wanted to know who the fuck had been in my house while I was gone. Especially since I hadn't asked anyone to do shit.

"Where'd the clothes come from?" I asked.

Her smile faltered and she glanced at the shirt she still held. "Killian stopped by earlier and asked if I needed anything. I told him I wanted my clothes, but that you'd asked me to stay put this morning. He went and packed a small bag for me."

"Killian was here?" I asked. "Did he say why he stopped by?"

She shook her head, then worried her lower lip. "Did I do something wrong?"

"No, sweet girl. This isn't your fault. I shouldn't have left you unprotected, not until I know who we can trust at the compound."

She twisted the shirt in her hands before shaking it out and putting in the dresser. She was tense, but her shoulders were hunched a little. I may not profess to know everything about women, but it was obvious she felt uncertain where she stood with me right now. I hated that, hated that one moment of weakness had done this to her. It wasn't fair, and we needed to talk, but not with an audience.

"Glad you're safe, Meg," Havoc said.

"Thanks, Havoc." She gave him a fleeting smile before glancing at me and then looking away.

Fuck. Why did shit always have to get complicated? This was why I didn't have a steady woman in my life. Too much damn trouble and drama.

"Everything okay?" Jackal asked from the hallway.

"She's fine," I said, turning to leave, but Havoc stepped in the way. He glanced at Meg, then gave me a pointed look.

"Remember who you're talking to," I warned him.

"I know exactly who I'm talking to, Pres." He lowered his voice. "Doesn't mean as my brother and my friend that I can't let you know that you're being a dick and hurting her feelings."

Jackal and Shade took a step back, but Scratch just leaned against the wall with his arms folded, probably waiting to see if there would be a show. I wasn't going to deal with this right now, not with Meg right behind me. After all the violence she'd seen, I didn't want her to watch me put my fist through Havoc's jaw.

"Get the fuck out. All of you. Shade, find the info I requested and call me when you have something. We'll figure out our next step after that," I said.

Havoc gave me a stony glare before walking off, and I knew I'd pissed him off. Not because of how I'd spoken to him, but because of how he perceived I was treating Meg. Truth was, I didn't want to talk to her around them. What I needed to say was better done in private. After they were gone and I'd made sure the front door was locked, as well as the back door and all the windows, I went back to Meg's room and found her sitting on the side of the bed, staring at the floor.

"We need to talk," I said.

"You don't have to say anything," she said. "I know that last night was just a one-time thing."

It was the fact she wouldn't look at me that bothered me the most, that and her dejected tone. She might know that last night wouldn't be repeated, but it was obviously not what she wanted. I'd been afraid of her getting attached. The last thing I wanted to do was hurt her, but maybe this little slight now would save her a lot of heartache later.

I ran a hand through my hair and looked around the room, hoping that inspiration would strike and I'd know exactly what to say to make her feel better. Didn't work. No matter how long I stared at her, Meg refused to meet my gaze. It made my gut twist, knowing that I'd done that to her, hurt her without meaning to. I'd known being with her last night was wrong, but I'd done it anyway. Now I was going to pay the price, and so was Meg.

"Meg, look at me," I said.

She slowly lifted her head and met my gaze, but she couldn't hide the pain she was feeling. Yeah, I was definitely the biggest asshole on the planet. Hurting Meg was like kicking a puppy.

"I told you that I don't do that happily ever after shit. Doesn't mean you won't make some guy a great girlfriend or wife."

"I knew last night that you wouldn't want anything permanent with me," she said. "But I don't regret what happened. At least now I know what it's supposed to be like."

"When this is over, when The Inferno are sent packing and you're safe, maybe you should consider going to live with the Devil's Fury or the Dixie Reapers."

Her face paled and I saw her hands shaking in her lap. "You're throwing me out?"

"No! Fuck, Meg. I'd never throw you out. I just thought you might be better off with one of the other clubs. Any of them would be lucky to have you."

She glanced over at the dresser and her lower lip trembled. This was why I shouldn't have fucked her. Any other woman would have thrown shit at my head for treating her this way. Not Meg. The only time I'd seen any fire in her at all was when she'd stepped in front of me last night, taking the punch meant for me. I'd thought maybe she was getting stronger, but now I had to second guess myself. Would Meg ever get better? She'd been with Silva the longest, had suffered the most abuse and trauma. It was possible the timid woman in front of me was all she'd ever be, and it broke my damn heart.

I moved in closer and reached for her. She flinched as my hand neared her face, then she turned those big eyes my way. I cupped her cheek and knelt in front of her. There was something about Meg that pulled at me. It wasn't just that I desired her, but I wished that I could make everything right in her world, take away the pain and bad memories. I knew that wasn't possible. Only Meg could battle those demons. I knew she was trying, searching for her place among us, but it couldn't be here with me. I was no good for someone like her.

"Sweetheart, you deserve someone better than me. I'm not the settling down type. I'm getting close to sixty, Meg. A family just isn't in the cards for me."

"Torch has a family," she said softly. "And Scratch. They're both around your age."

"Yes, they are. Do you think Torch would have settled down if he hadn't taken his wife in trade? The only reason that woman was inked as his property was part of a deal with her daddy. I know Torch loves her now, but she was just a duty back then. And Scratch has a hero complex. The second he took Clarity into his house it was only a matter of time that he claimed her."

"And you aren't like either of them?" she asked.

"I've seen a lot of fucked-up shit, Meg. I know that I'm not the only ex-military guy in any of the clubs we call family, but I've done things that would make most of their stomachs turn, all in the name of protecting my country and my family. You need someone who doesn't have so much blood on his hands."

Looking into her eyes, all I wanted to do was press my lips to hers, strip both of us naked, and claim her again. I knew it was the wrong thing to do, but it didn't stop me from craving her. Now that I'd had a taste, I wanted more. It wasn't fair to Meg, not when I couldn't give her more than that. She deserved the world, and all I could give her were some orgasms with no promise of tomorrow.

She leaned into my touch and her eyes slid shut. A look of bliss crossed her face, then she pulled away. Meg scooted back on the bed, putting more distance between us, which I fucking hated. I stood and went to the door. Looking at her one last time, I knew I was about to do something she might hate me for, but I thought it was the right thing. I shut her door behind me and went to my office, then pulled out my cell phone. I dialed Shade and hoped this shit didn't blow up in my face.

"What do you need, Pres? I'm still tracking the club sluts to see if anyone got a payday."

"I need you to look up something else for me, whenever you have a moment."

"Okay, consider me intrigued."

"I need you to look for Meg's family," I said. "She's been adamant about not going home, but I think it might be the best thing for her. Maybe if she sees her parents still love her, then she'll be willing to move on from here."

The line was so quiet I thought he'd hung up, but the screen said we were still connected.

"Shade?"

"I looked into each of the girls' pasts when we brought them here. Including Meg. I know you didn't ask me to, but I wanted to make sure trouble wouldn't come our way."

"And?" I asked.

"Her daddy was a cop. Got shot in the line of duty when she was just a kid. The mom died a few months after Meg was taken. It was ruled a suicide. She doesn't have family, Pres, except us. Her dad was Officer Parson Vickers. Her mom was Nari Lee Vickers."

"Korean?" I asked.

"Mom was full Korean and dad was half-white, half-African American. From what I can tell, they doted on her. I'm not sure why she didn't want to return home, unless she somehow knew her mom was gone."

I rubbed a hand down my beard and wondered what the hell I was going to do with Meg. Having her around the compound wasn't going to be easy, but I didn't want her to feel like I was tossing her out either. I'd hoped by finding her family that maybe she'd want to go home, but that wasn't going to happen now that I knew they were gone. I sighed and looked up, then my body tensed. Meg was in the doorway, her eyes filled with unshed tears.

"I need to go, Shade," I said, then disconnected the call. "Sweetheart, how long you been standing there?"

"Long enough," she said. "So now you know. I don't have anyone or anywhere to go."

"How did you know your mom was gone?" I asked.

"Because Silva showed me a video of her begging for her life. I bucked the status quo once and only once. He sent men to my mother's house, and then I watched as they slit her wrists and held her down in a tub of water until she bled out. He made sure I saw every second of it."

I swallowed hard and got up, going to her. I'd known she'd been through hell, but I hadn't realized just how far Silva had gone to rip her world apart. He had to have known somehow that her mom was all she had left of her family, and had found the woman. I hated to say the bastard was smart, but he had been. She'd mentioned a friend before. I'd bet money that Silva threatened to hurt her friend if she didn't toe the line. Sadistic as fuck, but smart. Then again, you didn't get to be at the top of the food chain without some intelligence.

"I was only trying to help," I said. "I thought maybe if I brought your parents here, then you'd see you had other options, other people who cared what happened to you. I didn't realize they were gone. I'm sorry, Meg."

"It's obvious you don't want me here," she said softly. "When it's safe, I'll leave. I'm sorry I stayed so long. You should have said something sooner."

She turned to go and I reached for her, then closed my fist and refused to make contact. Letting her go was for the best. She'd see that one day, understand after she found the man of her dreams. Being with her was amazing, and I genuinely cared for her, but it would never be enough. I didn't think I was capable of loving a woman, and that's what Meg needed.

I paced my office, feeling unsettled and on edge. I didn't like knowing I'd hurt her, that she didn't feel welcome. I'd gotten what I wanted. She was leaving. So why did I feel like such a shit? I hated the way she made me feel, all torn up inside and turned upside down. I'd always known what I wanted, what the club needed, and I'd made it happen. But with Meg, I didn't know a damn thing. She confused me, and made me sloppy. I couldn't afford to lose my focus or people could die.

My phone jingled with a text from Havoc.

Guests are here. Reckless Kings, Dixie Reapers, Devil's Fury, and Hades Abyss have all come to help.

Figured Torch would send someone anyway. I'd told him to focus on his own club in case he was targeted too, but the asshole never listened. Looked like it was time to figure this shit out with The Inferno and kick some ass. I wasn't about to sit around and let those fuckers hurt the women and kids I considered my family, mine to protect.

Chapter Six

Meg

It felt like my heart had been shredded and I had no one but myself to blame. I'd known what would happen, that Cinder didn't want me as a permanent part of his life. The fact he obviously regretted what happened between us was like a knife to my chest. It had been a special moment for me, and I'd felt closer to him than I'd ever felt to anyone. I should have known he wouldn't have felt the same, but some small part of me had held out hope, even as I'd told myself repeatedly it meant nothing to him. If he didn't want me at the compound anymore, then I wouldn't be here. I wasn't stupid enough to leave while there was a threat to my life, not unless I had some serious protection, but once I was able to, I'd find somewhere to go. Even living on the street was preferable to living in a place where I wasn't wanted.

I dashed the tears off my cheeks, but more just fell in their place. I'd left the house and he hadn't even noticed. Even though he thought there was a threat within the gates, I'd needed some space and fresh air. It was stupid, and I could admit that much, but I couldn't sit in that house with him another moment. I didn't want to be taken by The Inferno, or anyone else, but I also needed time to think and process everything I was feeling, and I couldn't do that with Cinder in the same house as me.

I walked along the path that went past the clubhouse and the gate. There were more bikes than usual and I remembered that other clubs might be coming to help end the threat to the women and children. A few bikers in cuts that read *Reckless Kings MC* loitered out front, as well as two members of Devil's Fury. One of them I'd met previously, Dingo. He was Jordan's brother and seemed nice enough.

He glanced my way and frowned, then shoved off the porch railing and came toward me. I didn't stop, hating that anyone saw me crying. Even when Silva had me, I hadn't cried in front of anyone after I'd watched his men murder my mother. Crying was a sign of weakness, and I couldn't afford to be weak.

"Meg! Hold up," he called out, and started jogging to catch up. "What's wrong?"

"Nothing," I muttered and kept walking.

"You're crying so it has to be something. Talk to me, Meg. My sister adores you, and she'd kick my ass if something happened and I didn't do anything about it," he said.

"Just leave it alone, Dingo. I was stupid, that's all."

He reached out and grabbed my arm, drawing me to a halt. I huffed out a breath and turned to face him. His eyes were full of compassion and worry.

"Meg, talk to me. Have I ever given you a reason not to trust me?"

"No," I said grudgingly. He really hadn't. For the most part, he'd kept his distance from me during his visits, but he'd always had a smile for me. Dingo seemed like one of the good ones, the type of guy a woman would be lucky to call her own.

"Come on. It's not safe for you to wander around alone. I'll walk with you if you really want to keep moving," he said, then slid his hand down my arm to grasp my hand. "We're friends, right? You know I would never hurt you?"

I nodded and felt a flutter in my chest. Other than the Devil's Boneyard women, no one had called me their friend in a really long time. Dingo tugged on my hand and I walked alongside him, trying to decide just what I would say. I knew he wouldn't leave it alone. For whatever reason, he was determined to help, even though there wasn't a thing he could do for me. Cinder had ripped out my heart and stomped on it, and only he could fix it. I knew he wouldn't, though. I'd just get some speech about how I'm better off without him, that he isn't the type to settle down, and the other crap that had spilled out of his mouth before.

We came to a small copse of trees and I sank to my knees in front of one. Dingo sprawled next to me, his legs outstretched, and he waited patiently. I could tell he wouldn't leave until I'd said something, explained why I was upset. It wouldn't do me any good. If he told Cinder, then the President of Devil's Boneyard would just watch me with pity, or even worse, he'd feel uncomfortable around me the duration of my stay. I didn't want either thing to happen.

"I can wait all day, Meg," Dingo said.

"I slept with Cinder," I said, blurting it out like ripping off a bandage.

"Did he..." He face flushed and his hands clenched into fists. "Did he force you?"

My jaw dropped. "What? No! Of course not! He would never do something like that."

"Then I don't understand. Why were you crying? Did it hurt?" he asked.

"It was wonderful," I said softly, and looked down at the ground. "And he never wants it to happen again. Regrets that it even transpired that one night. He told me how there can't be anything between us, and I overheard him on the phone. He tried to find my parents so they would come get me."

Dingo cursed and reached out to take my hand. "What do you want to do, Meg?"

"I need to leave, but it's not safe. I can't stay, not knowing how he feels. He'd told me up front that he didn't do forever, but I guess I was stupid and thought maybe it would bring us closer together anyway. It had the opposite effect. I'm such an idiot."

"No, you're not. You've been badly abused, Meg. It's only natural that you'd turn to someone who had shown you a bit of tenderness and caring. From what I've heard, Cinder could hardly keep his hands off you the night of your party. Is that when it happened?"

"Yeah. Now I'm wishing I'd just gone home and faced my nightmares. Or rather gone back to my hometown. There's nothing left me for there."

He pulled his phone from his pocket and started tapping on the screen. After a few chimes, I realized he was texting with someone, but I didn't know why or what it was about. When he shoved his phone back into his pocket, he stood and held out his hand. It was probably time to face the music, or rather Cinder. If he'd even noticed I was missing. At this point, I could probably stay hidden for a day or more and he'd just be thankful I wasn't reminding him of the mistake he'd made.

"Come on, Meg. My sister is going to your place to pack your things."

"What? Why?" I asked. "I already have most of my stuff at Cinder's place. I'm supposed to stay with him until everything is settled with The Inferno."

"Not anymore," he said. "I'm sending Jordan and Havoc to pack your shit, regardless of where it's located."

I tugged on him as he tried to lead me back the way we'd come, needing him to stop and explain what was happening. Dingo faced me, his jaw set and his lips pressed into a tight line. Whatever was going on in his head, it didn't seem he was going to take no for an answer. If I didn't know how sweet he was to Jordan, and how much she trusted him, I might have been a little worried.

"I'm getting you out of here, Meg," he said.

"Out? But… The Inferno!"

"Badger is coming with us, as well as Copper and Crow from Reckless Kings. The four of us can keep you safe on the way to the Devil's Fury compound. Grizzly will send someone else to help Devil's Boneyard."

"Leave?" I asked softly. "Now?"

"It's what you wanted, right? To get out of here? Away from Cinder and his bullshit excuses?" he asked.

"Well, yes, but I'd thought I'd have to wait. Are you sure this is the right thing to do?"

"I'll keep you safe, Meg. We all will. We'd die for you."

"Don't take things that far. Jordan would resurrect me just to kill me all over again if you died because of me."

He snickered, but I noticed he didn't deny what I'd said. Jordan loved fiercely and Dingo was one of her favorite people. Out of the two brothers I'd met, he was certainly her favorite. CJ tended to be a complete ass and I knew most of the club was getting tired of his shit. Couldn't blame them. He'd fucked up time and again, but I also knew it was because of Jordan and her tie to CJ that the Prospect hadn't been kicked out by now. Cinder had a soft spot for the women in the club, even if he wouldn't admit it. He might call Jordan a pain in the ass, but I knew he cared for her. Probably admired the hell out of her, she was so strong and independent. Nothing like me.

"How are we taking my things all the way to your compound?" I asked. "Not everything will fit on a bike."

"Reckless Kings brought a truck with them. You can ride with Crow and your belongings. The rest of us will surround the truck."

"With only three of you that's going to be difficult."

His phone started chiming again. It went off three times before he could even pull it from his pocket. He swiped the screen and then grinned.

"Looks like there will be more of us. Badger told the Dixie Reapers what was happening. Savior and Grimm are going to tag along, make sure we get there safely, then they'll come back to lend a hand here," he said.

"Fine. But if The Inferno comes to take me, just kill me before they get the chance. I've lived that kind of life before and I don't want to do it again," I said. "Promise me, Dingo. It's the only way I'll go with you."

"I promise," he said softly, then pulled me in for a quick hug.

I followed him down the road a ways before a black truck came hurtling toward us. I tensed, prepared to run, but Dingo lifted a hand and waved at the driver, even though I couldn't see who was driving. I hoped that meant he recognized the vehicle. When the truck came to a stop, a tall Native American man stepped out. He flashed me a tentative smile before focusing on Dingo.

"Jordan got what she could and swore she'd send the rest later. Cinder is in Church with everyone else, and he's asked where the rest of us are hiding. Not sure what bullshit excuse Hawk will give him, but the VP will come up with something," the man said before focusing on me again. "I'm Crow."

"Meg," I said with a little wave.

Crow motioned to the truck. "Your chariot awaits."

Dingo helped me up onto the passenger seat, made sure my seatbelt was fastened, and then he shut the door. He jumped into the bed of the truck and smacked the roof. Crow put the vehicle into gear and went back the way he'd come, pulling to a stop in front of the clubhouse. Havoc held a duffle bag in his hand and approached, then opened the back door and tossed it in before hefting a box and adding it as well. Dingo and the others going with us got on their bikes and surrounded the truck. Havoc gave me a lingering look, but I couldn't read his expression. With a slight nod, he shut the door and walked off.

I tensed as we approached the gate, wondering if they would just let me leave. Killian was there and he opened it up, then waved us through. My jaw dropped a little as I stared at Crow, who was silently laughing.

"Tinted windows, Meg. Did you notice that you couldn't see into the truck when I pulled up to get you? Dingo knew it was me earlier because he recognized the truck. No one can see in even though we can see out clearly," Crow said. "All that Prospect knows is that the Reckless Kings' truck is leaving the compound. He didn't see you get in. Doesn't know why I'm leaving or who is inside, and that's how we're going to keep it."

"Aren't you going to get into trouble for smuggling me away from the compound?" I asked.

"Nope. My VP gave me the order to get you to safety. Your life is in danger more than the others, and if you're feeling the need to escape your confines enough to walk around a place that isn't safe, then we need to get you somewhere secure where we damn sure know we don't have a rat."

"He didn't even notice I'm gone," I said, looking out the window.

Crow didn't say anything and silence reigned in the truck as the miles passed. We left the small Florida town I'd called home since being rescued, and eventually we left the state too. I didn't know where the Reckless Kings lived, and decided to nap. We made a few stops for bathroom breaks and food, but the men were always vigilant and made sure no one tried to hurt me or take me. When I saw the *Welcome to Tennessee* sign, I hoped we didn't have much farther to go.

I saw signs for the various towns and eventually it said we were nearing Nashville. Crow pulled off the highway and down a small road. Trees surrounded us and I had no idea where we were. Night had fallen and I could barely see anything beyond the headlights. We drove another twenty minutes before he turned down a path I hadn't even noticed. After what felt like forever, we came to a set of gates that said *Reckless Kings* above it. Crow waved at someone and a Prospect came forward.

"Already back, Crow?" he asked, then eyed the other bikers with us.

"Bringing precious cargo with me. Open the gates and let the others in too. They won't be staying but overnight, then they're heading back to Florida to deal with the Devil's Boneyard issue."

The Prospect nodded and pressed a button to open the gate.

We bypassed what had to be the clubhouse, but it looked nothing like the one at the Devil's Boneyard. This one looked more like a rustic lodge and was easily three times the size of the one I'd left behind. If I had to guess, I'd say the Reckless Kings had way more money than the Devils did. He continued down the road through the compound and stopped in front of a two-story home that resembled a massive cabin. Crow turned off the truck and got out, stretching before shutting the door. I hesitantly opened mine and stepped out.

"Where are we?" I asked.

The front door opened and one of the scariest men I'd ever seen stepped out. My steps faltered and my heart started pounding as I wondered if it was too late to run. Crow gripped my arm and tugged me forward. The giant smiled down at me, his features softening slightly.

"Welcome to the Reckless Kings, Meg. My name is Forge and I'm the Sergeant at Arms. We decided you'd be safest here."

I peered around him, hoping there would be a woman in the house, but I didn't notice one. My gaze landed on his again and he took a step back, motioning for me to go inside. Crow pulled me along, not stopping until he'd nudged me down onto a leather couch that was entirely too comfortable. He spoke quietly with Forge for a moment, then left only to return with my things.

I didn't know what to make of the situation, and I hoped I hadn't made a serious mistake. No one had hurt me or threatened me, but I was in a strange place with men I'd never met before. Maybe I hadn't made the wisest choice. The door opened again and Dingo strolled inside, a bag slung over his shoulder.

"Where you want me?" Dingo asked Forge.

"You can have the room next to Meg's. Since you're a familiar face, I'm sure she'll want you close by. You're both on the second floor."

"You're staying too?" I asked before Dingo could walk off.

He grinned at me and winked. "Can't leave my favorite girl among strangers. Besides, Jordan would kick my ass if I didn't send her regular updates on how you're doing. Once the threat has been neutralized, we can discuss something more permanent."

I nodded and watched him leave the room, meaning that I was now alone with Forge, a man who resembled more of a mountain than a human. The giant took a seat across the room and watched me. I took in the ink on his arms and peeking out of his shirt. He was intimidating, but if he could keep me safe, then I would adjust to his presence.

"Thank you for helping me," I said.

"Glad to do it," he said, smiling slightly. "Don't worry. Cinder will come to his senses and want you back."

I didn't think so. It was a nice thought, but not likely to ever happen. The man was probably glad that he wouldn't have to deal with me anymore, if he'd even noticed I wasn't there. For someone who had professed to be so worried about me, it was rather telling that I'd managed to slip away so easily. I only wished I could forget Cinder, but I knew that I would carry the memories for as long as I lived. I'd felt so safe with him, so cared for, until I'd learned he wanted me gone.

Even as my heart ached, I reminded myself that I was better off away from him. After everything I'd suffered, I deserved a bit of happiness, but not at the expense of someone else. If Cinder was miserable with me around, then it was a good thing I wasn't there anymore.

Chapter Seven

Cinder

I wasn't sure if I was relieved that it was time for Church, or disappointed that I was here and not discussing things with Meg. I hadn't missed the look on her face when she'd walked off earlier. Her bedroom door had been shut when I'd left the house, and I'd decided to give her some space. Hopefully, she'd be willing to listen when I was finished here. I hadn't meant to hurt her.

"What do you have for me?" I asked Shade.

"More like what do Wire and Outlaw have for you," he said. "They were able to remove Meg's picture from The Inferno's systems and took down that bidding site. Outlaw sent them a little present too, a virus that will disable their systems for a while. Not the perfect solution, but it buys a little time. Wire also said he was tracking where the photo originated, so he could have a name for us shortly."

"We need to send them a message," Scratch said. "Something that will make those fuckers think twice about coming after our women again."

"Meg's not mine," I said, "but I agree that we have to do something. This shit isn't acceptable."

Jackal snorted.

"What the fuck is that supposed to mean?" I demanded.

"Sure she isn't yours. No offense, Pres, but you've gotten closer to Meg than anyone here. You're the number one person she trusts, and that's saying something after the hell she's survived." Jackal shrugged. "If she's not yours, then I don't think she'll ever belong to anyone."

I didn't like what he was saying, but I couldn't exactly refute his words either. Meg really wasn't mine, would never be mine, but I knew he was partially right. If I didn't claim her, then she might not ever let someone get that close to her again. The woman had a lot of love to give, if she'd just allow some of those walls to come down. It was understandable why she felt the need to protect herself, to keep distance from everyone, but it was no way to live.

Havoc folded his arms and glared at the table, his muscles tense and his teeth grinding together. I didn't know what the fuck his problem was, but I'd gotten the biggest *fuck you* look when he'd stepped into Church. No one else had noticed so I'd let it slide until I could talk to him one on one. It wasn't like my Sergeant at Arms to do something like that, which meant something happened to piss him the fuck off, and he seemed to blame me for it. Havoc was too valuable to the Devil's Boneyard to start a fight over some bullshit, so I'd wait and hear him out before I decided if I was going to rip the fucker's head off for that disrespectful shit.

"Any other news?" I asked.

Cowboy lifted a hand. "I know I'm not an official Dixie Reaper anymore, but I help where I can… as long as that help isn't going to put a target on my wife and kids."

"From what we can tell, they're just after the Devil's Boneyard women," I said. "I can't guarantee they won't turn to the Reapers if they find out you're helping us. If you want to go home to protect your woman and kids, then I'd understand."

He shrugged and looked at the other Reapers. "I'll stay, unless I feel my family is in danger."

Hawk rubbed the bridge of his nose before pushing off the wall. The Reckless Kings were taking this threat seriously and sent their VP from Tennessee along with two other club members. I'd thought there were more coming, but something seemed to have come up last minute.

"I think it's safe to say The Inferno is a pain in all our asses," Hawk said. "Taking them down will be next to impossible, but if we tackle them one fucking town at a time, then we might make some headway. They don't have a big foothold in this area yet, but it's not stopped them from fucking with y'all."

"So take care of the issue here, then what?" Bats asked. "The Dixie Reapers haven't had an issue with them yet. I know we're family in a sense, but that doesn't mean we'd have been hit by The Inferno. By being here, we've put a target on our club, but no way we were going to sit out while women and kids were threatened."

Bats hadn't been around our club much, but right now I was glad the Reapers had sent him. He'd brought Cowboy, Zipper, and Flicker with him. Again, I'd thought there were others, but for some reason I had a half dozen men missing from the other clubs. I didn't know what emergency had cropped up, and I hadn't had time to ask. At the moment, my focus was making sure the women here were safe. After I dealt with this shit with my club, then I'd lend a hand to the others.

"If we stop them from infiltrating this area," Hawk said, "then we can handle another area, then another. Reckless Kings has a chapter in nearly every state from the east coast to the west coast. I've been told by my President that all the chapters are on board for taking out the trash."

I nodded. "So we need to come up with a plan to get rid of these fuckers in a way that will guarantee they don't darken our doorstep again. They're pissed we thwarted their plans before. Even though those weren't official Prospects or patched members, The Inferno is still seeing it as an attack on their club."

"They snatched Janessa and were going to kill her," Irish said, his face flushed in anger. "They didn't suffer nearly enough."

"Agreed," I said. "They came after us first and we were defending our own. They don't care, though. The Inferno don't give a shit about family, and especially don't care about women. They treat theirs like trash."

"How do you know that?" Cowboy asked.

Rocket stepped forward. "Because I know one of their women. She knows I'm Hades Abyss and doesn't want to bring trouble to the club, but she's given me some intel on what happens to women with The Inferno."

He gave a nod to Shade and a folder slid down the table. I flipped it open and wished I hadn't. Hearing what those fuckers did and seeing it were two different things. Picture after picture showed one abused woman after another. Each one tortured in a way that made my stomach turn. There was no way some of them had survived their injuries. I didn't know if these were club whores, their old ladies, or just random women they'd picked up to play with, but whoever they were, they needed help. I hadn't left Meg and the others in Colombia, and I knew I wouldn't sit back and let this stand in my own fucking country, a country I'd signed a contract to protect when I'd joined the Marines. I might not be active duty anymore, but as Meg had said... once a Marine always a Marine. It wasn't something you just shut off.

"Jesus," Hawk muttered as he looked at the pictures.

"Some are club whores," Rocket said. "Most are random selections. The ones who don't end up in the ground are sold to the highest bidder, no questions asked. I know you took down Silva in Colombia, but this is on our own soil."

"This shit can't stand," I said. "Hawk, I don't think going after them one at a time is going to be an option. If the sadistic fuckers are capable of this, and considering their substantial numbers, they'll just regroup, recruit more members, and be an even bigger threat than before."

"I'll call Beast," Hawk said, mentioning their President. "Whatever is decided, the Reckless Kings will help any way we can."

The VP for Hades Abyss ran a hand through his hair. "We're with you too, however far this goes, we're in it for the long haul."

"Thanks, Fox," I said.

"We have a new chapter," Fox said. "Based in Mississippi -- small place outside Jackson. I can contact their VP and give them a heads-up. I have a feeling they'll want in on this, even though their numbers are still fairly small. All of their officers are ex-military. Like you, they took an oath and still plan to uphold it."

"I'll take as many hands on deck with this shit as I can get," I said. "Contact anyone you can, see who you can get on board for a nationwide attack. If we take them on one chapter at a time, we leave ourselves vulnerable to retaliation. We'll strike all of them at the same time, not give them a chance to scramble and call in reinforcements. I want these fuckers in the goddamn ground. Hear me?"

I looked around the room and saw everyone nodding or acknowledging my words in some way. I wasn't playing with these assholes anymore. No one came after my family. The attack on Janessa was random at first, or so we'd thought. I'd assumed, incorrectly it seems, they went after her a second time because her vehicle was familiar. Now I wondered if they'd known she had a tie to this club or the Reapers and had sought to send a message to us. Now that the others in the club were targeted, I believed that had been phase one of their plan. Retaliation didn't seem as likely anymore, and if this was retaliation, then they were taking it too fucking far. Maybe the wannabes weren't acting entirely on their own. I now believed that someone higher up was pulling the strings and setting their little puppets off to create chaos. Even if they were coming back on us for taking out their men, this shit was intolerable. I'd been around too fucking long to take this lying down. No more. Not in my fucking town!

"We'll reconvene tomorrow morning, same time. That should give everyone a chance to discuss this shit with their clubs. Anyone in a day's driving distance who wants to join us, we'll find room for them." I banged the gavel. "Now get the fuck out of here."

Havoc remained behind and I studied him. I could tell there was something weighing on him, something that had infuriated him. He didn't say a fucking thing, just glared at me. He might be a big bastard, but I hadn't held my own as President of the Devil's Boneyard by my charm and good looks. If I had to, I could knock Havoc on his ass. Might be time I reminded him of that.

"You going to stare at me or tell me what the fuck is wrong with you?" I asked after another five minutes passed.

"What you did to Meg was wrong," he said. "I know you're my President, and you know I respect you, but that was fucked up, Cinder."

"What are you talking about?" I asked.

"You fucked her, then made her feel like a damn club whore," he said. "If you weren't going to start something real with her, then you should have scratched your itch with someone else."

I stood and placed my hands on the table, leaning into his space. Didn't matter that he was right. No one spoke to me like that. "Let's get one thing straight, boy. I'm the President of this fucking club, and a damn sight older than you. Unless you want me to kick the shit out of you, you'll keep a civil tongue in your head when speaking to me. What happened between me and Meg is exactly that… between us. I don't need you or anyone else telling me how to treat her."

"You sure about that?" He stood, then walked out.

I didn't know what the hell that last comment was about, but I was going to find out. I left the clubhouse and went home, intending to have a heart-to-heart with Meg. If she was upset and telling everyone else about it, then that shit was going to stop. She needed to talk to me and not my Sergeant at Arms. Or more likely, she'd confided in Jordan, which was about the same thing since that woman never kept shit from Havoc. I knew that Meg had been dealt a rough hand, and I'd gone along with everyone else and babied her, given her the space I thought she needed. Then she'd come to me and I'd taken her to my bed. I'd made it clear, repeatedly that I didn't do forever, so if she got it in her head that sleeping with me would change my mind, that was on her.

I stepped into my home, shut off the alarm, and found the women in the living room. All of them except Meg. Even the kids were accounted for, all staring at some cartoon on my sixty-five-inch TV. Not my intended use for it, but as long as they weren't screaming or tearing shit up I couldn't complain. Kids weren't my thing, never would be.

"Where is she?" I asked, wondering if Meg was still hiding in the bedroom.

Jordan crossed her arms over her chest and tilted her chin at a stubborn angle. "Not saying."

Clarity glanced at Jordan, then gave me a sympathetic look. Always the sweetheart of the group. She had some iron to her when she needed it, but for the most part, Clarity was a little angel. Her sweetness had attracted my VP and won over the hearts of every man in my club.

"She's not here, Cinder," Clarity said.

"Not. Here." I looked at each of them. "Where the fuck is she?"

Since they hadn't called anyone, I had to assume she'd left of her own accord and hadn't been snatched from my damn house. How the fuck she'd gotten out when the alarm was set I didn't understand. No one knew the passcode except me and Havoc. Unless... shit. With the way Havoc was acting, I could see him trying to help Meg out and turning the alarm off. It wasn't smart, though. There was too much danger out there for her, even inside my own gates.

"She left after you treated her like trash," Jordan said. "She's not on Devil's Boneyard property anymore. She was off the property before your precious Church even started."

I staggered back a step and looked at each of them, seeing the truth of Jordan's words in each of their faces. Meg had left the compound, knowing how dangerous it was out there. She'd preferred that to staying here with me? I hadn't meant to hurt her that badly, but I'd wanted to be honest with her. It had seemed like the right thing to do at the time, even if I hadn't maybe put it as gently as I should have, but now I had to wonder just how badly I'd fucked up.

"I've looked up to you," Jordan said. "But what you did with Meg was wrong, and you know it. She's fragile and you used her. If you didn't intend to keep her, then you should have never touched her."

Damn. Jordan and Havoc both saying the same fucking thing to me. I was pissed, but at the same time, I had to admit that they were both right. I'd known from the beginning I couldn't offer Meg a future, not at my side. I'd taken her anyway. I'd acted selfishly in that moment, and it had hurt a good woman.

"You're right," I said. "I shouldn't have touched her. I'll have to look for her. She can't get very far without any cash. I'll bring her back and talk to her, make her understand that it was never my intention to hurt her or treat her badly."

"Too late," Josie said. "She's not in Florida anymore."

Not in Florida? What the hell? And then it all made sense. All the missing men from today's meeting. They weren't on a sudden errand for their clubs. They were getting Meg out of here, away from the Devil's Boneyard, and away from me. It hurt, and I couldn't deny that I was scared as shit that something bad would happen to her. Just because I didn't plan to marry the woman didn't mean I wanted her to come to harm, get captured, or even killed.

"Where?" I asked.

"None of us will tell you," Jordan said as she brushed past me. "Not until you get your head out of your ass. When you can admit that Meg means more to you than a quick fuck, then maybe I'll tell you where she went. Don't bother asking the other women. They don't know anything other than Meg went away and left the state."

Jordan started to leave and I reached out to grab her arm, gripping tighter than I'd intended if her surprised cry was any indication. My Sergeant at Arms growled from the doorway and physically removed my hand from his wife before pulling her into his embrace.

"Havoc, what the fuck?" I asked.

He placed a hand on her belly and looked her over, and it suddenly made sense, his overprotectiveness, the rage I'd seen simmering just under the surface. The last time Jordan had been pregnant, he'd been in Colombia. He'd missed everything except the last part of her pregnancy, and it seemed he was a bit out of sorts this time around. This wasn't entirely about the way I'd treated Meg. He'd knocked up Jordan again, which meant he'd be a damn bear to live with until the kid was born. Fucking perfect.

"Congratulations seem to be in order," I said.

"We didn't want to say anything until the time was right," Jordan said. "I just found out two days ago."

"I wasn't trying to hurt your wife, Havoc, and you damn well know it," I said.

Jordan patted his chest and smiled up at her husband. "He's been like that with everyone. Poor Jackal gave me a hug when he dropped off Josie and the kids, and I thought Havoc would tear his head off."

"Can someone please tell me where Meg is? I need to make sure she's safe."

Jordan shook her head. Havoc glanced at me, then shrugged. "She made it to her destination in one piece without any trouble. That's as much as I'm saying right now."

Fucking fantastic. I should make an example of him, but part of me admired that he was trying to keep Meg safe, even if the asshole *was* protecting her from me. I let them leave and made myself scarce when the others came for their women. Should have known my VP wouldn't just leave shit alone. Scratch found me in my office, and he shut the door behind him.

He didn't say anything at first, just watched me. The man wasn't going to make me flinch, and he fucking knew it, which meant he was trying to figure out exactly what he wanted to say and how he wanted to say it. Scratch had never been one to sugarcoat shit, but I didn't know if he was about to talk to me as my VP or as my best friend. We'd been through a lot of shit together over the years, and I was closer to him than anyone.

Which also meant he knew me too fucking well. With just the two of us in this room, he would be more likely to speak his mind. It wasn't like I was going to beat the shit out of him or toss him from the club. The only way that would ever happen was if he turned traitor, and Scratch was the one man I knew I could count on, even if I'd had a quick flicker of doubt when I'd learned I had a rat in the club.

"Just say it already," I said.

"The women aren't too happy about how things went down with Meg," he said. "They liked her and were hoping she'd stay here indefinitely."

"I thought Jordan said no one else knew where Meg went."

"They don't, but they know something happened between the two of you, and that Meg is now gone. They heard what Jordan had to say, and Clarity is especially upset."

I closed my eyes a moment. "I'm sorry your wife isn't happy about this, Scratch, but what happened with Meg is no one's damn business. It seems Jordan stuck her nose where it didn't belong, and now Meg has vanished. I have no way to keep her safe if she's not here."

"Maybe it's for the best," he said. "You didn't want to claim her, and I know she was always underfoot. It's probably a good thing she's moved on. Eventually she'll trust someone else enough to let down her guard. It's her chance to find someone to give her forever and not just right now."

"Are you saying I can't give that to a woman?" I asked.

He snorted. "You keep saying it, have been saying it for years. I'm sorry that women tend to fuck you over, but Meg isn't like that and you damn well know it. I'm not here to bust your balls about it, but I wanted to let you know that the ladies aren't feeling particularly kind toward you at the moment."

Fucking great. Nothing caused trouble faster than pissed-off women, and now every last one in my club hated me. They didn't understand that I'd never lied to Meg, had never given her false hope. Whatever future she'd dreamed up was completely on her. Even if I should have kept my dick in my pants, I'd been as transparent as I could be, telling her from the start I wasn't the forever kind of guy. I didn't see how all this shit was now my fucking fault. And yet, I knew damn well if she were still here, still under my roof, I'd want her again.

Women. Pains in my Goddamn ass.

After my VP left, I shifted in my seat. I was beyond irritated that Meg had run, and that someone here had helped her. Just the thought of everything we'd done the night she'd been in my bed was enough to make me hard again, which made me all kinds of fucked-up. She was gone, in trouble, and here I was thinking about fucking her again. I closed my eyes and focused on the sounds she'd made as she came multiple times, the way she'd screamed my name. Before I even stopped to think about what I was doing, I had pulled the lube out and had my dick in my hand, stroking one out.

I'd find her, one way or another. And maybe when she came back, I'd get her back into my bed. Pound her sweet little pussy so good until we were both spent. Shackle her to my bed and do every filthy thing she'd allow. I bit my lips as I remembered how tight she'd been, how fucking perfect. A few more strokes and I came, groaning with my release. I cleaned up and shoved my cock back into my pants.

"Where the fuck are you, Meg?" I muttered to myself. I looked around my office, hoping I'd find a clue, or that inspiration would hit me and I'd suddenly just know where she was. None of that happened.

Instead, I went to stretch out in bed. My fucking sheets smelled like her and I closed my eyes and breathed her in. I'd screwed up. Even I could admit as much. I didn't have forever to give a woman, but maybe we could have come up with some other arrangement. I knew that I still wanted her. My cock twitched just thinking about being balls deep inside of her again.

"Face it, old man," I said to myself. "You're fucked and not in a pleasant way."

I closed my eyes a moment, trying to convince myself it was better that she was gone. Instead, I just imagined all the ways The Inferno could get their hands on her, and what it would mean for her. If those assholes dared to touch her, I'd rip them apart.

Chapter Eight

Meg

I'd had a fitful night of sleep, being in a strange place, and the scary looking Forge under the same roof hadn't helped my nerves any. Even though I knew Dingo was close and would watch over me, it had still been hard not to be afraid. Once I'd been shown to my room last night, I'd stayed here. It was silly -- probably. I didn't know Forge, or the Reckless Kings, but they seemed to want to help me, to keep me safe. I'd thought Cinder would do that, but I'd been wrong. Well, sort of wrong. He'd kept me safe from everyone else, but he hadn't protected me from a broken heart.

My eyes misted with tears and I placed a hand over the ache in my chest as I thought about his words. He'd never lied to me, never made promises of any kind other than he would protect me, but he hadn't protected me from himself. The fact he'd slept with me and then pushed me aside hurt more than anything I'd suffered before. I could admit it was because I was falling in love with the man.

There was a knock on the door and I held the covers up over my chest as I sat up in bed. "Come in," I called out tentatively, unsure who was on the other side.

Dingo popped his head around the door as he pushed it open and gave me a smile. He didn't cross the threshold, but the smile slipped from his face as he saw the first tear slide down my cheek.

"Meg, what's wrong? Did I scare you when I knocked?"

I shook my head and pressed my lips together, not wanting to admit how foolish I'd been to fall in love with a man who would never want me. Not for more than a quick fuck here and there, although the one night and morning seemed to have been more than enough for him.

"I know you've had a rough time of it recently, and the stress can't be good for you. The Reckless Kings would like their doctor to check you over, make sure everything is all right. He has a small room in the clubhouse where he treats people."

I snorted, having been around the Devil's Boneyard long enough to know what types of treatment the bikers would need. Stitches and removal of bullets were on the top of the list.

"He's a good guy, Meg," Dingo said. "Graduated from Johns Hopkins, which I've been assured is a top-ranking medical school."

"Then why is he working with bikers?" I asked. "No offense."

"None taken. As brilliant as they say Dr. Kestral is, I'm sure he had his pick of any hospital in the country. And to answer your question, his baby brother is a Reckless King."

I didn't know what to make of that. I'd never given their families much thought, to be honest. It made me wonder if Cinder had family out there. Were there siblings, parents, or nieces and nephews he'd never mentioned? Of course, we hadn't exactly discussed much. I hadn't even been completely honest with him about where I came from, but that had only been because it was too painful. I'd known my parents were gone and that I didn't have anyone left to care if I was alive or not.

"I'll see Dr. Kestral," I said.

"Get showered and dressed. I think Forge is cooking breakfast," he said. "Or someone is. I smell bacon and eggs."

I nodded, and after he shut the door I gathered my clothes and went into the hall bathroom. As much as I'd have liked to linger in the shower, I washed quickly and pulled on a pair of jeans and a plain long-sleeved tee. My hair was still wet and I didn't see a hairdryer, so I braided it to keep it out of my way. I carried my pajamas back to the guest room and set them on the foot of the bed, then straightened the covers. There was a chill to the wood floors of the house so I quickly grabbed some socks and my shoes. After smoothing on some lip balm and a little moisturizer, I headed downstairs.

Forge was sitting at the table with a cup of coffee and Dingo was across from him. A tall woman with blonde hair stood at the stove, but she didn't acknowledge me when I entered the room. Her rumpled barely-there clothes made me wonder if she'd stayed over, not that it was any of my business. Forge hadn't seemed to have a wife or old lady, but it didn't mean there wasn't a steady woman in his life. Unless… I swallowed hard. He wouldn't ask a club whore to cook for us, would he? I hadn't seen much of those women at the Devil's Boneyard. I knew they were there, but they didn't live at the compound. Whenever the sun set and the music started pumping at the clubhouse, they'd come in droves to try and snag the attention of one of the guys. I'd seen them from a distance but had never spoken to one.

Considering my past, I had a hard time imagining anyone wanting that kind of life. I didn't look down on her for her choices, I just didn't know why she'd pick that type of life. Even though I had learned to trust the Devil's Boneyard members, it didn't mean I wanted to hop into bed with them. Well, except Cinder. I'd gladly get into his bed again, but not as one of the women he'd toss out the next day. I wanted to be there every night and wake up to him every morning. Wouldn't happen, but it didn't stop me from yearning for it. Now that I'd had a taste, I wanted more.

The woman scooped something out of the skillet and set it on the plates, then turned off the burner. She turned with two plates in her hands, and I could tell that she'd had a hard night. Possibly several. She served Forge and Dingo, then cast a glare at me before stomping out of the room. I went to stand and retrieve the other plate, but Forge reached out and placed a hand on my arm, making me jolt.

"Sorry," he said, as he released me. "You're a guest so you're damn sure not getting your own plate."

I didn't know what to say, so I just sat quietly. He turned his gaze toward the door where the other woman had vanished and his jaw tightened.

"Bunny!" he yelled. "Get your ass in here."

She appeared in the kitchen doorway, arms folded as she stared at him.

"What the fuck was that shit?" he demanded. "I have more than one guest. I'd suggest you serve her food as well."

She sneered at me and didn't move. "I'm not serving the whore. She can get her own damn food. Bad enough I had to cook it."

Forge stood, his chair scraping against the floor. As he moved toward her, I saw her pale a bit and her lower lip started to tremble. Dingo ate his food, ignoring the drama, but I couldn't stop looking their way. Forge was a bit taller than her, but the way he stared down his nose at her, and the contempt rolling off him, would have made me flinch if it'd been directed at me. He was menacing even if he wasn't as big as Havoc. I could see why he was the Sergeant at Arms.

"The only whore in this house right now is you," he said. "Get the fuck out. As of this moment, you're no longer permitted in my house. You don't touch me, don't even fucking look at me."

"Forge, I…" She clamped her lips tight when he growled at her. After a slight squeak, she scurried out of the room and I heard a door slam.

Forge ran a hand through his hair and sighed, then got the third plate from beside the stove and set it down in front of me. His touch was light as he patted my shoulder, then reclaimed his seat, eating as if nothing had just happened. Is that how Cinder saw me? Disposable? I looked down at my plate, but I suddenly wasn't very hungry.

"Sometimes the club whores forget their place," Forge said. "Shouldn't have asked her to come into my house. Won't happen again. I'm sorry she disrespected you, Meg."

"It's fine," I said softly.

"No, it sure as fuck isn't," he said. "I don't know what's going on with you and the Devil's Boneyard President, but I have no doubt he's going to come looking for you sooner or later. If he'd seen Bunny slight you like that, or call you a whore, I can only imagine how he would have reacted."

Dingo snorted. "Never seen him violent with a woman, but he definitely wouldn't have let her get away with that shit. The man is in denial that he cares about Meg, but it's clear for everyone else to see."

"He doesn't want me," I said, picking at my food. "He wanted me gone, so I left. He won't come looking for me."

"We'll see," Dingo said.

After we finished eating, what little I could manage to swallow, Dingo took me to the clubhouse. I hadn't known what to expect, but my jaw dropped at how beautiful it was on the inside. The floors, ceilings, and walls were all a gorgeous pine, and polished to a high shine. Natural light came in from windows that were high up across the front, and I saw a balcony overlooking the main floor, the railing across made from what seemed to be tree limbs, also sanded and polished to match the rest of the clubhouse. I was in awe.

"I've never seen anything like this place," I whispered to Dingo.

He chuckled. "Yeah, it's something. I was told the doctor's room was back this way."

I followed him to the back of the clubhouse, down a hall with several doors. I heard a buzzing and we passed an open door where a man was getting a tattoo. It looked like a professional set-up inside. There was another room that said *Massage* on the door, and then we approached one that said *Dr. Kestral.* The other doors didn't have any writing and were all shut, so I had no clue what was behind them.

Dingo knocked on the doctor's door. The young-looking dark-haired man who opened it wasn't what I had expected. But then, nothing around this place was what I would have imagined. The doctor didn't seem old enough to have completed medical school, but he wore a lab coat and had a stethoscope around his neck. There was kindness shining in his eyes and he gave me an easy smile.

"You must be Meg," he said.

I nodded and stepped into the room when he motioned me inside. I glanced at Dingo, a mild panic seizing me when I realized he was still in the hall.

"You might want privacy," Dingo said. "I'll hear you if you call out."

I swallowed hard and got onto the padded table as Dr. Kestral closed the door. I noticed he didn't lock it, which eased my fear a bit. The doctor wasn't as heavily muscled as most of the bikers I'd been around since being saved, but he seemed trim and fit.

"I'm Martin Kestral," he said, holding out his hand.

I shook it, not bothering to say my name since he already knew it. I spent the next twenty minutes answering questions. Anything pertaining to sex or my period made my cheeks warm, but I gave him truthful answers.

"Meg, I requested your files from the doctor you saw after coming back to the United States. You mentioned that you thought you were barren because you'd never conceived."

I nodded.

"Were you not aware you'd been on birth control?" he asked.

"Birth control?" I blinked. "But I never took pills or anything."

"The files I received show that you had received shots in Colombia. Is that correct?"

"Yes. They said it was vitamins or something."

"How often did you get them?" he asked.

"Every three months."

He tapped his lips with his fingers and shook his head. "Meg, I don't know how to tell you this, but I think they were giving you doses of birth control in your injections. You aren't barren. In fact, all the scans and blood work done by your doctor in Alabama show that you're perfectly healthy and capable of having children."

I felt the blood drain from my face and I placed a hand over my belly. If that was true, then I'd inadvertently lied to Cinder and could very well be carrying his baby. My hands shook and the room spun a little. What had I done? He would be furious if he ever found out. A whimper escaped my lips and I swayed.

Dr. Kestral reached out and gripped my arms, keeping me upright. "Meg, I need you take some deep breaths and calm down."

"I told him I couldn't get pregnant," I said softly.

"It was an honest mistake. I'm sure Cinder wouldn't hold it against you. You said that your last period was three weeks ago. If you're still here in a week and you miss your cycle, let me know and we can do a pregnancy test. We can do both blood and urine just to be safe."

I felt a tear slide down my cheek and I hastily wiped it away. Tears hadn't gotten me anywhere in life, and they certainly wouldn't change the fact I was pregnant. Or not. Maybe I wasn't pregnant. Plenty of women had trouble conceiving, so it was possible I was one of them. There was no point panicking until I knew something for certain. Like Dingo had pointed out, I'd been under a lot of stress and it wasn't good for me.

Dr. Kestral checked my eyes, ears, and nose, then gave me the all clear. He helped me off the table and opened the door, letting Dingo into the room. Jordan's brother clasped my arm and led me back through the clubhouse and out into the fresh air. We didn't immediately go back to Forge's place, but Dingo let me just stand there and decompress for a moment.

"Better?" he asked.

"Yeah. Thanks."

"Bad news?" he asked.

"Maybe. I won't know for a bit."

His gaze dropped to my stomach and I knew he understood what I meant. Part of me wanted to ask if anyone from the Devil's Boneyard had contacted him, but if Cinder was relieved that I was gone, I wasn't sure I wanted to know. Some small part of me hoped that he hadn't really wanted me to leave, that he was looking for me, wanted me. I knew it was stupid to dream such things. Women like me didn't get a happily ever after with the man of their dreams. As far as I knew, none of the other women from Colombia had found their Mr. Right, even though a few had been brave enough to start dating. Some of them kept in touch with the Devil's Boneyard, but not all of them did.

Dingo and I walked back to Forge's house in silence, and the Sergeant at Arms didn't say a word as I entered the house. He did give a nod of his head toward the living room and I went to sit down. He sat in a chair a few feet away from me and Dingo claimed the other end of the couch. Forge reached for a remote and started a movie. His selection made me laugh a little.

"Heard you were partial to this one," he said as one of my favorite movies from the eighties started.

"You heard right. But you don't have to watch this with me. I know most men don't care about romantic movies," I said.

"Do I look like I'm worried about losing my man card?" he asked.

"Um, no?" I looked him over and had to admit that no one would ever accuse him of being anything other than manly.

"Enjoy the movie, Meg. Don't ever hesitate to ask for what you want. I might be a hard-ass, but I want you to be comfortable while you're here," Forge said.

"Is that why you're letting Dingo stay at your house?" I asked.

He nodded.

"Thank you," I said after a few minutes. "For helping me, for giving me a place to stay, and trying to set me at ease. Being around strange men is still something I struggle with, but I'm getting better. I think."

Forge cleared his throat. "Listen, my Pres chewed my ass out after you left earlier. I'm sorry I had that club girl in here. Won't happen again. I'd already decided not to have them over, but he pointed out that those women might make you uncomfortable, and that's the last thing any of us want."

"I'm sorry you got into trouble over me," I said.

"Not over you. Over my stupidity. He made a valid point and I feel like an asshole for not thinking with my head instead of my dick when I asked her over last night."

"I don't want you to change how you live your life just because I'm here," I said. "That wouldn't be fair of me."

Forge smiled faintly. "I'll be fine. Probably wouldn't be a bad idea to lay off the women for a few days or so anyway. Those girls come around because they want to. None of us would ever force any of them, but there are rules they're supposed to follow and sometimes they forget that. They tend to create more drama than any man wants to deal with, so taking a step back isn't a hardship."

I didn't like that Forge felt like he needed to change his habits just because he was letting me stay in his home. It didn't seem right, but I wasn't going to argue with him. It sometimes still stunned me just how sweet the bikers could be. They looked all gruff and fierce, and some were the very same in personality, but I'd found that most had a soft spot when it came to women and kids.

As I'd watched the couples at the Devil's Boneyard, I'd also discovered that those men loved hard when they found the right woman. I'd hoped to be that woman for Cinder, but maybe he had been right when he said he'd never settle down with anyone. I wanted to argue with myself that if I'd believed him I would have stayed out of his bed, but I knew better. Those moments, even if they would never happen again, were precious to me. I'd remember him forever, whether there was a baby or not. Deep down, I knew if I was pregnant that I would need to tell him. No matter how angry he got, he had a right to know he had a kid out there in the world. I didn't expect him to take care of us, but I wouldn't take away his choice to know his child either.

"You're thinking too hard," Dingo said.

"If I'm pregnant, I have to tell him," I said.

He grumbled under his breath. "No offense, but you don't owe him shit. He made you feel like you had to leave the only home you've had since being rescued. It was a shit thing for him to do. The man is one hell of a president, but he doesn't seem to know a damn thing about how to treat a woman."

"Probably been with club whores too long," Forge muttered. "Doubt I'd know how to treat a good woman either. Too used to women just spreading their legs when they see me."

"I'm no better than those women," I said.

Forge paused the movie and leaned forward, staring at me hard. "I want to be real clear on something, Meg. What happened to you is far different from the women who come here. They're here because they want to be, they like getting fucked by multiple men, showing off their bodies. You weren't given a choice. Not to discount any of the club girls. There's nothing wrong with what they're doing, but they're free spirits who don't want to be tied down. There are some who are here giving it up to anyone and everyone just because they're hoping one of us will decide to keep them. I have no doubt if you'd been left alone, allowed to grow up in your loving home, that you'd have gone to college or married some nice guy and settled down. You're the forever kind of woman, and Cinder knows that. Anyone who meets you can tell that right off."

"He doesn't want the forever kind of woman," I said. "Or kids. He likes his life the way it is and doesn't want any complications."

"Then maybe you need to work on forgetting him and move forward. Cinder isn't the only man in the world, baby girl, and I can promise that some guy would feel like the luckiest bastard if you gave him a chance," Forge said.

There was a knock at the front door and Forge stood. I couldn't see who was on the front steps, but I could hear another man's voice. Forge returned with Dr. Kestral on his heels. The young doctor gave me a tentative smile, as if he weren't certain I was all right with him stopping by. I didn't have any say in the matter. It wasn't my house, and I wasn't a part of the

Reckless Kings. Forge gave a subtle nod of his head and Dingo got up and followed him out of the room. I watched them, curious what was going on.

"You seemed upset earlier," Dr. Kestral said. "I wanted to make sure you were all right."

"I'll be fine," I said. "Just processing everything."

Dr. Kestral waved a hand to the chair Forge had vacated. "Mind if I sit?"

I shook my head and he walked over to the chair and eased down, almost as if he were worried any quick movements would scare me. He wasn't completely wrong about that. I did still flinch sometimes. The doctor had been kind, though, and I didn't think he'd do anything to hurt me. Not unless it was a painful medical procedure that couldn't be avoided.

"I hope you don't mind, but I called the Devil's Boneyard to ask a few questions about your past," he said.

I tensed and he reached for me, but stopped a few inches shy of touching me.

"Not the President," he said. "I spoke with their Sergeant at Arms, who helped get you set up here. He told me about your time in Colombia, the things you were forced to endure, and how very brave and strong you are. I would have to agree with him."

"I'm not either of those things."

"You are," Dr. Kestral insisted. "Meg, you're an incredible woman to have faced that and still be standing. From what I heard, you were even happy until this latest development. It's not your fault you trusted your heart to the wrong man."

I chewed on my lip a moment. "Dr. Kestral --"

"Martin," he said, making my head jerk a little. "Call me Martin. Please."

I was getting a feeling that he wasn't here for medical reasons at all, and I recalled what Forge had said right before that knock at the door. Had he somehow known the doctor was stopping by? Had he been trying to tell me that I should give Dr. Kestral a chance? I wasn't ready, might never be ready, to be intimate with another man. It had taken me a year to get to that point of trust with Cinder.

"Martin, it was really sweet of you to come and check on me, but if you're hoping there can be something between us --"

"Meg, no. I … I mean, I'd love for you to consider dating me, if you decide to stick around, but I mostly wanted you to know that I can be your friend. If you need anything, want to talk, or just need a shoulder to cry on, then I'm happy to be there for you. In any capacity you'll allow. You seem like a sweet woman who's had a hard road to travel."

"All right. Martin."

He smiled, and I had to admit he was a very good-looking man. Maybe if I hadn't shared that experience with Cinder the cute doctor would have given me a spark, or at least a faint tingle. But I didn't feel anything. I worried that Cinder had ruined me for all other men. Too bad it didn't go both ways. I seriously doubted I had ruined him for other women. I didn't doubt that he wouldn't hesitate to sleep with someone else. I wasn't special to him. It still hurt, and I didn't know how long before I was able to move past the pain of rejection, but I knew I couldn't wallow in self-pity.

"I can always use a friend," I finally said, giving him a slight smile. "But I know I'm not ready for anything beyond that, and I may never be ready."

"No pressure," he said. "Just know that I'm here if you need anything."

He stood and left the room. I heard him speaking to someone softly before the front door opened and shut. Dingo came back into the room and reclaimed his spot. He didn't say anything, but his expression was shuttered, which was unusual for him. Normally, I could see exactly how he felt.

"Dingo, everything okay?" I asked.

"Cinder knows you're gone. He demanded to know where you were, said he couldn't protect you if you weren't there with him. Havoc and Jordan aren't saying anything. No one is."

"How long did it take before he realized I wasn't there?" I asked.

"After Church. He went back to his house to talk to you. Guess he figured you were hiding somewhere inside before he'd left. When Jordan told him you weren't there anymore, weren't even in the same state, I heard he got a little angry."

"He'll get over it," I said. "Probably went about business as usual last night and this morning."

"And if he didn't? What if he really does miss you, Meg? What if he just needed time to realize how important you are to him?" Dingo asked.

"Then he'll come for me. And if he doesn't, then I have my answer."

He nodded and sighed. For the first time since leaving the Devil's Boneyard compound, I had to wonder if I'd done the right thing. What if Dingo was on to something? What if Cinder really did want me there and I'd overreacted? No. I remembered his words, the way he'd tried to push me away. Regardless of what he said now, he hadn't wanted me there. I'd given him exactly what he wanted. I'd just have to wait and see if he changed his mind.

And if he never came for me, then I'd have to figure out the next step in my life. There could very well be another person growing inside of me right now. It might not just be me that I had to worry about from now on. Whatever happened, I knew that I had to push through the pain. I'd survived worse than a broken heart.

Chapter Nine

Cinder

Wire had contacted Shade with information on our rat three days after I discovered Meg was gone. It shouldn't have surprised me, not really, and yet I'd stared at CJ as Havoc restrained him. Even knowing that he'd monumentally fucked up, the Prospect glared at me with nothing but hatred.

"Why, CJ?" I'd asked. "You even sold out your sister."

"All those bitches were welcomed into this club with no questions asked, and that fucking Meg was the worst. Spending all that time at your house, winning you over. I've paid my dues and busted my ass to be patched in, and here I am, still fucking waiting."

I'd glanced at Havoc and the other officers gathered around CJ. They looked every bit as furious as I felt, and as much as I wanted to take vengeance for Meg, she wasn't mine. Not really. Scratch and Havoc had families who required justice. CJ wasn't leaving the compound, not in one piece anyway. I knew Havoc would cut up his body and have him dumped in several areas.

"See that it's done," I'd said before walking off.

That was two weeks ago. It had taken a damn week to get shit organized nationwide, and another to gather supplies and set everything into motion. Every chapter of the Reckless Kings was ready to go, as were their allies. Dixie Reapers, Hades Abyss, and Devil's Fury were on board too. There would be a massive strike against every chapter of The Inferno that we could locate. I'd heard rumblings there were some that were underground, so I knew there was a chance these assholes would pop up again, but hopefully we'd put the fear of God into them and send a message they couldn't ignore. Don't fuck with one of us, or you fuck with all of us. While my club took care of the issue here, everyone else would handle The Inferno in their own areas.

I'd spent nearly every fucking night wide awake, smelling Meg on my sheets, and worrying if she was safe. I should have changed them, but something had held me back. I hadn't wanted to lose that last little bit of my connection to her. I knew there were people here who could tell me her location, but short of torturing it out of my own men and those who had come to help, there wasn't a damn thing I could do. Part of me had to admire that they were protecting her, but I wanted to be the one to keep her safe.

She'd been gone three nights before I realized how much I missed her. The way she sang as she cleaned and cooked, her scent, the sweet smile she always gave me, and the feel of her in my arms. We'd only had that one night together, but it was enough for me to know that I didn't want another woman. I'd fucked up, pushed her away and made her feel unwelcome. Now I was paying the price, and so was she. This was her home and I'd driven her out of here into the unknown.

"Pres, need your head in the game," Jackal said softly as we stared at the building we were about to attack.

I tried to shake thoughts of Meg from my mind. Jackal was right. I needed to focus or I'd get people killed, possibly even myself. Then who would keep Meg safe? Once this was over, I was going after her.

One way or another, I'd get someone to tell me her location. I needed to make things right with her, tell her that I missed her, needed her, and I had to hope that she'd agree to come home where she belonged. Not just at the compound, but under my roof and in my bed.

"Everyone remember what they're supposed to do?" I asked, looking at the men with me. Everyone nodded, and I motioned to proceed.

I crouched as I slowly made my way toward the house, my gun drawn. The safety was already off and I was prepared to fire when necessary. Havoc hunkered down under a window on one side of the house, and Scratch did the same on the other. They tossed smoke bombs inside, and as I'd hoped would happen, the men inside ran out.

Just one problem. There weren't nearly as many of them as there had been when we'd done our recon. Where the fuck were the others? I circled the building and checked the perimeter. Jackal, Cobra, and Irish crept into the house, protective gear over their faces and their bodies. I heard shots fired and wanted to rush inside, but the smoke hadn't cleared. More shots and then silence. My men came out, not a mark on them. Irish removed the mask over his face and his gaze met and held mine.

"Pres, we have a problem."

"What is it?" I asked.

"There are pictures inside on the walls. They know where Meg went, and I think they sent men after her," Irish said. "There's shots of her at one of the Reckless Kings' compounds. I don't know how they found her, but we need to find out. If there's another rat, better to know now. Looks like they used a telephoto lens so no telling how far or how close they were when the pictures were taken."

I scanned the men with me, my hand still gripping my gun tightly. Movement in the trees caught my attention and I took off. Whoever was out there, they were moving fast and with purpose. I was getting too damn old for this shit, but I pushed myself, refusing to back down and let the man escape. I fired off a few shots and hit him in the leg. It slowed him enough that I was able to tackle him to the ground. After a few fists to the face, the man just groaned and didn't fight back.

"Where are the others?" I demanded.

He spat at me. "Not telling you shit."

I smashed my fist into his jaw again. "Where. The. Fuck. Are. They?"

He grinned, blood coating his teeth. "Going after your whore."

My body tensed and I went ice cold. The fucker just grinned up at me like he hadn't a care in the world.

"Boss has plans for her," he said, then bucked his hips a few times. "Lots of plans."

A red haze covered my vision and the next few minutes passed in a blur. The next thing I knew, Havoc was prying me off the man who was now covered in blood, both eyes blackened and swelling, his nose broken, and a few teeth missing.

"Easy, Cinder," Havoc said. "If you kill him, then we can't get information from him. Think of Meg."

I growled and tried to get to him again, but Havoc refused to let go. I'd beat that fucker to death if he thought for one second he was going to hurt Meg. I knew exactly what he'd meant. They were going to rape her before they sold her, and I wasn't about to let that shit happen.

Havoc turned his head and yelled over his shoulder. "Tie him up and get him to the compound. We'll find out what he knows. Someone call Reckless Kings and give them a heads-up."

"On it," Phantom said.

Scratch moved up beside us and placed a hand on my shoulder. I met his gaze and the compassion I saw there was enough to deflate some of my fury. They were going to hurt my Meg. I hadn't thought I wanted her, hadn't wanted to keep any woman, but she'd slipped beneath my defenses and now I couldn't imagine a world without her in it.

"We'll save her," Scratch said. "She'll be back with you where she belongs."

"'Bout fucking time," Havoc muttered before he released me.

Phantom moved closer and cleared his throat. "Um, Pres. The Reckless Kings aren't answering. She's at their Tennessee compound, or she was. What do you want to do?"

"Get answers from the asshole that was just hauled away," I said. "Then I'm going after Meg, wherever she may be."

We walked back to our bikes and rode to our compound. When I cleared the gates, I kept going. Unlike the barn the Dixie Reapers kept at the back of their place, and the shithole we'd had at our old compound, I'd put in an underground dungeon of sorts. It was well hidden by what appeared to be an innocuous building, a warehouse where we kept extra stock of basic shit like toilet paper, paper towels, and anything else the clubhouse might need. Or so it would look to anyone who decided to snoop. Nothing incriminating.

I activated the hidden compartment in the floor and the door slid open. As I descended the stairs, I could hear the asshole we'd captured cussing everyone out. The underground area encompassed a space big enough for three cells, and a special room that Havoc liked to call his torture chamber. Except this time, he wouldn't be the one dealing with the trash we'd hauled home.

The man had been stripped of his clothes and strapped to a chair over a drain. One wall and a table were filled with different tools Havoc liked to use when *negotiating* with prisoners. The idiot just grinned at me, a wild look in his nearly shut eyes as if he didn't fear a damn thing. And maybe he was so batshit crazy that he really didn't. No one sane would ever join The Inferno. When we'd done our recon, we'd only seen Prospects and some hang arounds who were hoping to have that honor. But this guy… he was a patched member, and I'd felt like I'd won the damn lottery. The slippery bastards hadn't come this close before, always sending the minions to do their dirty work.

"You're going to tell me what you know about Meg," I said.

"I ain't telling you shit," the man said.

"Oh, you'll tell me."

I started stripping off my clothes until I was only in my boxers. No sense getting blood on my clothes and ruining them. The man scanned me, his eyes landing on the tattoo on my bicep. It was the first sign of hesitation I'd seen in his eyes. Whoever he was, he now knew what I'd done for my country. I wasn't just a Marine. I'd been part of a special team, the kind you didn't fuck with and live to tell the tale.

"They said you were just some old man," he muttered.

"You really think some old man could hold my position in this club as long as I have?"

"Still not saying anything."

"Oh you will. I have all the time in the world."

The leer he sent my way made my blood chill in my veins.

"You might. Your precious whore doesn't," he said, then cackled. "She's gonna be broken in real well, then a special buyer has won the pleasure of her company."

I took several deep breaths and tried to lock down all the shit brewing in my mind and my soul. I couldn't help Meg if I let my emotions rule me. I hadn't been the best at what I'd done by being sloppy. I cleared everything from my head and focused on the man in the chair.

I walked over to the wall and table of various instruments and picked up a set of pliers. When I approached the man, he just smirked, not a fear in the world. Or someone else would have thought. I saw the look in his eyes, saw what he tried to hide from everyone else, but I wasn't fooled. He was about two seconds from pissing himself. I moved to the side, in case he did exactly that, and gripped the hand fastened to the arm of the chair. One at a time, I pulled off his fingernails. The man's jaw tightened and his body tensed, but he didn't give me the satisfaction of hearing his screams.

I tossed the pliers aside, knowing that anything I used would need to be cleaned before it was put away. I picked up a small knife with a blade so dull you'd have to saw through whatever you wanted to cut. Making sure the asshole saw it, I went to work. Took some doing, but I carved off his nipples, enjoying the sound of his screams and the begging he did.

"There's only one way to end this quicker," I said. "You're not getting out of here alive, but you can die faster. Tell me where to find Meg and how you fucking found her to begin with. Reckless Kings aren't answering the phones."

"My club diverted their attention," he said.

I threw the knife to the side and picked up one a bit sharper, then started making shallow cuts. After the fourth swipe, he whimpered and begged for a reprieve.

"Then tell me everything," I said.

"Your girl was left with only five men protecting her. The Inferno went in and captured her. The men who took her weren't as sneaky as they thought. The Inferno has eyes everywhere. Just because we didn't snatch her off the road didn't mean we had no idea where she'd been taken. A bunch of bikers surrounding a blacked-out SUV? Didn't take a genius to figure out precious cargo was on board, especially with multiple clubs guarding it."

"And the men with her?" I asked.

"Left for dead."

I glanced at Havoc and he stepped away, pulling his phone from his pocket. I wanted to go make sure those men were okay, but I needed more information. He'd said that The Inferno had taken Meg, but not where.

"Your whore is locked up tight," he said after a few more slices along his stomach. "They want to make a deal."

"Deal?" I asked.

"You turn yourself over to them and they won't sell your girl. Without a president over Devil's Boneyard, this territory will be easy to take over." He blinked and I could tell that he was close to passing out from the pain I'd inflicted.

"And Meg goes free?" I asked.

He gave a humorless laugh. "Not a chance. She's going to be well fucked, if they haven't started already. But she won't be sold to The Butcher."

"Butcher?" I asked.

"Man overseas. He breaks them down, makes sure they have no hope left, and then the carnage starts. Broadcasts it, takes bids on what happens to her. Highest bid wins."

I wanted to throw up, but I held it together. I had to save Meg, one way or another. If I turned myself over to The Inferno, maybe it would buy some time for someone else to get Meg out of there. Right now, I didn't give a shit what happened to me. I'd lived a long life, and I'd had an amazing woman in my arms even if it was just the one night. But Meg had her entire life ahead of her.

"Where do I go?" I asked.

"Map is in my pants pocket," he said. "Go alone or she suffers even more."

I glanced at Havoc who was already pulling the paper out. He glanced at it before handing it over, and I knew he'd memorized the location with that one look. It was one of the things he did best.

"Kill him," I said. "But not too fast."

He nodded and I heard the man screaming as I gathered my clothes and went back upstairs to the warehouse area. There was a small bathroom up there and I quickly rinsed off before tossing my bloody boxers in the trash and pulling my clothes on. When I went to get on my bike, Scratch placed a hand on my arm.

"We're going to come for you," he said. "Both of you."

I glanced at the phone in his hand and knew he'd activated the cameras down there and seen and heard everything. I gave him a nod, not really caring one way or another if they saved me, as long as Meg made it out of there alive. I got on my bike and didn't stop riding until I'd pulled up to the gates at the place on the map. Despite the long hours to reach my destination, I hadn't dared stop for more than gas along the way, not wanting to leave Meg waiting another moment. Men immediately surrounded me, cuffing my hands and shoving me to my knees.

A gun was placed against the back of my head but I wouldn't give them the satisfaction of hearing me beg, or of closing my eyes. I'd been through too much shit in my life to be weak now. A whimper drew my attention and my head whipped in that direction. One of the brutes had Meg held tightly in front of him. Her clothes were dirty and torn, but she seemed to be in one piece. Her gaze met and held mine, and my heart nearly stalled in my chest.

"Don't make her watch," I said. "If you're going to kill me, then do it, but don't make her witness it."

"Aww. So sweet," the asshole with the gun said. "Bring the whore over here."

Meg was shoved forward, then forced to the ground in front of me. Tears slid down her cheeks as she reached out, her hands shaking.

"Tell him, bitch," her captor said, giving her a shove so that she fell against me.

It felt good to have her hands on me, and part of me was happy I'd gotten to see her one last time. I just hoped they wouldn't make her stay while they executed me. The man smacked her in the back of the head.

"I said tell him," he demanded again.

"Cinder, I..." She licked her lips and gave me a pleading look. "I love you."

The man smacked her harder. "That wasn't what you were supposed to tell him, you stupid cunt."

More tears trailed down her cheeks.

"Whatever it is, Meg, it's okay. I'm sorry I pushed you away. I'm sorry for everything, and I don't want you to think any of this is your fault."

"I'm pregnant," she said softly. "The baby is yours."

The men around us laughed. It felt like the earth had been jerked out from under me and I was free-falling. Pregnant? Meg was carrying my kid? I dropped my gaze to her still flat belly and tried to imagine her swollen with my child.

"I didn't lie," she said. "I really thought I couldn't have children."

"What... How?" I asked.

"The Colombians were dosing me with birth control and I didn't know it. The injections stopped after you saved me. I was never infertile. I'm so sorry."

"Meg, you have nothing to be sorry for," I said. I swallowed hard, knowing that I needed to tell her. It might be the last thing I ever got to say to her. "I love you, sweetheart. I should have never pushed you away."

She wrapped her arms around my waist and cried against me. I wanted to comfort her, but with my arms shackled behind my back it was hopeless. I rubbed my cheek against hers, trying to give her at least a little comfort.

"Any last requests?" the man behind me asked, pressing the gun tighter to my head.

"Can we have one more night together?" she pleaded. "If you're going to kill us, can we at least have that?"

One of them grabbed his crotch. "Oh, you're precious. You aren't going to die. I have first dibs on fucking you. Every man here will have you, over and over."

She paled and pressed her lips together, then her gaze met and held mine. I saw the resolve there, the determination, and I knew she'd try to survive anything if for no other reason than our child was growing inside of her. She'd told me before she didn't want to live if she faced this kind of life again, but I knew that baby was a game changer. I couldn't tell her that Havoc was coming, that the club would rescue her. I didn't want to alert The Inferno to anything.

"One night, bitch. Then you belong to us and this fucker dies," one of the men said.

Meg and I were hauled to our feet and shoved down a dirt path. There was a concrete building ahead of us, and when they pushed us inside I saw that it was a single cell with a mattress on the floor and a bucket in the corner.

Someone removed the cuffs on my wrists and threw a blanket onto the bed. I didn't know why they were offering us that one piece of comfort, but I wouldn't argue. The only thing that made a little sense was that they planned to use it against Meg in some way after they took my life. The thought of Meg lying on that stained mattress made my stomach turn. Who knew what fluids had been spilled there. I doubted those who had found themselves in these accommodations were overly hygienic.

"When the sun rises, she goes into service and you die," one of the men said.

The door slammed shut and I heard a bolt being thrown to lock us in. There was a dim light overhead and no windows. The place smelled and it was the least romantic spot ever, but Meg threw herself into my arms, not seeming to care.

"You told me to stay at your house so I'd be safe, and I didn't listen," she said. "Now I've put our baby in danger."

"Not your fault," I said. If I was going to die tomorrow, I didn't want her feeling guilty for any of this. I was the one who had been an asshole to her. If the blame lay anywhere, it was at my feet.

I set her away from me and spread the blanket over the mattress, thankful it was thick and smelled like detergent. At least it would be clean. I held my hand out to Meg, then wrapped my arms around her waist, kissing her softly. If all we had was this one night, then I wanted to make it a happy memory for her.

"Did you mean it when you asked them for one more night with me?" I asked. "Or were you just stalling?"

"I want you," she said. "I know this isn't exactly a five-star hotel, but the fact we're together is enough."

I placed my lips against her ear and dropped my voice low enough no one could hear, even if microphones or cameras were planted in here. It would only look like I was nibbling on her ear and getting her in the mood. I had no doubt that once she was rescued, Shade would make sure any video footage was wiped.

"They're coming, Meg. You'll be rescued tomorrow."

She looked up at me, her lips parting, but I kissed her before she could ask anything. Despite our situation, my cock hardened in my jeans. I slowly removed her clothes, then my own. There wasn't a place for my cut, so it dropped to the dirty floor with everything else. Nothing mattered right now except the woman in my arms.

I laid her down on the blanket, then covered her with my body. I trailed my lips along the column of her neck, rubbing my beard against her soft skin. Her fingers slid through my hair and her thighs cradled my hips. I worked my way down, sucking and nipping at her breasts before spreading her open wide and dragging my tongue along her folds. She whimpered and arched her back.

"Cinder," she said, sounding breathless. "I missed you."

"Not Cinder right now, sweetheart. It's just us, and what did I tell you to call me when we're alone?" If anyone learned my name at this point, it wouldn't much matter. Once I was dead, the name Vincent wouldn't mean shit to anyone but Meg.

I hadn't realized until just then how much I wanted to hear her say my name. My real name. To everyone else I was Cinder. Meg was special. She was mine even if only for a few more hours. I knew that once Havoc and the others came to save her that they would protect her and my kid. She'd never want for anything. It was about all that kept me together right now. Otherwise I'd be losing my shit. Even though there was a chance they would get here before I died in the morning, I couldn't count on it. My men were good, but I didn't doubt for a second The Inferno would come for me once they knew the Devils had breached their territory. I'd do everything in my power to protect Meg until I drew my last breath.

"Vincent," she said, her gaze holding mine.

As I looked at Meg, I wondered how I could have ever been so stupid as to think I didn't need her, didn't want her, or love her. My heart swelled with everything I felt in that moment, and I wished that we had a million more nights together. Instead, I'd have to make this one good enough to last her a lifetime.

"I..." She stopped and bit her lip. "I wanted you to know that no one's touched me since our last time together. They scared me and threatened to make me service all of them. Even before you got here they were saying vile things to me. I didn't want you to worry that they'd hurt me."

I rose over her body, running my fingers through her hair. Even now, when she faced an uncertain future, she was still trying to protect me. I'd never met anyone as incredible as Meg, as giving and loving. I couldn't believe I'd wasted so much time. If I'd tried to get closer to her sooner, then we could have had a year of happy memories. Instead, I'd been a dick to her time and again, allowing her to stay yet making it clear I didn't care either way. Until the day I'd run her off with my careless words.

"I would give anything to have kept you out of their hands," I said. "I promised you were safe when you came home with us from Colombia. It seems I've broken that promise."

She placed her fingers over my lips. "You gave me more than I thought I'd ever have. And now we're going to have a baby together. There's no greater gift than that."

"The club will take care of you," I said.

She shook her head, tears gathering in her eyes again.

"Meg, you have to listen. I'm a realist, sweetheart. There's no way they're letting me walk out of here."

A sob caught in her throat and I pressed my lips to hers. "Always remember that you were loved, so damn much. I'm just an old fool who was too stupid to tell you sooner."

"I love you," she said, her voice breaking.

I wanted to make the moment perfect for her, but I also knew that wasn't necessarily what she needed right now. I could make her scream in pleasure, but I thought she needed the same connection I was craving. With our gazes locked, I eased inside of her. Even though I'd hardly done more than kiss her, she was so damn wet. I made love to her slowly, savoring every second. Every stroke of my cock had me grinding my pelvic bone against her, pressing against her clit. Meg gripped my shoulders, never looking away from me. Her eyes remained open and all the passion and love I saw in them made my heart pound in my chest.

I felt her pussy tighten on me. She was close.

"Come for me, Meg."

Her thighs locked against my hips as I drove into her, taking her harder and faster. She tossed her head back, but as she shattered, coating me with her cream, her gaze found mine again. I didn't stop, didn't slow, and managed to hold off my own orgasm until she'd come at least once more. I filled her with my cum, my cock jerking with my release, and I couldn't resist the sweetness of her lips another second. I kissed her thoroughly, trying to show her everything I was feeling.

Neither of us could sleep, not even after that. We talked for a while, and made love three more times before the sun started coming in under the door. My arms tightened around Meg, knowing that it was almost time. I didn't know how to prepare her for what would happen soon. I only hoped she didn't try to save me like she had the night of her birthday. If Meg got hurt in an effort to protect me, it would gut me. As long as she was safe, I could face my death without any fear, even though I'd have a ton of regrets.

I heard the bolt being slid and pressed my lips to her temple, thankful I'd insisted we both get dressed an hour ago. I closed my eyes and breathed her in, letting her scent calm me.

"I love you, Meg. Always remember that."

She clutched at me, but one of The Inferno members threw open the door and dragged me away from her. Meg cried and reached for me, but I gave her a quick shake of my head.

"Be brave, my sweet girl." I smiled at her as the man shoved me to my knees. "Close your eyes, Meg. Don't watch."

She sobbed and scrambled across the floor toward me, throwing herself into my arms. I held her a moment, savoring the feel of her, and then gently pushed her away. I gave a nod toward the bed and she backed away. As she sank onto the mattress, I watched her take a shuddering breath and close her eyes. The tears streaking her cheeks made my heart ache.

I felt the gun press against the back of my head, and I kept my eyes on Meg, wanting to see her beauty until the last moment. The hammer cocked and I took a breath, ready for what came next. Except the blast of a gun wasn't the one against my head. Meg screamed and her body jerked, but I was focused on The Inferno member collapsing on the floor next to me, a hole through his head and blood pooling on the concrete floor.

I looked over my shoulder to see Renegade grinning at me.

"Miss me?" he asked.

"Fucking Christ," I muttered as I stood.

"Nope, not Jesus. Though I am your savior today." He winked and I shook my head at his nonsense.

I heard Meg gasp and I looked over at her. She was pale, too damn pale, but she gave a cry and came running toward me. I wrapped her in my arms and cradled her close.

"I'm fine, honey. Renegade got here in time to save both of us," I said.

"Pres, I suggest we get the fuck out of here," he said. "We have a full crew here cleaning house, but in case there are any stragglers, I'd prefer to get the two of you to safety."

I lifted Meg into my arms and carried her, following Renegade who had to shoot two more men along the way. I saw one of the club trucks idling outside the gates and I climbed into the backseat. Renegade got behind the wheel, but didn't say anything. Meg remained in my lap, crying softly as I tried to soothe her fears. It had been close. Really fucking close.

"I'm going to need a status report," I said.

"Our family, Reckless Kings, and their allies are rounding up the last of The Inferno members and hopefuls. By nightfall, all those fuckers should be in the ground or burned to a crisp," Renegade said.

"Take us home. I'm ready for a shower, some hot food, and then I just want some quiet time with my woman," I said.

I saw Renegade smirk in the rearview mirror. "You got it, Pres. Someone will get your bike home for you."

I held Meg close and shut my eyes. I'd nearly lost my life today, nearly left behind the woman I loved and our kid, all because we had a fucking rat in our club. From now on, anyone who wanted to join would have to more than prove themselves before they even put on a Prospect cut. I was sick of this shit, and too damn old for it.

"Hey, Pres," Renegade said softly. "Sorry you didn't get to take them all out."

"As long as they're dead, I don't care who did it. The only thing that matters is that our women and kids are safe."

I placed my hand over Meg's belly and thought about the baby growing inside her. My life was about to drastically change, but for once, the thought of a kid running around my house didn't scare the shit out of me.

Chapter Ten

Meg
Two Months Later

I washed the breakfast dishes, a set Cinder had insisted I pick, and set them in the drying rack. It wasn't my favorite thing to do and I had a tendency to put it off as long as possible. The dishwasher had died a few days ago and a new one had been ordered, but the one I'd wanted was out of stock. I'd tried to tell Cinder that I didn't need that specific one, but he'd been spoiling me a bit. If I so much as mentioned liking something, it was delivered a day or two later.

I heard cussing from down the hall and smiled, knowing that he was more than a little frustrated with the baby furniture I'd selected. Granted, if I'd known that the company who delivered it wouldn't also set it up, I would have gone elsewhere. Cinder had looked resigned as he watched box after box come through the front door. I'd mentioned letting the Prospects handle it, but he insisted that he would take care of his own kid.

When the last of the dishes were finished, I dried my hands and headed toward the angry grumbles. The nursery door was open and I leaned against the frame and peered into the room. The baby bed looked like it had exploded out of the box with parts everywhere. So far, he'd managed to get the underbed storage together, but the bed itself still lay scattered.

"Are you sure I can't ask Killian and the new guy to come help?" I asked.

"Bane? You think he'd cuss any less over this disaster?" Cinder grinned. "The man was in the Navy. He may know words even I haven't heard yet."

I narrowed my eyes, seeing right through him. "You don't want him here because he flirted with me."

He shrugged, not denying it. Bane had been accepted into the Devil's Boneyard as a Prospect two weeks after The Inferno was destroyed. Fresh out of the Navy, he'd been eager to join a brotherhood that wouldn't send him all over the world. He also met Cinder's new requirements. After CJ's betrayal, he was only accepting ex-military or ex-government personnel, anyone who had received a certain level of security clearance and had commendations out the ass. I knew that Bane had been thoroughly vetted, and that Shade and the other hackers had torn his life apart and analyzed every detail. I hated that he didn't trust anyone, but it made me feel all warm inside that he was so protective.

"He should be glad Magnus was there to stop him from grabbing your ass," Cinder said.

Reed, a Prospect who had helped me when I'd first been brought here, had been patched in about five months ago and now went by Magnus. I still had trouble remembering that at times and had slipped up more than once. Magnus had assured me it didn't bother him, but I knew he'd earned his new name and I didn't want to offend him by not using it.

Cinder sighed and tossed aside the pieces he'd been trying to fit together, then stood and stretched. "I'm too old for this shit."

"Not old," I reminded him. "There's a difference in seasoned and old. Far as I can tell, you're just right."

Cinder smiled as he came closer and wrapped an arm around my waist. He pulled me tight against him, and I felt his cock press into my hip. My breath caught as I saw the wicked gleam in his eyes. Something told me the baby furniture would have to wait, not that there was a rush. I wasn't even showing yet, and had a long way to go before the baby arrived.

I loved seeing this side of him. Nearly dying, and seeing me in the clutches of The Inferno, had changed him. He hadn't wasted a moment of our time together, always showering me with affection, whether we were in private or not. We'd only been back a few days when he'd surprised me by dropping to one knee in the middle of the clubhouse and asking me to marry him. I'd cried so damn hard. Poor man had gotten scared and thought he'd done something wrong with all my blubbering, but I'd finally managed to say yes. He'd tried to rush the wedding, but I'd refused. It wasn't that I didn't want to be his wife, and after nearly losing him I could understand why he wanted to get married quickly, but I only planned on getting married once and I wanted to do it right.

Jordan had offered to watch all the kids twice a week for a few hours while Clarity and Josie helped with wedding plans. Instead of going to the Justice of the Peace, or using the clubhouse, I'd asked for tents so we could have an outdoor wedding. It also meant we had to arrange to rent tables and chairs for the event, and hope the weather wasn't too bad. I knew there was always a chance it would storm, but I was hoping the day would go according to plan.

Cinder smoothed my hair back from my face. "You feeling okay?"

I nodded. Morning sickness had hit me a month ago, and while I still had trouble with it, I'd learned that gingersnaps helped. The cabinet was filled with tins of them. Of course, Cinder had also stocked the freezer with pineapple sherbet since I craved it. Thankfully, I hadn't wanted any strange combinations of food. He was probably getting a little sick of pasta, though. I'd wanted it almost every meal the last few weeks.

My stomach rumbled and my cheeks warmed. He chuckled and pressed a kiss to my forehead. "Why don't you call and beg Killian to come put this crap together, and I'll have your favorite restaurant deliver something for lunch. What type of noodles do you want today?"

"They aren't all noodles," I said. "And I want lobster ravioli. With extra shredded parmesan. Oh, and garlic knots!"

He gave me a tender smile, pressed his lips to mine, then pulled his phone from his pocket. While he ordered our food, I used the cell phone he'd insisted I have to contact Killian, who had promised he would show up with reinforcements and get the nursery together in no time. I hoped he was right because after I ate and took a nap, I knew I'd be reaching for Cinder, and not in a PG kind of way. I'd had a rather insatiable sexual appetite for the last month.

The Prospects arrived before our food so I showed them where everything was and wished them luck. Killian took one glance at the mess Cinder had made and started mumbling under his breath. It didn't take long for our food to get dropped at the front gate. Cinder left long enough to get it and bring it home to me. It was a mild day in Florida so I carried two glasses of sweet tea out to the picnic table on the side of the house, another addition he'd made for me.

I'd also had most of the rooms repainted in something more cheerful than beige or gray. The nursery was going to be a pale yellow since we didn't yet know if we were having a boy or girl. I hadn't bought bedding or clothes yet, even though I'd really wanted to. Cinder had pointed out if I was just a little more patient we wouldn't have to select gender neutral items. There was only so much white, yellow, and green I could stomach, so I'd conceded his point.

He gave me a wink as he set the sack on the picnic table and started pulling out the containers of food. The lobster ravioli smelled like heaven, and I grinned when he opened a round tin and showed me the dozen garlic knots, but it was the raspberry cheesecake that made me lean across the table and kiss him long and hard.

"Woman, if you want to eat, you need to keep your sexy self over there."

"Just telling you how much I appreciate the way you take care of me."

He shook his head. "Yeah well, I have some making up to do."

I wasn't going to argue with him, even though I didn't feel the same way. I'd learned already that nothing I said would change his mind. To Cinder, he'd failed me by not admitting his feelings sooner. While it had hurt being away from him, and I'd been scared to death when that man had held him at gunpoint, the fact we were together now was all that mattered to me. Yes, I still woke from nightmares about that day, but the moment Cinder wrapped me in his arms everything was right in my world.

The day Cinder had nearly lost his life everything had been pure chaos. The clubs were still reeling from the events that occurred, but the Reckless Kings more than anyone. While Cinder had been told the men watching me had been killed, only one had lost his life. The others who had been left for dead spent some time in the hospital, but they survived. I didn't know what had happened to the bodies of The Inferno members, and I didn't want to know. Cinder had assured me they wouldn't be an issue anymore, that clubs had banded together to strike every Inferno holding nationwide. I was hoping our future would be peaceful, but living with an outlaw club, I knew that wasn't likely. For now, I would be grateful I had the love of a good man, and we were starting a family together.

"I think I'm going to put up a fence around the back," he said as he took a bite of his spaghetti. "Eventually our kid will need room to run, where they can be safe. I don't want you worrying about turning your back for half a second and losing them."

"What kind of fence?" I asked, my brow furrowed. Part of what I loved about his house was all the open land behind it. I liked seeing that view when looked out the back windows.

"Maybe one of those white picket things. I thought I'd do a big enough area to add a patio so you'll have a place to sit, and maybe put in a sandbox. Eventually the kid will need a swing set or something."

"You know, for a man who never wanted children, you've put an awful lot of thought into what's going to happen two or three years from now."

He stopped chewing and stared for a moment, then swallowed and reached for my hand. "I didn't want kids, never saw the appeal. Then I learned you were pregnant with my baby and all I could think was that you'd be beautiful as your stomach stretched to accommodate our kid. I'm going to be there for every appointment, not just now but after the baby gets here too. At my age, it's doubtful I'll have another one."

"Are you saying you only want one?" I asked.

He looked at me and didn't say anything for several minutes. "Do you want another one?"

"I don't know. Let's get through this pregnancy first, then we can talk. After the birthing videos I saw, I'm not even sure I want to have this one."

"You can hold my hand and scream all you want when we're in the delivery room. I'll let you call me every name you can think if it will make the moment more bearable."

"Love you," I said.

He winked. "Love you too."

We finished our meal, and after throwing away the trash, made our way to the nursery to check on the progress. There were three Prospects in the room and nearly everything was finished. They were putting the last of the screws in the changing table, which seemed to irritate Cinder.

"Told you I was too damn old for this shit," he muttered as he watched them.

"You should make them leave."

"Why?" He looked down at me and I leaned up to whisper in his ear.

"So I can prove just how old you *aren't*. Right after a nap, of course," I said, fighting back a yawn.

"Nope, after that comment, you can nap after."

He swatted my ass, then chased the men out of the house, locked the door, and carried me into our bedroom. When he reached for the hem of my shirt, I slapped his hand away and went into the bathroom.

"Where are you going?" he asked.

"I haven't had a shower today. I smell."

He leaned against the bathroom doorway and rolled his eyes. "Woman, you never stink."

"Maybe you could scrub my back, make sure I get really clean."

He smirked and started removing his clothes, setting his cut on the bathroom counter. His shirt came off, and I reached out to trace his newest tattoo. It was my name in a script with a thorny rose under it. I'd asked about the rose and he said that I was beautiful but could be a thorn in his ass just like the rose. After giving him an angry glare, I'd kissed the hell out of him.

I started the shower after I stripped off my clothes, making sure it wasn't too hot or too cold. The doctor had told me to avoid extra hot showers or baths. Even though Cinder liked taking a shower so hot I worried the paint on the walls would peel, he never once complained about the cooler temp when he showered with me.

I soaked my hair but before I could reach for the shampoo he already had it in his hands. He massaged it into my scalp and down the length of my hair before helping me rinse. His hands were just the right amount of rough as he soaped my skin. My nipples puckered as his fingers danced across them.

He backed away, making me whimper and reach for him.

"Uh-uh. Not this time." He leaned against the tiled wall and folded his arms over his chest. "Pinch your nipples, Meg. Show me how much you need to be touched."

I cupped my breasts and tugged at the dusky tips. His cock jerked and I watched as pre-cum gathered on the head. Licking my lips, I wondered if he'd let me taste him. He chuckled, drawing my eyes back up, and he gave me a wink before stroking his shaft.

"All in good time, sweetheart."

"Please, Vincent." I wasn't even entirely sure what I was begging for. To suck him, or to have him touch me.

"Does my sweet girl need to come?" he asked.

I nodded eagerly.

"Show me how much you want it," he said, his voice getting deeper with more growl to it.

I slid my hand down my body and parted the lips of my pussy so he could see how hard my clit was and that I was more than just slick, I was dripping for him. He tipped his head toward the bench along the left wall and I propped my foot on it, opening myself farther. He groaned as he watched me stroke my pussy. I'd already learned when I ached this much, my hand would never be enough, but I did it for him. I rubbed my clit, then dipped two fingers inside before swirling them around the bud again.

"It's not enough, is it?" he asked, his lips tipping up on the corner. "Not what you need?"

"No. I need you. So much."

"You need my cock filling you?"

I nodded.

"Then come show me how much you love it."

I dropped my foot back to the floor of the shower and crossed to Cinder. Kneeling at his feet, I licked the pre-cum off his slit and then wrapped my lips around him. I licked and sucked, loving the taste of him, the way he filled my mouth and slid along my tongue. He didn't touch me, never once reached toward me. His arms remained folded over his chest as I pleased him, the heat burning in his gaze telling me just how much he loved what I did to him.

"Stand up and face the wall, Meg," he said.

I released him and stood. He shifted out of the way as I leaned forward, placing my hands on the tiles.

He gripped my hips and pulled me back until I was angled just the way he wanted. I felt the head of his cock slide against me before he slammed into me, hard and deep. I cried out, my eyes shutting in pure bliss. We'd learned quickly that I enjoyed it when he was a little rough with me. I trusted him, more than anyone ever before. No matter what he did, I knew he would never truly hurt me.

I jolted when his hand slapped my ass.

"Focus, Meg. Get out of your head."

He pounded into me, but my orgasm stayed just out of reach. When he slid from my body, I cried out in dismay, but he quickly shut off the water and dragged me to our bed, not caring that we were both soaked. Cinder lifted me and set me down in the center of the bed. Before I could even blink he'd shackled one of my wrists to the headboard, then the other. When he opened the bedside table drawer, I knew I was in trouble.

The whir of my favorite toy both excited me and put me on edge. I knew exactly what it meant. He held it up, making sure he had my attention.

"You don't come until I say you can. What happens if you don't obey?" he asked.

I licked my lips. "You'll punish me."

The second the toy touched my clit it felt like pleasure was zinging through my body. I didn't even last to the count of twenty before I was coming, screaming out his name. My heart raced as he turned the toy up higher and tormented me some more. If I came before he permitted, then my punishment was to keep coming until he said to stop. He was relentless as the toy pulled one orgasm after another from me. My body trembled, my thighs shook, and I didn't think I could handle much more.

I bent my legs and dug my heels into the mattress, hoping it would shift the pressure a little, but Cinder wouldn't allow that to happen. He cupped my ass with his hand and a moment later, he drove into me, his cock filling me up as the toy made me come yet again. He fucked me, hard and ruthless, as he took what he wanted from me. I jerked at the cuffs, wanting to reach for him, to touch him.

Every time he got close to coming, he'd pull out and grip his cock tight. Then he'd slam back inside of me and drive me to the brink of madness. It felt like hours had passed when he finally shut the vibrator off and reached up to uncuff me. I'd thought it meant I'd finally have what I wanted, him taking me until he filled me with his cum, but I was so very wrong.

Cinder withdrew from my body and flipped me over, only to cuff me to the headboard once more. He positioned me so that my knees were under me, my thighs pressed together, and my chest against the mattress. He'd told me before that it made me even tighter and let him slide in deeper. All I knew was that I loved it when he did this. In the past two months, I'd cast away any fears I had in the bedroom and gladly explored things with the man I loved more than anything.

He wasn't gentle as he fucked me, driving both of us to the brink. He slid a hand between my body and the bed, then pinched down hard on my nipple. I screamed out as my orgasm rushed through me. He pounded into my pussy, the hot jets of his cum filling me up. I felt his cock twitch inside of me, even after he'd stilled. I could hear his ragged breathing and my heart thundering in my chest.

Cinder set me free, then cuddled me against his chest.

"I didn't take it too far, did I?" he asked.

"No. It was just right." I smiled faintly. "Every time with you is amazing, and you know it."

He pressed a kiss to my neck and just held me as I slowly started to drift to sleep. I was all warm, and safe. He always made me feel safe. Even the first time he'd cuffed me to his bed, I'd known that he would make sure nothing ever hurt me. He'd broken my heart when I'd left, but now that I knew how much he loved me, I would never leave his side.

"Love you, Vincent," I murmured.

"You're my entire world, Meg, you and our kid." I felt his hand caress my belly. "Sleep, love. We have the rest of our lives together. You won't miss anything if you take a nap."

I smiled and sighed happily as his arm tightened around me. It still baffled me that someone like him could ever love someone like me, but I was so grateful to have Cinder in my life. He was just the right amount of rough and tough, and knew exactly when I needed him to be all soft and loving. Our lives might be far from perfect, but we were perfect together, and that was all I needed.

Cowboy (A Bad Boy Romance)

Harley Wylde

Jacey: Marrying Beck was a mistake, one I can't get away from no matter how much time passes. I can't leave him. It's not just that running might cost me my life. I have no idea what he would do to the kids if I weren't here to protect them. I can't leave them vulnerable to a monster like him. I've never once strayed from Beck, even when he's broken bones and done unspeakable things to me. My life is one never-ending horror movie. But now I have Ty… he's everything I've ever wanted in a man, and I'm not sure I'm strong enough to walk away.

Ty: The beautiful, sweet mom who comes to my ranch has a haunted look in her eyes that I want to chase away, and bruises she tries damn hard to hide. Kissing her might have been a mistake, but maybe it wasn't. I've wanted Jacey Lane since the day I first saw her, and knowing her husband abuses her just infuriates me. Ty the cowboy might not be able to do much of anything, but Cowboy the Dixie Reaper sure as hell can. If keeping Jacey safe means I need to go home, then so be it. My brothers will stand beside me and help me guarantee that Beck Lane never draws another breath.

Chapter One

Jacey

His lips were warm and firm against mine. I couldn't remember the last time I'd truly been kissed, and I'd never had a kiss as memorable as this one. The feel of Ty's arms around me, his strength, made me want to melt against him. His tongue flicked against my bottom lip and I opened, letting him in, needing to taste him. Ty fisted his hand in my hair, not tight enough to hurt but just enough that it turned me on.

I hadn't felt desire for anyone in a really long time, or had anyone desire me. His mouth devoured mine as he walked me backward until I pressed against the wall. I could feel the hard ridge of his cock as he pushed his hips tighter against me, and my panties grew damp. I wanted to rub against him, to beg for more. I hated to admit that I'd never had an orgasm, not even self-induced. How pathetic was that?

But I had to put a stop to it. This. Whatever it was. What we were doing wasn't right, no matter how much I wished it could continue. I'd let things go too far, and I knew it. My only excuse was that Beck had been in rare form last night, even worse than usual. I lived with a monster, a man who made me do horrible things and wouldn't hesitate to end my life. I was terrified of him, with good reason, and I was trapped in a nightmare. Just once, I wanted a moment of happiness. A few minutes where I was desired and treated with care. Didn't make it any less wrong, but I could never regret this moment with Ty. I'd gladly burn in the eternal fires of hell for just this one taste of Ty, to have him hold me just once.

Pulling away, I placed a hand on his chest. His heart was thumping every bit as hard as mine. It was the first time we'd crossed the line, and it would have to be the last. My heart ached as I fought to say the words that would bring it to an end. I wanted him, more than just physically, but I knew it could never happen.

"Ty, we can't."

"I know, but I couldn't resist anymore. Do you know how long I've wanted to kiss you?" He moved his thumb in a slow caress along my jaw. "Ever since our eyes met that first time, I knew you were special."

"I'm married, Ty."

He snorted and ran a hand through his hair. "I've met your husband. You can do better. And I honestly wouldn't call what you have a marriage. More like a hostage situation. You and I both know you're just too scared to leave him."

"Be that as it may, we've been married for twelve years. We have two kids! It's not like I can just walk out." I knew it was a feeble attempt at putting things back to friendship level. Guilt ate at me. Even though I didn't love Beck anymore, hadn't for a long time, I was still a married woman. At least on paper. I hadn't had a true marriage with Beck in a really long time, if ever. What Ty said was true. I was scared shitless to leave the monster I'd married. I'd tried it before and paid dearly. I wasn't sure I'd survive the next attempt.

"That isn't a good enough reason to stay married, Jacey. You were only eighteen when you met Beck, just out of high school. People change. I know you aren't the same, though I have my doubts Beck was ever anything other than rotten to the core, and it's time you moved on. You can't tell me you're happy with him."

I knew the feelings I'd been developing for Ty were wrong. At least, by society's standards they were. In my heart, I knew that the love I felt growing for Ty could never be anything but incredibly right. He was just so sweet… so good to me. Far different from the way Beck treated me. There were times I'd close my eyes and imagine what life would be like if Ty were my husband and not Beck. It was the only way I could stay sane, to take a trip to another world, even if it was only in my mind. A place where the man lying next to me loved me and treated me right. Not someone who left bruises and humiliated me. No one knew about the pictures and videos. Or I didn't think they did. It was stupid to daydream about a life with Ty maybe, but it helped.

His jaw firmed. "I've seen the bruises. I know you try to hide them, but I don't understand why. He should be in jail. Men like him don't stop with one hit, Jacey. If he's done it once, he'll keep doing it."

Ty was right and I knew it, but that didn't change the fact that I *was* legally married, and I couldn't afford a divorce anytime soon. And it wasn't just the bruises. Beck's depravity went way deeper. Regardless of how it looked, I stayed to protect my children. Beck had threatened to take the kids if we ever split up. I was sure he'd do it, too. To the rest of the world, he was a hero, the type of man you could count on and call in an emergency. That's the Beck the public saw. No one knew what he was like behind closed doors. I knew a very different Beck. I knew the monster. The man who would make his wife pose naked so he could sell the pictures online, minus my face of course. Couldn't have anyone finding out what he was up to. I'd refused once, and only once. I hadn't been able to leave the house for nearly a week he'd beaten me so badly. After that, he'd started taking videos and selling them. I was beyond humiliated. It was one thing to do that sort of thing because you wanted to, and another to have it forced on you, and by the man who was supposed to love and cherish you.

"Please understand, Ty. There's nothing I can do right now."

Or ever, for that matter. If I tried to leave, he'd haul me back and beat me again. Maybe next time he'd kill me. Then my kids wouldn't stand a chance. At least I could do my best to shield them when Beck went into one of his rages, which happened more and more frequently. And as long as he had me to pose for his little side business, then I didn't have to worry about him using our kids. I didn't think for one second that he loved our daughter and son. I wasn't sure Beck was even capable of the emotion. Whatever mental issues caused his problems, they were getting worse and I worried that he'd be completely unstable soon. Not that he'd admit he had a problem, and he'd somehow lied his way through the psych evaluation for the department.

Ty sighed. "You know I love Jackson and Danica like they were my own. It eats at me knowing the three of you are with that asshole."

I smiled. Ty was amazing with my kids, and not just because he spoiled them rotten. He had befriended them, and had even let the kids ride the stable mounts free of charge. Both of my children had fallen in love with horses, just like I had as a little girl. And I worried they were falling a little in love with Ty too, much like their mom.

"Those kids took to riding like ducks to water. They earn their keep, helping with the horses. Hell, I wouldn't charge you for Reaper, but I know you wouldn't accept my offer."

I looked away, feeling a flash of insecurity. Money was a touchy subject for me. Beck gave me enough to cover the stable fees for Reaper each month, and to buy groceries. Honestly, I didn't know why he let me keep Reaper, except it made him seem like a doting husband. If I needed clothes or shoes, I practically had to beg for them. He always seemed to have plenty of money for whatever he wanted, though. Like a new gun, a night of partying with his friends, or anything else that struck his fancy. Wouldn't surprise me at all if he bought some time with prostitutes, although I didn't know why when he'd just take whatever he wanted from me. He didn't know that I asked my doctor to test me regularly for STDs in case Beck gave me something. After Jackson was born, I'd also been sneaking birth control so I wouldn't get pregnant again.

"I should be paying you for their riding lessons," I said.

"I don't want your money, babe. If I need more money, I'll go back on the circuit."

"Do you think I want to see you get hurt?" I cupped his cheek, moving in close again. His crisp, clean scent teased my nose, and I wished I could burrow into him. When his arms had been around me, it was the safest I'd felt in a long time. I'd give anything to feel that every day.

When Ty had first told me about his rodeo days, I'd found it exciting. I'd always enjoyed watching the different events whenever the smaller circuit came to town. Then he'd told me why he'd quit. It scared me that he could be hurt again, or even killed, all to chase after another buckle. Ty might be a three-time World Champion bareback bronc rider, but he wasn't invincible. To me, he was sexy, the epitome of what a man should be, but I knew most rodeo cowboys were in their teens and twenties, and Ty was quite a bit older.

"You're important to me, Ty. I couldn't have made it this past year without you. If things were different..." I knew he wanted more than I could give, and if I were honest with myself, I'd admit I wanted him just as much. But it was never going to happen. If Beck ever found out about the kiss... No, I wouldn't even think about that. If Beck thought for one second that I had feelings for Ty, he'd do his best to ruin Ty's life, and mine. I could only imagine the ways he'd decide to punish me.

He studied me, his jaw working back and forth as if he were trying to contain his irritation. I knew that it wasn't likely he'd ever be satisfied with just friendship, and sooner or later, I'd have to let him go. It wasn't fair to hold on when I couldn't take that next step, could never be with him the way he wanted. The day I'd said "I do" to Beck had been the beginning of the end. And even if I could go back and change things, walking away from Beck's proposal would mean walking away from my kids. No matter what hell I'd suffered, I'd never want to lose them.

"Is Beck working tonight?" he asked.

I tried to recall which shift Beck was working. He'd still been in bed when I'd left to take the kids to school. I sometimes thought he'd asked for that floating schedule so I wouldn't know when it was safe to try to escape. "He's pulling a double and won't be home until close to midnight. Why?"

Ty checked his watch. "Let's go get a treat for the kids before we get them from school. Then I'm taking y'all somewhere fun. I'll have you home before they need to wind down and get ready for bed. Just leave your car here and we'll come back for it later."

Leaving my car here meant that if someone were spying on Beck's behalf, they wouldn't be able to find me around town. No one ever came to the stable to look for me. For whatever reason, Beck didn't see Ty as a threat. They'd only met once, when I'd first come to check out the stable. Beck told me later Ty was weak and pathetic. I should be grateful that Beck thought so little of him. It meant I had one refuge where I could hide for a bit, decompress, and just breathe without the constant worry and fear.

I knew I was going to give in to Ty, how could I not? *Jacey Lane, you're a sucker for that slow southern drawl of his and those baby blues.* "All right. Where are we going?" I asked.

He grinned, a dimple flashing in one cheek. "The mall, of course. Didn't Danica say something about wanting some new bear they have at that specialty store? I figure we can find something for Jackson there too. Can you imagine their faces when they crawl in the back seat and see those bear boxes just waiting to be opened?"

I bit my lip and placed a hand over my belly as it cramped a little. I'd barely had time to shove a muffin in my mouth on the way to the elementary school and I hadn't been back home since. That was five hours ago. If I didn't eat soon, I'd get lightheaded.

"Do we have enough time to grab some lunch while we're out? I'm starving."

"We can eat at the mall food court, or we can grab something along the way." He looked at his watch again. "It's only twelve. If we hurry, we might even be able to sit down somewhere."

"Just let me grab my purse from the car."

He followed me out of the office, locking the door behind him. Even though Ty kept any payments in the safe, he made sure no one could access his workspace when he wasn't around. There were also cameras in the stable hallway, which meant the horses were safe as well. If anyone tried to steal one, it would be easy enough to turn them over to the police. It was one of the features that had sold Beck on letting me keep Reaper here. Or maybe he'd hoped Ty would let him access the feed on occasion to make sure I wasn't flirting with anyone.

We walked down the dusty barn aisle, horses sticking their heads over their doors in curiosity. My fingers twitched, wanting to reach over and take Ty's hand, but I knew I couldn't. Not out here in the open. Anyone could be watching, and then Beck might find out. I hated living every second of my life in fear, but I didn't know what else to do. I couldn't go to the police. He *was* the police.

In the heat of summer, the fans along the barn corridor would be on, but it was cool enough now they weren't needed. The stalls were insulated so the horses were comfortable regardless of the temperature outside. I could smell the sweet scent of hay and that underlying musk of horse that made me feel like I was in heaven. People gave me strange looks when I said my favorite smell was horses and dirt, but it was true. I could bury my face against my horse and just breathe him in for hours and be perfectly content.

I paused in front of Reaper's stall and rubbed his head a moment. "I'll see you tomorrow, big boy."

The horse nudged me with his nose and I laughed before giving him one last pat. I'd named the tall black horse The Grim Reaper, but he was really the sweetest thing. I would trust him with either of my children, and that was saying something. People were scared of him because he was so broad and tall, but I knew Reaper had the heart of an angel. Much like the tall, handsome cowboy walking beside me.

At my car, I snagged my purse, then reset the locks and alarm. When I reached Ty's truck, he held the door open for me and I climbed into the monstrous thing. I settled into my seat and fastened my seatbelt as Ty got in. Glancing his way, I admired the way the sun glinted on his golden-blond hair. His skin was tanned from working outside all the time, and I knew his hands were rough and calloused from a hard day's work. When he smiled, his blue eyes flashed with humor, shining with the brightness of the sky. And earlier, when he'd kissed me, his eyes had darkened with passion, like the stormy sea.

Someday, he'd make some woman a wonderful husband. My heart ached, knowing that woman would never be me. Until the day I died, or Beck did, I would be forever tied to the father of my children. I only hoped that living with him wouldn't warp my kids and turn them into replicas of their dad, or even worse, instill a fear so deep inside them they never learn to trust someone.

It took around forty minutes for us to reach the area by the mall. Without even asking, Ty immediately drove to my favorite Mexican restaurant. Even though I didn't dine in town with Ty often, for fear of Beck finding out, I'd confessed how much I loved their enchiladas and cheese dip. Ty was always doing sweet things for me -- picking my favorite restaurant, bringing me chocolates for Christmas and Valentine's Day, giving me a small gift on my birthday. It was always something easy to hide from Beck. We were seated quickly and it only took us a half hour to eat and pay the bill. Once we were done, we drove over to the mall and went in search of the bear store.

"You really don't have to do this," I said, as we made our way down to the lower level. Ty was forever buying my kids things. "You spoil them already."

"I like spoiling them."

I knew arguing with him wouldn't do any good. Sneaking Ty's presents into the house wasn't always easy, but I hadn't been caught yet. Beck didn't pay enough attention to Jackson or Danica to notice if they had a new toy or outfit. It was sad that the man who should love them unconditionally, should protect them and provide for them, would rather tear them down and scream how worthless they were, while the man who had only known them a short time made sure they had what they needed and wanted. Ty had been so kind to me and the kids, giving us far more than he should, and he'd never crossed the line until today.

When we entered the store, I searched the shelves for the precious bear Danica had so desperately wanted. I couldn't remember the name of it, but it had been purple and wore some sort of crown. Maybe a princess of some sort? But by the time I reached the end of the aisle, I hadn't seen the bear. There were a few empty shelves so I supposed it could've been in one of those spots.

"No luck?" Ty asked.

I shook my head. "I know she'll be happy with something else, I just wish we could've gotten her that particular bear."

"What about this?" he asked, holding up a sparkly pink bear that looked like it had strands of glitter in its fur.

"Perfect! You know how much she loves pink."

It took us another minute or two to decide on something for Jackson, but we finally settled on a plain brown bear. My son was very practical for someone so small and preferred animals that looked more like the real thing. He'd always turned up his nose at bears that, as he said, were non-bear colors.

Once the animals were stuffed, we went to pick out clothes for them. Jackson's was easy -- a cowboy outfit, since he'd said he wanted to be like Ty when he grew up. Danica's was a little harder. I never knew what my daughter would like, since her tastes seemed to change from month to month. I finally decided on a pink-and-teal sundress. We made our purchase and hurried back to the truck with only thirty minutes to spare before the kids were out of school.

The elementary school was decent and near my house, even though it wasn't on par with one of the local private schools. It wasn't near enough to the police station that Beck would see me picking up the kids with Ty, if he even recognized Ty's truck, but it was close enough that if the car broke down, me and the kids could walk home if we had to. So far, that hadn't happened, and I hoped it never did. Jackson might be tall for a kid his age, but he was still only six, and seven blocks was a long walk when you had to keep an eye on a rambunctious boy.

Ty reached over and took my hand. "I'm sorry I upset you earlier with the kiss."

He seemed so sincere, but I could tell by the look in his eyes that he felt ashamed. Even though he claimed Beck wasn't a real husband to me, and he was right, it didn't make me any less married. In the eyes of the law, I was Beck's wife. Even though I hadn't felt like one in years, if I were caught fooling around, Beck would use it against me. Ty was the decent sort of guy who would never poach another man's wife.

"You didn't upset me. It's just..."

"Just what?"

I smiled at him sadly. "There's no point wanting what I can't have. It just hurts more at the end of the day."

"I may not have ever done the relationship thing before, but you know I would commit to you in a heartbeat, if you'd just give me a chance. I haven't even been on a date since the day we met."

"I never asked that of you, Ty. I don't have that right." I pulled my hand free from his. I had to fight back the sting of tears as I realized that Beck wasn't just ruining my life and that of the kids, but he was ruining Ty's life too by keeping us apart. I had to let him go, make him see that there would never be a chance for us, but it hurt. My heart felt like it would break into a million pieces if I were to push Ty away.

It was painful, knowing how much he wanted me and knowing I couldn't act on it. I craved love and the kindness that Ty showed me, but Beck would never let me have that. He'd never divorce me, not unless he was the one moving on to greener pastures. And even then, he'd make sure to belittle me and tell everyone what a horrible wife and mother I'd been, that he was trying to improve his life by seeing someone else. And he'd likely take the kids with him. Not because he wanted them, but because he knew I did.

"Jacey, you have every right."

"Tyler Adler, you may say that now, but in another year, you're going to be tired of being home by yourself at night, not being able to kiss me or hold me. You'll get tired of me going home to my husband every night and not being able to give you the kind of relationship you want. You know I can't leave Beck."

Ty's jaw tightened and he stared at me, the blue of his eyes blazing a brighter hue. For a moment, it was like looking at a very different Ty, a man I didn't know. The intensity of his gaze should have frightened me, but a little shiver raked my spine and hardened my nipples. I'd never seen this alpha version of the man I'd been calling my friend, the guy who looked ready to kill on my behalf. That look on Beck would scare me spitless, but on Ty... I kind of wanted to swoon a little.

"He isn't going to get the kids. I won't let him," he said. "I may just look like some broken-down cowboy, but I have connections, Jacey. I could make that man disappear if that was what you wanted."

I bit my lip. "Ty, he's a well-respected police officer with the Mayfair Police Department. He's been on the force for the past ten years. I don't have a job -- Wait. What do you mean make him disappear?"

Maybe there was more to my sweet cowboy than I realized. That thought still didn't scare me. There might be plenty I didn't know about Ty, but I did know that he would never hurt me.

"Don't worry about it. Just know it's an option, and yes, you do have a job. You review books and blog about them. Even if you don't get paid for it, it's still work. And you create wonderful works of art."

"I can't sell my art in a gallery to make money. I enjoy doing that type of thing, but I don't know that I would want to do it as a full-time job."

"Doesn't mean it isn't art. I still say you should make bookmarks or brochures or something. You're really talented, babe. I know that idiot husband of yours says otherwise, but Beck is an asshole. Everyone loved the brochures you designed for the Wolf Creek Stables."

My cheeks warmed at the compliment. I was so used to hearing how I couldn't do anything right that it was nice to have someone say they appreciated something I'd done. When Beck had given far less money one month and I'd been short on the stable fee for Reaper, Ty had offered me a deal. He needed a way to promote the Wolf Creek Stables, and he'd heard that I knew how to design stuff on my computer. It had been nice of him to take the brochure in trade for that month's fee.

"It isn't just the job, Ty, and you know it. I suffer from depression and he'll hold it against me. I told you about my trip to the psychiatric hospital. You don't think that's going to count against me in a custody hearing? They'll look at that stay and my current medications and treatment schedule, and decide I'm an unfit parent. Face it, Beck looks good on paper and I look like a train wreck. He has commendations, has been in the newspaper labeled as a hero, and people love him."

Beck was very careful not to let his true self show in public. If only I'd known twelve years ago that he was such a competent actor. Maybe I wouldn't have fallen for his charm and let him slowly pull me into his web. It had started small, and before I knew it, I was married and he was controlling every aspect of my life, and I'd lost all my friends. Even the little family I had left wanted nothing to do with me because they felt I hated them. Beck had ensured that I missed every holiday gathering, every birthday party, and any other family event.

"You're not a train wreck. Ever since they got your meds right, you've been fine. Better than fine. No one would ever guess you're depressed." He reached over and squeezed my hand. "And if you weren't with Beck anymore, I bet that depression would slowly fade. He makes you miserable, Jacey."

"I still have bad days; just not that many of them."

He gave me a tender smile. "We all have bad days. You think there aren't days I don't want a drink? I've been sober for ten years now and there are still times I think 'man, a beer would be great today.'"

Ty had shared his battle with alcoholism the first time he'd noticed my bruises. He'd taken a guess as to what happened. Ty was quite a bit older than me, though his boyish charm often made him seem younger than his forty-five years.

"We're a pair, aren't we?" I asked.

"Who better to understand you than someone who's been fighting a disease themselves? If you really want a job so bad, I'll hire you at the stable."

I laughed. "Yes, I can see lots of work getting done in that scenario. Just look, you've spent half the day out of the office already."

Although, it would mean spending a lot more time with Ty. I wasn't certain if that was good or bad. As much as I'd love to spend every day of the week with him, I didn't think I'd be able to work in close quarters and not want to touch him.

"You know I don't have to be there every day. I have someone in charge of lessons, someone in charge of boarding, and the cleanup crew. The stable is well taken care of in my absence. The only reason I show up every morning is in hopes of seeing you."

My cheeks warmed and I looked away. When he said things like that, I wanted to kiss him. Now that I'd felt his lips against mine, the urge to be closer to him would only grow worse. Beck hadn't kissed me in years, and the last time he had, it had been brutal and a show of dominance, not love. He'd even drawn blood, then given me the coldest smile ever.

We pulled up at the school at the back of the line, but had a clear shot of the door. I pulled out the visor label I'd gotten for Ty's truck when he'd started making it a habit of taking me to get the kids. I hung it from the visor, indicating which kids were being picked up. The teachers stood on the walkway with a walkie-talkie and called out each child's name. Until the car pulled up closer to the door, the children would be kept inside. It was a safety measure, and one I appreciated.

"We need to stop talking about this before the kids get out. I don't want to upset them," I said. Their father upset them often enough already.

"Fine. We'll table the discussion for now, but it's far from over. I'm not giving you up without a fight, especially now. We've become good friends, but I want more, babe. I want a relationship with you and the kids, one that includes you coming to my house, not sneaking off to the barn under the guise of visiting your horse."

He had a point. In the year we'd known one another, Ty had been to my house, outside it, a dozen times or so, but I'd never been to his. It had started when my car had gotten bogged down in mud at the stable. He'd given me a ride to pick up the kids and dropped me by the house. Since then, he'd found other reasons to stop by, but I knew better than to let him inside. Whoever watched the house would tell Beck a man had been inside. Even if he didn't feel Ty was a threat, it didn't mean he wouldn't make me pay for letting the cowboy into our home.

I knew the stable was on Ty's personal property, but I also knew he had a hundred or more acres of land. Only twenty of that was used for his business. The truck he drove was five years old and comfortable but not flashy, so I tended to forget that he had money. It was days like today, when he was able to buy something for my kids that I just couldn't afford right now, that I was thankful for his generosity. While the bears were cute, they weren't cheap. The two stuffed toys with clothes had cost seventy-five dollars.

When he'd seen how much my kids loved being at the stable, and how eager they were to learn to ride, he'd taught them both on Sugar, the most docile horse he owned. After that, he'd let them use the stable mounts every time they came with me. While I rode out on the open land, Ty would watch my kids in the corral. Then he'd bought them mounts of their own. I'd been floored when we'd reached the stable after school one day and found a pony and horse standing in the aisle near Reaper with bows in their manes. Ty had come around a corner and smiled warmly at us and asked the kids if they liked their surprise. I'd wanted to protest, but how could I when I saw the joy on my children's faces?

The bell rang and a moment later the door opened. As the car line moved forward, more and more children were sent out to their parents. I spotted a familiar splash of blue and smiled as my kids tried to break from the teachers and race over. They didn't even question why he was the one in the pick-up line. It happened often enough now that it was becoming habit.

Ever since Ty had given Danica a blue T-shirt that said "Cowgirl Up" on the front, she'd worn it every week, sometimes twice a week. Both of my kids loved Ty, but did they love him enough for me to get into a custody battle with my husband? Or risk my life, or theirs? It wasn't the first time I'd thought of divorcing Beck. We'd grown apart, if we'd ever even been close. The first year or two, I'd made excuses for his behavior, but it had only gotten worse. I'd learned the hard way that I couldn't leave. He was too controlling for that, and he'd never let me go and have the department see him as being weak. Too weak to hold on to his woman. No, I was trapped, and I felt like I was slowly dying.

We moved up in line, inching our way closer and closer to my babies. When we stopped a few feet away, both kids bounced over to the truck and a teacher helped them climb in, making sure they were buckled before closing the door. Ty had even purchased a booster seat for Jackson to make sure my baby boy was safe. He was almost too perfect. If he hadn't told me about his struggle with alcoholism, I might have thought he was entirely too good to be true. Now I knew he had faults like everyone else.

"Hey, guys," Ty said. "Did you have a good day at school?"

"Yes," they chorused.

"What's in the boxes?" Danica asked, eyeing the one on her side of the truck.

"A little surprise. Why don't you open them?" Ty said.

Both kids popped the boxes open. Danica squealed when I saw her pink bear and I heard an "awesome" from Jackson as he pulled his cowboy bear out of the box. I had to admit that Ty'd had a wonderful idea. It wasn't often my kids received bears from that place because the cost was just ridiculous. Getting Ty to stop spoiling them was impossible, but I tried to steer him toward cheaper things, like a candy bar or soda after school. I was a little nervous about what he'd planned next. Between our lunch and getting the bears, he'd already spent over one hundred dollars on us today. Sometimes that was as much money as I had for a week's worth of groceries.

"Thanks, Mr. Ty," Jackson said.

"Yeah, thanks," said Danica. "She's the prettiest bear ever!"

Ty smiled at the kids in the rearview mirror. "You're welcome. Now, are you guys ready to have some fun?"

"Are we going riding?" Danica asked, starting to kick her feet in excitement.

"I thought we'd do something different today. Why don't you two sit tight and we'll be there in about fifteen minutes or so. Then you can tell me what you think of my idea," Ty said.

I gave him a curious look, but he just smiled and wouldn't give anything away. After driving back toward the mall, then continuing past it, he pulled into *Pirate Pete's*. Both kids started bouncing and talking at once. I couldn't remember the last time I'd been able to afford to bring them to this children's paradise.

Both kids scrambled out of the truck once it was parked, and we followed. I had a strong dislike for the place, but only because it was so loud it gave me a headache. My kids adored *Pirate Pete's*, though, and that's what mattered most. They had so few happy moments, or they had until Ty came along. With all the bad things going on at home, I hated to take away a moment of happiness if they could find it elsewhere.

My kids had learned early on to speak as little as possible to Beck, which worked in our favor. I didn't worry about them slipping up and talking about the time we spent with Ty. They knew that Beck would hurt me, and possibly them, if he thought for one second the cowboy was acting in a way he shouldn't. I'd kept them in the dark as much as I could about what really happened when Beck got his hands on me, but I knew they'd heard my screams in the past.

I'd enjoy this afternoon with Ty and the kids, then I'd face reality when I went home. I didn't know how much longer I'd survive with Beck, but what other choice did I have?

Chapter Two

Ty

I hated watching Jacey and the kids leave at the end of the day, knowing they were going home to a man who would possibly kill them one day. I'd asked a friend to do a little digging, and what he'd found on Beck Lane wasn't the least bit reassuring. I didn't know how the man managed to be a police officer, unless the majority of the Mayfair PD was as dirty and crooked as Jacey's husband. The only reason I hadn't brought it up to Jacey was because she thought I was some sweet guy. I didn't have the heart to let her find out the truth. Yeah, I'd been a rodeo cowboy for a lot of years, but there was another part of my past that I kept hidden. I hadn't always walked the straight and narrow. Once upon a time, I'd ridden a steel horse more often than the ones with hooves. I'd found it humorous Jacey called her horse Reaper, since my club was the Dixie Reapers.

I'd walked away when things had gone sour, and my President, Torch, had let me. A drug deal had gone sideways and a rival club had put a price on my head over a decade ago. Sometimes it felt like a lifetime had passed. If I'd hung around, I could have ended up dead. My brothers had my back, and the threat had been dealt with, but it had been a wake-up call about the type of life I was living. None of my brothers had old ladies, and only Bull had a kid. I hadn't wanted to end up like that, alone. At first, I'd traveled, riding my bike from city to city. After a while, it got tiresome and I wanted to put down roots. Of course, from what I heard, a lot of my brothers had settled down and started families since then. The club sounded like a different place from before, but there was no way I could go back and leave Jacey behind.

I'd moved to this area and opened my stable about three years ago, stashing my old Indian motorcycle in a shed out back of my house. I took it for a ride every now and then, but it didn't feel the same when I wasn't wearing my cut. Torch had told me to keep it, that I would always be a Reaper, so it hung in my closet. A reminder of the brothers I'd left behind. Sometimes I pulled it out and just held it, remembering the good times and the bad. The name *Cowboy* was stitched across the front, the name my brothers had called me. Now I was just Ty to everyone. It didn't feel right to wear it when I wasn't an active part of the Dixie Reapers. They might still call me brother, but I knew the truth. I was just like everyone else now, an everyday guy.

I wanted to be more than just Ty to Jacey, though, to her and her kids. Even though they weren't mine, I wanted them to be. I'd contemplated handling Beck myself, but I didn't know what kind of backup he had. A man couldn't be as rotten as he without at least a few of his friends being cut from the same cloth. It was laughable that the man who was supposed to walk on the right side of the law, a hero for the people, was a monster when no one was looking. Then there was me… I'd done some bad shit in my life, hadn't even pretended to be on the legal side of things when I'd been a Reaper, and yet I'd treat Jacey and the kids with the love and respect they deserved, protect them, and let them know every day that they were cherished.

I sat down at the desk in the office I kept at home and flipped open the file I had on Beck Lane. The man wasn't just getting paid by the MPD, not according to the bank statements Wire hacked. He was making some on the side too. Quite a bit, actually. I was still trying to track it all down, but I knew for certain some of it came from Maurice Salazar, a known drug dealer who was slowly moving up the ranks. Beck's bank account was way too flush for someone earning the shitty pay of a peace officer, and it pissed me the fuck off that he gave so little of it to Jacey.

Even still, the payoffs he was getting from Salazar didn't match all the cash deposits going into his account. There was way more and I knew it was coming from somewhere illegal. Beck's salary showed as direct deposits from the City of Mayfair, but these others were over the counter or funds transfers from accounts that didn't seem to really exist. Wire had also found another account, one that was supposed to be hidden, that was flush with several hundred thousand. Beck wasn't entirely stupid. He didn't dump large amounts into his regular account in any kind of pattern, or all that close together. If he were stupid, it would be easier to take him down. He had everyone fooled, except for those who had looked evil in the face before, or who were just as crooked as him. I'd taken one look at the man and known that he was evil. When I'd noticed the bruises on Jacey's arms, it had confirmed my suspicions. I had to wonder just how much the kids saw, or whether they received any of those punches. Jacey was a good mom, and I had no doubt she protected them as much as she could, but even she couldn't stop a force like Beck Lane.

I didn't know what sources Wire had used to get the dirt on Beck that was stuffed inside this folder, but I appreciated it. In most places, the money from Salazar would be enough for Internal Affairs to get involved. But Mayfair wasn't just any town. I had a feeling the corruption went pretty high up. I just wished it were more, something I could take to the police chief or mayor, if they weren't in on everything. It was times like this I missed being part of my club. The guys would have my back, and Wire would give me everything he could, even more than what he'd found so far. And if he couldn't find what I needed, then he'd look for someone who could. I wanted to get rid of Beck by any means necessary, anything to free Jacey from the nightmare she was trapped in.

I knew guys like Beck. They lured sweet women in, women like Jacey, then they turned on them when it was too late. He'd made sure Jacey didn't have a support system. No family or friends to come to her aid. It hadn't happened over night, which meant he was a patient fucker. He'd known what the hell he was doing when he'd set everything into motion, but I just didn't understand why. I knew power was the biggest part, and some evil inside the man genuinely enjoyed hurting Jacey, then making her feel like she'd deserved it. I wondered if he'd picked her long before he'd spoken to her, watched her, and waited to make his move. It seemed like the type of thing he would do.

The only way to save Jacey was to either pack her up and get her the hell out of the state, or get rid of Beck. To eliminate Beck, I had to figure out how far the corruption ran. Just how deep were the criminals in the sleepy little town of Mayfair? It looked like a quaint place when you drove down Main Street. It had been a selling point for me, but now I had to wonder about the sinister side of things. The drug dealers, pimps, and who knew what other types of people we had in Mayfair, people who were apparently well connected and didn't fear prison.

Getting Jacey to leave wouldn't be easy, and there wasn't a guarantee her crazy-ass husband wouldn't follow. He wouldn't take it well if she made him look like a fool, running off with another man. And I *would* be going with her. No way I'd send her off on her own. The only place I knew I would be able to keep her safe was the Dixie Reapers' compound. I had no doubt Torch would welcome us and help sort this shit out, but I couldn't very well tell Jacey about Torch and the Reapers without confessing about my past. The last thing I wanted right now was for her to run from me.

I turned another page, studying every detail, hoping that I'd notice something new, something I'd missed previously. Anything! Even a crumb that would put me on the right path. But if I found it, found proof that Beck belonged behind bars, who the fuck was I going to tell? I couldn't trust any of the city officials, or anyone at the police department. I needed to call Torch, explain what was going on, and see if he had any suggestions. I didn't know if Wire had told him about my situation, and I hated to keep asking my brother for info that could get him into trouble with the Pres. The last thing I wanted was to keep secrets from the club, even if I wasn't an official member anymore. If Torch couldn't spare anyone to come help me keep an eye on Beck and make sure Jacey stayed safe, then maybe he would point me to a club who could. It wasn't unheard of for clubs to work together in certain instances, but usually money was involved. I just didn't know if this would qualify.

After another half hour of looking over all the documents and not getting anywhere, I shut the file and tossed it aside. I needed more. I picked up my phone and called Wire, even though I'd told myself I wouldn't. He'd already done enough for me. I glanced at the clock and saw it was just after dinner. I didn't know if he'd be partying with the club sluts and our other brothers, or if he had someone serious in his life. We hadn't really discussed his personal life that much. He hadn't volunteered the info and I hadn't asked.

On the sixth ring, he picked up.

"Cowboy, good to hear from you again," Wire said.

"I've told you I'm just Ty."

"Nope. You'll always be Cowboy around here. Need more help with that situation you were checking into?" he asked.

"Yeah. I've been looking over everything you sent and it's not all adding up. There's money coming from somewhere else and I want to know where."

"About that… I kept working on it after I sent over that stuff. You're not going to like what I've found so far. This guy is a serious piece of work, and the fact he's a cop just makes it even worse. He's been uploading videos to porn sites and charging perverts to watch him, or someone, fuck a woman who clearly doesn't want the attention. The classier sites won't touch that shit, but you know there are places deep enough on the Web that won't care if the woman is being forced. Hell, they get off on it. No faces or distinguishing marks, just a dick fucking a pussy."

My stomach knotted and I thought I might throw up. I had the horrible feeling that it wasn't just some random woman Beck was uploading to those places. Jesus! Even thinking that he might be raping her and then profiting from it made me want to hunt him down and set his ass on fire. Dick first. What kind of sick bastard were we dealing with?

"There's more," Wire said. "He's also been selling pictures of a woman in various poses, again with no face or distinguishing marks. He makes her sit or stand where her pussy lips are parted, or he forces her to hold herself open. From what I can tell between the video and the pics, I think it's the same woman."

I tossed the phone on my desk and threw up in the trashcan. I dry heaved a few times after I had nothing left in my stomach, then picked up the phone with a shaky hand.

"Jesus Christ, Cowboy. Is he posting that shit of your woman?" Wire asked.

"I don't know for sure, but yeah, I think it might be her. You said he's forcing her in the videos?"

Wire was quiet a moment. "I'm sorry I said anything. Fuck. Yeah, it looks like she's not a willing participant. He's telling her to hold still and take it, and saying shit like she'd better not fucking cry. In some of them she's screaming for him to stop. He's a really sick fuck, Cowboy. You need to get her and those kids out of there. And I mean now."

"I don't have a way to keep them safe here. He's on the local police force and has friends in all the right places. I'm a no one here."

"Then you get them out of there and bring them home. Your real home, you fucker."

"Wire, if I do this, if I get them away from here, you know we can't stay at the compound indefinitely. After everything she's been through, I need to keep her safe. The club might not be into heavy shit, but you and I both know trouble finds the Reapers even when we aren't looking for it. I can't do that to her or those kids."

Wire sighed. "Yeah, I get it. You're somewhere outside of Nashville, right?"

"Yep. About an hour from the city limits, more in traffic."

"Puts you around six hours from the compound, if traffic laws were something we worried about. I'm going to talk to Torch and Venom, let them know what's going on, and we're going to send some guys your way. Try to act cool until they get there. No heroics, Cowboy. I know that woman means something to you, but you'll get both of yourselves killed if you don't wait."

"I hear you. I'll sit tight. Jacey usually gets here in the mornings after she takes the kids to school. Only times she doesn't show up, she claims she's been sick, but now I'm thinking otherwise."

"We're going to protect them, Cowboy. Whatever it takes. I'll be in touch."

The line went dead and I set the phone aside. Waiting wasn't my strong suit, but I didn't want to risk Jacey or the kids. I didn't know how the fuck she'd survived this long, but I hoped like hell she'd make it one more day.

I got up and went to the bedroom. Pulling my old rodeo bag from the top of the closet, I dumped out the gear I likely wouldn't use again and loaded it with a week's worth of clothes. I tossed in other important shit, like my toothbrush and a few weapons, some stacks of cash, then zipped it shut. Staring into my closet, I slowly reached in and pulled out my cut. I'd been through some serious shit while wearing it, and it seemed fitting that I had it on when I dealt with the Beck issue.

It felt like forever before the sun started to rise. Sleep had been impossible. Even if I hadn't seen the video Wire had talked about, I could imagine it. I wanted to kill Beck with my bare hands, but I wanted him to suffer first. Jacey was going to have justice, Reapers style. I only hoped once she saw that side of me, realized who I really was, that she wouldn't run. I didn't want her to lump me in with the likes of Beck, but I knew it could happen. It's why I'd kept my past a secret.

Maybe it was wrong of me, but I hoped that fucker followed us. He'd have no jurisdiction in the Reapers' territory, and my brothers would help me capture him. Once I had Beck right where I wanted him, I planned to inflict as much pain on him as possible. I wanted him to know what it felt like to be helpless, to be abused and left to suffer, to pray for the end and only hurt more in the hours to come.

Oh, yes. I was going to make Beck pay. And when I was done, I'd make sure he could never hurt another woman or child ever again.

Chapter Three

Jacey

Beck hadn't come home last night. I'd lain awake until it was time to start the day, and he'd never come in from his shift. I hadn't received a call about him being injured, which meant he was out with the guys or doing God only knew what. If it involved a woman, I hoped she was smarter than me and would run far and fast. No matter how much I wanted away from Beck, I wouldn't wish him on another woman. Not ever. No one deserved to live the way I had over the past twelve years.

My hands shook as I went to wake the kids, and I paused in the process of going to their rooms. I didn't know what kind of mood Beck would be when he came home, or what he'd want from me. It was possible he'd come home drunk, and that always made for a day of misery and humiliation. He was at his cruelest when he'd been drinking. For some people, alcohol lowered their inhibitions and let them have fun. With Beck, it lowered his and let more of the darkness out. He'd often told me that he'd had offers from men to fuck me, but he'd like rubbing it in their faces that I belonged to him. I often worried that one day he might change his mind.

I knew I needed to get away, to save my kids. There was no way I'd survive this relationship long enough for them to move out on their own. For now, Beck was content to humiliate me and exploit me in any way he could. Someday that could change, and I didn't want to be around when he decided his kids were fair game. No one meant anything to him, only money.

I was about to open Jackson's door when I heard my cell phone ring in my purse. I never received calls this early in the morning unless it was Beck, and he always called the home phone, expecting me to be here to answer it. I pulled it from my purse and my eyes went wide when I saw it was Ty. Not the stable number, but the personal one he'd programmed in a few months ago. It had been the day he'd noticed the bruises on my arms, even though he'd tried not to make a big deal of it at the time.

"Ty?" I asked softly. "Is everything all right?"

"No, everything is far from all right, Jacey. I'm on my way to you right now, with some friends. I don't want you to be scared when you see us. You trust me, don't you? You know I would never hurt you or those kids?"

I swallowed hard, his words causing me a moment of panic. "Ty, what's going on? Why would I ever be scared of you?"

"There are things about me you don't know, Jacey, a part of my past I've left buried. I can't do that right now, though, not and keep you safe. I'm getting you out of there, you and those kids. Pack light if you can, but make sure you each have a week's worth of clothes and anything else you need."

"Ty, I can't just..."

"Yes," he said harshly. "You can and you damn well will, Jacey."

"Ty."

I could hear him breathing in the silence, and then he uttered the words that completely tore me in two.

"I know, Jacey. I know what he makes you do, and I'm not standing by and letting it happen anymore. He will never touch you again, and I will make damn certain he never gets those kids. Do you hear me?"

I gasped and choked back a sob. I closed my eyes and let the tears fall. My worst nightmare had come true. Ty, my sweet cowboy, the man I was falling in love with, knew about the pictures and videos, had possibly even seen them. I felt like my entire world was unraveling, and the only good thing I'd ever had would be ripped away. How could he possibly ever want me after seeing that?

"Jacey." His voice was softer. "Babe, what he's done to you changes nothing for me. I will protect you and those kids at all costs, and we *will* finish what we started yesterday. You deserve so much more than life has given you. Don't fight me on this. I'm coming for you, and you're going to leave with no questions asked."

"All right, Ty," I said softly. "I do trust you, and you're right. I can't stay here, can't wait for the day he kills me and turns on my children."

"Hold tight, sweetheart. I'll be there soon."

He ended the call and I stared at my phone a moment. I took a shuddering breath and wiped the tears from my eyes, then went to wake up the kids. I told them Ty was going to take us somewhere, on an adventure, and we needed to pack quickly. Danica was old enough that she seemed to sense something else was going on. There was a look in her eye that said she didn't for one second believe we were going on a vacation, especially after I said we had to hurry before their dad came home.

Neither of my kids were anxious to see Beck, and both were packed in record time. I was just placing our bags in the front entry when I heard the sound of motorcycles coming down the street. I'd never seen many bikes in this area and my heart kicked up a notch as I wondered if my husband had anything to do with them. Three bikers pulled up out front of my house, just past the driveway, and stopped farther along the curb in front of the house. I saw that each wore a leather vest with a grim reaper emblem on the back. I couldn't read the text from my front door, but my hands were shaking as they got off their bikes. A truck pulled up behind them and another guy in the same vest got out.

As the one who seemed to be the leader approached, he pulled off his helmet and sunglasses, and my heart stuttered and nearly stopped. *Ty*? My Ty was a biker? I opened the door and stepped out, not sure what to say to him or how to react. I knew that not everyone who was part of some sort of biker club was a bad guy, and Ty had never struck me as anything but good. As he drew closer, I saw the word *Cowboy* stitched on his vest along with the words *Dixie Reapers*.

"Ty, what's going on?" I asked, then looked past him at the other men and the motorcycles parked at the end of my driveway.

"This is part of my past that I haven't told you about, but it's a part that will let me keep you safe and get you away from Beck. The men behind me are part of the Dixie Reapers, a club I belonged to for a lot of years. I walked away over a decade ago and never looked back, but I can't protect you from Beck on my own, and it's not safe for you to stay here."

I glanced at the men. They'd removed their helmets and sunglasses as well. They didn't seem frightening, except for their size. Each of them was large and heavily muscled, as big as Beck if not more so. The one who'd gotten out of the truck came up alongside them, and I saw *Prospect* on his vest. I didn't think they were called vests, though. Beck had watched one of those motorcycle shows one time, but I hadn't paid much attention to it. I preferred lighter things that were more appropriate for a younger audience. There was enough darkness in my life already.

"Jacey." Ty's voice snapped my attention back to him. "These men are here because they want to keep you safe. They're my brothers, even if they aren't blood. I want you to come with us. You can ride on the back of my bike and the kids can go in the truck with your bags."

"Your bike?" I asked and looked at the yellow motorcycle he'd ridden here. "You want me to…"

"Yeah, babe, I really do." He leaned in closer and dropped his voice to a low growl that had my panties getting wet despite the seriousness of my situation. It was Ty. My Ty, so how could I not get turned on when he went all alpha and sexy on me? "Want to feel your body pressed close to me, your arms tight around my waist."

"Danica and Jackson might be scared riding with someone they don't know," I said.

The man who'd been in the truck came forward, moving slowly. "Ma'am, my name's King, and I promise to protect your kids with my life, but if they want you to ride along with them, at least for the first little bit, then I'm all right with that if Cowboy is. He's calling the shots."

"And the other two?" I asked, glancing their way again.

The tallest one stepped forward. He hesitated only a moment, glancing at the others. "My name's Grimm. We don't like to use our real names for various reasons, but I can tell you're scared, and knowing what I do of the situation, I'm going to share that part of myself with you. Before I became a full-fledged member of the club, my name was Ivan Volkov."

"Russian?" I asked. "You don't have an accent, other than southern."

He smiled a little. "My parents were Russian, but I mostly grew up here in the States. These men already know that, except Cowboy, so what I've shared with you is special. Not everyone knows where I came from or who I really am. Same for everyone else in the club."

The other one came forward and gave me a warm smile. "They call me Sarge and I'm ex-military. I will do everything I can to assure that you and your children arrive at the Dixie Reapers' compound safely."

"Compound?" I asked, looking at Ty again.

"Think of it as a gated community that is heavily protected," he said. "Beck at work? How much time do we have?"

My body tensed as I jerked my gaze down the road. For a moment, I'd forgotten that he'd been gone all night and could return any second. I rushed inside and shooed the kids out the front door, then tried to carry out our bags. Grimm came inside and hefted them with ease. I picked up my purse but set my cell phone on the table along with my car keys. I didn't know if Beck could use them to track me, but I didn't want to take the chance.

"Jacey, leave the purse," Ty said.

"But… I'll need my ID and money." Not that I had more than forty dollars in my wallet, and that was only because Beck had asked me to pick up beer and some other things for him.

"Get your license out of your purse, and get all your birth certificates and social security cards. You won't be coming back here, Jacey. I don't trust Beck not to have somehow hidden something inside your bag."

I nodded. I'd had a feeling we wouldn't be returning so I'd already packed anything important, like the kids' shot records and birth certificates. I took my license out of my wallet and shoved it into my front pocket, then closed the front door for the last time. My hands shook and Ty reached for me. I went willingly, needing the comfort of his arms around me.

"You can ride with the kids until we reach the next town," he said. "Then I want you on my bike. I've been dreaming of taking you for a ride."

"The kids… they get bored on long trips." I hadn't had time to go buy them anything like coloring books, new novels to read, or anything that might entertain them. Nor did I really have the funds for that, but I didn't know how long we'd be on the road.

"We'll take care of it along the way, Jacey. We need to leave. Now," Ty said, his voice brooking no argument.

I nodded and let him guide us down to the end of the driveway. The men introduced themselves to the kids and explained that we were going on a long road trip, but we'd stop soon for snacks and anything else they may want or need. I buckled into the front seat of the truck and noticed that there was already a booster seat for Jackson. Once everyone was situated, King put the truck into gear and pulled away from the curb.

My stomach was doing somersaults as I waited for Beck to appear and go into a rage. As the blocks passed and nothing happened, I eased my hold on the door and tried to relax back into the seat. When Mayfair was in the rearview mirror and only the open highway lay before us, I breathed a little easier, hoping that just maybe we'd managed to pull it off, that we'd finally escaped Beck.

"Darlin', no one's going to catch up to us now," King said, giving me a smile. "Even if your husband has discovered you're missing, it will take him a while to figure out where you're going."

"But what if someone on the street got a good look at your…" I waved at the black vest.

"Our cuts? It's possible. He'd still have to do a little digging to figure out where we're located and then get there. We have an officer who is aware of your situation and he'll make it damn hard for your husband to get any help from the local law enforcement," King said.

"Momma," Jackson called from the back seat, his voice soft and a little hesitant. "Are we leaving Daddy?"

I swallowed hard and then turned to smile at my kids. "Yeah, baby. We're leaving Daddy. Mr. Ty is going to take us somewhere safe, okay?"

Danica heaved out a dramatic sigh. "Finally."

I blinked at my daughter. "What?"

She fastened her gaze on me, looking far more like a wizened adult than a kid. "Jackson and I pray every day that you'll leave Daddy and take us with you. We know he hurts you, and we don't like it. We've heard you cry and scream, beg him to stop."

I turned to face the front and tried really damn hard not to cry. King reached over and squeezed my hand briefly. Ty was riding out in front of us and had turned to look our direction. I wondered if he'd seen the move and didn't approve. I reached up and wiped a stray tear off my cheek, hoping my kids didn't notice. We traveled another half hour before everyone pulled off the road and into a little town.

We stopped in front of a diner that said *Betty's* on the window. Ty helped me out of the truck, wrapping his arms around me. His lips brushed my cheek, then he placed them against my ear.

"I see King lay another hand on you, and that kid won't live long enough to patch in."

I gasped and blinked up at him, but he gave me a smirk that said he wasn't serious. At least, I didn't think he was. His lips pressed against mine and I couldn't help but melt against him. Ty growled a little and deepened the kiss, his hold tightening on me. A throat cleared, and we pulled apart in time to see Grimm wink at us as he passed with a kid holding onto each of his hands.

My cheeks flushed as I looked up at Ty, but he seemed rather pleased by our public display of affection. "Been waiting a really damn long time to kiss you like that, whenever I want. Expect plenty more where that came from," he said.

"Ty, I..." I shut my mouth, not knowing if I wanted to deter him, or beg for more.

"That asshole is in your past now, Jacey. He's a dead man walking, babe. The second I found out what he'd done to you, he'd sealed his fate."

"Y-You'd k-kill him?" I asked, my heart thumping hard in my chest.

Ty leaned in closer and dropped his voice to a harsh whisper. "He raped you, then filmed it and sold it. He forced you to expose yourself for pictures to line his pockets, then left you without enough money to take care of your kids. Not to mention the beatings. What else has he done, Jacey? So yes, I'd fucking kill him if given half a chance, and I wouldn't regret it for one second."

I trembled and I wasn't sure if it was because his words scared me -- that Ty could be capable of something like that -- or if it worried me more that the thought of a world without Beck sounded like heaven.

"Jacey," he said, his voice softening. "I will never, *never* hurt you or those kids, but yes, I will kill to protect you. I'm sorry if that means I'm not the man you thought I was, and I hope it won't change the way you look at me. But I will do whatever it takes to make sure you never go through any of that again."

"Ty, I..." I licked my lips and then pressed my mouth to his. I didn't know how to put into words what I wanted to say, but I hoped he understood that I wasn't scared of him. I could never fear Ty.

"Let's get something to eat, then find some stuff to keep the kids busy."

He wrapped his fingers around mine, then frowned at our clasped hands. He lifted them up to eye level, then narrowed his gaze. Before I realized what had upset him, he pulled my wedding ring off and threw it in the gutter. He linked our fingers again and led me into the diner.

I didn't know what to do with this version of Ty, but I had a feeling I might like seeing the alpha side of him. He wasn't scary and out of control like Beck. Even when he was speaking about killing my husband, the way he looked at me... there was still tenderness in his eyes, and something more.

I'd almost go so far as to say Ty loved me, and maybe he did.

Whatever the future held, I hoped that I would finally get a chance to find out what life would be like with Ty. Or Cowboy. Whatever he wanted to be called.

And I hoped I got a chance to find out if the heat between us extended to more than just kissing. If anyone could give me an orgasm, my money was on Ty.

Chapter Four

Ty

We'd been on the road for five hours by the time we reached the Dixie Reapers compound. Lots of new faces, and quite a few familiar ones too. Jacey had ridden on the back of my bike for a while, but the last hour she'd slept in the truck. As much as I wanted to introduce her and the kids to everyone, I didn't want to overwhelm them, not after the emotional day they'd had.

Torch gave me a hug, which surprised the fuck out of me.

"Good to see you, boy. I knew you'd find your way home sooner or later," he said.

"I'm not home, Pres. This is just a layover while I make sure Jacey and the kids are safe."

He grinned. "We'll see about that. If your brothers can't convince you to stay, then the women and kids will convince your family this is where you belong."

"My f-family?" I asked, hating the stutter.

"You called her your woman when you talked to Wire, which means she's yours, and so are those kids. There are a few unclaimed homes here. Had a few of the guys make sure one was ready for you. Fully furnished, and King texted the ages of the kids, so there's toys and shit for them too."

I looked around, noticing way more houses than had been here when I'd left.

"A lot's changed," Torch said. "Some things are the same, but we're a lot more cautious these days, and we have the backing of three other clubs. We're tied to the Devil's Boneyard, Devil's Fury, and Hades Abyss by blood or marriage, and each club will have our backs if we need the help. What happened to you won't ever be an issue again. Clubhouse these days is just as wild at night as it used to be, but the prospects all room there now. We've got nine patched members with old ladies, and ten with kids. Excluding you, unless you decide you're ready to stay."

I swallowed a knot of emotion and gave him a nod. "Thanks, Pres."

Torch slapped my shoulder. "You're still one of us, Cowboy. Always will be, and that makes that woman and those kids part of us too. You know damn well we protect our own. King will show you the way to the house. Get them settled and have a night with your woman. Be in Church at nine o'clock in the morning."

"Yes, sir."

I got back on my bike and followed the truck to a two-story home that was a robin's-egg blue with black shutters and a red door. No way in hell any of my brothers came up with the paint scheme for this. Must have been one of the old ladies Torch had mentioned. I knew he and Venom had settled down, and Wire had mentioned Tank recently found someone. It made me wonder who else had paired up while I was gone. I looked at the house again, and had a feeling Jacey would like it. The place looked like a nice family home, not something that should be in the middle of a biker compound. I shut off my bike and walked over to the truck to help Jacey and the kids out.

King carried their bags inside, placing them just beyond the door, then he gave me a quick salute and made himself scarce. The kids looked around and seemed hesitant. I could understand. Their lives had been turned upside down today. Even if Beck was a monster, he was still their dad. It had to be confusing, just packing up and walking away without a word. And while I'd spent a lot of time with them at the stable and occasionally going to eat or out somewhere fun, leaving town together like this just wasn't something they would have expected. Not to mention the fact I'd kissed their mom every chance I'd had once we were free of Mayfair.

Yep, I needed to sit down and have a talk with everyone.

"Everyone inside," I said, motioning toward the house. "Have a seat in the living room and I'll try to answer some questions."

The kids scampered inside with Jacey moving at a slower pace. I shut and locked the door, knowing my brothers were the type to come barging in unannounced, especially when they were curious. I stood in front of the three of them, my arms folded as I studied my little family. Yeah, Torch wasn't wrong. They were mine, even if I hadn't officially claimed them. Jacey's marriage wasn't a deterrent at this point, not with my current knowledge of what Beck had done to her. If I'd known what she'd been suffering all this time, I'd have gotten her away from him sooner.

"I'm sure you kids are confused right now," I said, addressing Danica and Jackson.

"Not really," said Danica. "You're trying to save our mom, right? Because you love her?"

My eyebrows rose as I looked at Jacey. I knew Danica was smart, but I hadn't realized just how smart until this particular moment. The kid saw more than I gave her credit for, which made me wonder what she knew about her dad. Her brother didn't seem bothered by Danica's question. I just wasn't entirely certain how to answer her. I could tell her the truth, but I didn't know exactly how much they knew. I didn't want to bad-mouth their dad if they admired him like the public did, or if they knew exactly what their mother had been through.

"Yes, I'm trying to save your mom, and both of you," I said.

Jacey dropped her gaze and squeezed her hands together. It made my heart ache, knowing she wanted more from me. I just hadn't wanted to tell her how I felt in front of the kids. Not for the first time anyway.

"And yes, I love your mom. I would do anything for her, and for the two of you," I said. "Your dad isn't a nice man, and I --"

"They know," Jacey said. "Danica said they know he hurts me. You don't have to hide it from them."

"Are we going to live here?" Jackson asked. "Are you our dad now?"

Danica eyed her brother. "It doesn't work that way."

Jackson looked disappointed, his lower lip protruding and his gaze shifting away. I wanted to tell him that I would be honored to be their dad. Even more, that I wanted their mom by my side for the rest of my life, but I knew now wasn't the time. It might never be the right time. Once I handled Beck, Jacey might very well see me as every bit as monstrous as her husband and take off. I wouldn't blame her in the slightest.

"Why don't the two of you go upstairs?" I suggested. "There are two bedrooms that were prepared for you. I need to talk to your mom a minute."

The kids shot off the couch and went running for the stairs. When I heard the squeals as they found their bedrooms, I focused on Jacey. She rubbed her hands up and down her thighs before standing and coming closer to me.

"Ty, what you've done for us… I can't ever repay you."

"I didn't ask you to. All I want is for you to be safe and happy. If you're talking about the expense involved in all this, don't worry about it. Money isn't a problem."

She looked around, then her gaze focused on my cut. "The money you used to open the stable, and for all the things you've bought the kids… It wasn't all from the rodeo, was it? I know champions can make a good amount, but it goes beyond that, doesn't it?"

"No, I didn't just use rodeo money. When I was an active part of the club, I earned a cut of the profits like the others. Didn't touch much of it and just added it to my winnings. I may have done some bad things in my life, Jacey, but I'm not like Beck."

"I know," she said softly. "I've known you're nothing like him since the day we met."

"You can have your own room if you want," I offered, even though it about killed me to say the words. As large as this place was, there had to be several bedrooms. Even if the kids had to share one, I knew they wouldn't mind if their mom felt better in her own space.

She pressed her body to mine and curled her hand around the back of my neck. "I was hoping I'd get to share yours."

God, this woman! I wanted to kiss her, claim her, press her against the wall and take what I've wanted for a damn year. The only thing holding me back were the kids upstairs who could appear again at a moment's notice. Maybe it was being here at the compound again, but I could feel parts of my old self creeping in already, the man who would have made a move on Jacey long before now, the guy who'd always taken what he wanted. If I'd done that months ago, I could have saved her so much pain.

"You're welcome in my bed anytime, Jacey, but I don't know that I can have you lying next to me and remain a gentleman. I know you have this image of me, the do-good cowboy who is sweet and charming, and maybe that's a part of me… but I'm also a man who's used to taking what he wants. I only held back because of Beck, and now that I know what he's done to you, I won't be holding back anymore. I wish I had gotten you away a long time ago."

She pressed her lips to mine in a brief kiss. "It's not your fault. I didn't tell anyone what was happening. The neighbors, Beck's coworkers… none of them would have believed me, and I was too humiliated to tell you. I didn't want you to look at me and see… see…"

She swallowed hard and couldn't even finish her sentence, which was just as well since it was complete bullshit. If she thought for one second I saw her as less than before, then she was wrong.

"I meant what I said to the kids. I love you, babe. I think I have for a while, but I kept my distance out of respect for you. I knew that Beck didn't deserve you, but I could see you were the type to be loyal. Don't ever for one second think you're less in my eyes because of what happened to you. You're a victim, Jacey, and none of that shit is your fault. You trusted the wrong man. That's your only crime in all this, and I've seen Beck in action. He's good. Damn good."

"But you knew, didn't you? Knew who he really was?" she asked.

"Yeah, I did, but then I've dealt with monsters most of my life. People don't see Beck for who is truly is because they expect him to be good. If you can't trust a cop, then who can you trust? They want him to be a hero, so that's what they see when they look at him. They can't see the darkness inside."

"I was so stupid falling for all his lies," she said.

"No, honey. You weren't stupid. You thought you were in love. Men like Beck can spot someone sweet like you a mile away. You were like a little lamb being led to the slaughter. I don't blame you, and no one else will either, not if I have any say in the matter."

"I wish I could have met you before Beck." She ran her hands up and down my chest, pausing to run her fingers across the name *Cowboy* on my cut.

I smiled at her and smoothed her hair back from her face. "Sweetheart, when you were eighteen, I was thirty-three. You wouldn't have looked twice at me back then."

"Then I would have been an idiot," she said. "Age is just a number, Ty. Or am I supposed to call you Cowboy?"

"You can call me Ty. To you, I'll always be Ty. I wouldn't have it any other way."

"What happens if Beck finds out where I am?" she asked.

"I'll handle it. He's not getting anywhere near you."

She nodded and cuddled against me, pressing her cheek to my chest. I wrapped my arms around her, holding her tight and wishing I could take all the pain and suffering away. I hadn't seen the videos Wire mentioned, and I didn't think I could stomach watching them. It was bad enough hearing what was in them. Knowing that countless men had watched those, had listened to her scream and gotten off on it, made me want to track each and every one down and make them suffer. It sickened me that men like that were out there in the world. I was no angel, but I'd also never hurt a woman or kid, and I never would.

There was a knock at the front door and I reluctantly released Jacey to see who it was. When I opened the door, a petite woman and two little girls were standing on the front walkway.

"I'm Ridley, Venom's wife, and these are our girls. I don't know if Torch mentioned it, but there's a playground here at the compound and we thought we'd see if your kids wanted to come run off some energy. After being cooped up in a car all day, I thought they might want to stretch and play."

I motioned for her to come in. She eyed me up and down and smiled a little.

"So you're the infamous Cowboy. I've heard mention of you a few times over the years, along with Joker and Hammer. Incidentally, I've heard Hammer may be returning to us soon. Venom says his time is up, but Joker has another year or so," Ridley said.

Jacey came closer and leaned against me.

"Sweetheart, this is Ridley and her girls. They belong to Venom, who you haven't had a chance to meet, but he's the VP for the club. She wants to take Jackson and Danica to the playground."

I felt Jacey stiffen and I held her closer.

"It's okay. Ridley says they've added a playground to the compound so it's inside the gate and the kids will be safe," I assured her.

Ridley nodded. "Venom plans on joining us too. He just had to talk to Torch for a minute. I saw Dad and Darian with their two kids over there already, so they can play with Isadora and Foster too. Um, I should mention I'm Bull's daughter. I don't remember if you were around back then or not, but I used to come to clubhouse sometimes when I was little."

"Bull has more kids?" I asked, vaguely remembering a blonde little girl.

She nodded. "Oh yeah, and he's such a teddy bear with them. He missed out on a lot not getting to be around me when I was younger, so he's making up for it. I like to give him shit about his wife being younger than me, but I honestly like Darian."

"Your dad has little kids?" Jacey asked.

"Yep," Ridley said. "Foster is getting close to six and Isadora is not quite three. They're adorable, and nothing at all like my two hellions."

Jacey blinked at the little girls standing docilely by their mom. "Hellions?"

"Don't let them fool you. These two terrors strike fear into most of the guys around here. Just ask Tank. One of my girls jumped at him from a tree, and that's one of the milder things they've done," Ridley said.

I snickered because I could honestly see Venom having kids like that. He'd been something of a hell-raiser from what I remembered, and Wire had already told me what a firebrand Ridley could be. There was no way in hell two people like that would produce meek kids.

Jacey seemed to make some sort of decision about the woman and girls standing in our entryway, and called up the stairs to Jackson and Danica. The kids came racing down, then halted when they saw the girls.

Ridley waved. "Hi. I'm Ridley and these are my daughters, Mariah and Farrah. Farrah's the oldest, and the most trouble, so don't do anything she suggests or your mom might kill me."

Danica tipped her head to the side and studied Mariah and Farrah, and Jackson hid behind his sister a little.

"I'm Danica and this is my little brother, Jackson," she said, moving closer to the girls and Ridley. "I'm ten and he's six."

Farrah smiled, showing off a missing tooth. "I'm ten! Mariah's six."

"Six and a half," Mariah corrected.

"Do you want to come to the playground with us? There's swings, a slide, and stuff we can climb on," Mariah said.

Danica and Jackson looked up at Jacey and she gave a nod.

Ridley herded all the kids outside, then paused in the doorway. "Venom and I thought you could also use some adult time to work things out between you two. I'll keep them occupied for a while."

I shut and locked the door behind her and turned back to Jacey.

"She's…" Jacey didn't seem to have the right words for Ridley, and I wasn't sure I did either, other than devious. Winning her way in here claiming to want to let the kids stretch their legs, and then that parting shot. Yeah, I knew why she'd come by. Everyone at the compound probably knew by now how I felt about Jacey and that I hadn't made much of a move before now.

"She's one hundred percent right. We could use some adult time," I said, gathering her in my arms again. "As far as I'm concerned, you're no longer married to Beck. In fact, I bet Wire could make that a reality with a few keystrokes."

"Who's Wire?" she asked.

"The best hacker in the damn country, possibly the world, and he's a Dixie Reaper. Say the word and you'll be legally divorced from Beck by nightfall."

She blinked up at me. "Really?"

I nodded. "Pretty sure he could handle something like that."

I could tell she was tempted. Even if she stayed married to Beck, she'd be a widow before long. I knew he'd come for her, and when he did, I'd make sure he never left. Just one problem. There wouldn't be a body so any life insurance he had wouldn't do Jacey and the kids any good. I had more than enough money to support them, and if it ran out, I'd earn more. It just felt wrong cheating them out of something Jacey had literally earned through blood and tears. Wire could probably hack into Beck's accounts and siphon the money into one for Jacey, but I didn't think she'd touch that money.

"Do it," she said, her jaw firming. "Make it go away, make *Beck* go away. I don't want to be his wife anymore, not even on paper."

"You sure, Jacey?"

She nodded.

I pulled my phone from my pocket and shot off a text to Wire.

Jacey wants to be officially divorced from Beck. Can you make it happen?

It only took a minute before I got a response.

Consider it done. Give me an hour, two tops and she won't be married anymore.

I smiled and showed the message to her. Jacey relaxed, the tension easing from her. I knew it wouldn't be that simple, that Beck Lane wouldn't care if they were legally married still or not. I knew it made a difference to Jacey, though. She'd held back in my office because she was a wife, but I'd just taken that issue off the table. Or rather, Wire would. I wasn't going to ask how he accomplished it because I really didn't want to know. All I cared about was the end result.

"I'm really free?" she asked.

"In a matter of speaking. He's not going to back off, Jacey, not until I make him."

"But… I'm free… to be with you," she said softly, her curves melting against me.

"Yeah, babe. You're free to be with me, and keep a clear conscience."

"Then take me to the bedroom, Ty. I don't want to waste any more time. We've already lost a year that we could have been together."

She didn't need to tell me twice. I lifted her into my arms and carried her up the stairs. There were three doors on the right of the landing, one directly across from the stairs, and another to the left. Instinct made me go left and I nudged open the door with the toe of my boot. The master bedroom was spacious and done in muted blues and gray.

I kicked the door shut and managed to twist the lock, just in case. I carried Jacey over to the bed and let her slide down my body. The pulse in her throat fluttered and her lips parted. I loved that she wanted me every bit as much as I wanted her. Slowly, I reached for the hem of her shirt and started to lift it. Her hand shot up and she wrapped her fingers around my wrist.

"Wait."

"If you don't want to do this, just tell me, Jacey. I would never force you to be intimate with me."

"It's not that." She licked her lips. "I'm not eighteen anymore, Ty. My body isn't... it's not as pretty as it used to be."

"Jacey, you are gorgeous and sexy, and I will love every part of you because I love *you*."

She nodded and released me. I finished pulling her shirt up and over her head, then couldn't contain the growl that erupted at the sight of what Beck Lane had done to her. There were scars along her torso, some looked like knife wounds and others were burn marks. Wire hadn't mentioned this shit when he'd told me about the videos. My gaze locked with hers as I sank to my knees in front of her, then gently kissed each and every mark on her body. Her skin looked like a roadmap of pain, but also survival. Despite everything he'd done to her, she was still standing, and she was here with me.

Salty tears dripped from her cheeks onto my face, and it nearly ripped my heart in two, seeing firsthand what that monster had done to her, and knowing that no one had treated her right in a really long time, if ever. I vowed that no matter what it took, I would make sure this incredible woman knew that she was loved, appreciated, and that what Beck had done to her was far from all right. She should never have had to suffer for so long, not even for one second.

I worked her jeans down her legs and pulled her shoes off before removing the denim all the way. There were more marks on her thighs and I traced them softly. I wished that I could erase every one, and the memories that went with them. I hoped there would be a day that she wouldn't think of Beck, wouldn't remember the horrors she'd faced, but I knew that was a long road to travel. She'd taken the first step when she'd left him.

Her bra and panties were plain, but the curvy woman standing in front of me was mesmerizing. I wouldn't have cared what she was wearing; she still would have been the most beautiful woman I'd ever seen. I traced the lines of her body with my hands, marveling at how damn soft she felt. When my gaze met hers, I could see the vulnerability there, as well as the trust and love. The way she stood, bare and open to me, not trying to hide, told me everything I needed to know. Jacey knew that I wouldn't harm her or humiliate her.

I took my time, worshiping every inch of her body, teasing her with kisses and little licks as I worked my way from her hip to her breasts. I slowly removed her bra and panties. Her nipples were hard and I couldn't resist taking a taste. I lapped at the first one before sucking it into my mouth. I flicked it with my tongue until she was trembling, then switched to the other side. When she was whimpering with need and begging for more, I stood and removed my boots and clothes. My lips crashed down on hers, and I kissed her until we were both gasping for breath.

I needed to go slow, to make this really good for her, but it had been so damn long since I'd touched a woman and I've been craving Jacey for a year. I was worried I wouldn't be able to hold back and would disappoint her. I'd never cared before, not really. Yeah, I'd made sure my past lovers, even one-night stands, had a good time, but it hadn't mattered if I'd made it the best they'd ever had. Not until Jacey.

"Make love to me, Ty," she said.

I closed my eyes a moment, reality setting in. I was far from prepared. In the old days, the clubhouse kept a fishbowl of condoms, but I wasn't about to get dressed and head over there for a condom. It was no one's business what happened in this house, not when it came to Jacey, and if I went fishing in the bowl of rubbers, then everyone would know what was happening right now. Just because Ridley had taken the kids so we could have some adult time didn't mean that we were necessarily getting naked. If I went to the clubhouse, then everyone would know for sure what we were doing.

"Jacey, I don't have condoms with me. I haven't been with anyone since the day I met you."

"I'm clean and on the pill," she said. "And I trust you. Maybe I shouldn't, not with my past, but I do."

It humbled me that she could say that, and mean it. I tumbled her to the bed, and her legs wound around my hips. My cock brushed against her slick folds and I groaned as I sank into her. She was so damn wet, and we fit together perfectly. I wasn't a small man by any means, but she didn't flinch or utter a word of protest. I felt her nails bite into my shoulders as she lifted her hips, silently asking for more. I gave her every inch of my cock, then held still, just taking in the moment. I'd thought we'd never make it to this point, and I wanted to savor it, to savor *her*. Our gazes locked and my heart raced at the love I saw shining in her eyes.

I took her slowly, drawing it out as long as possible. The slick clasp of her pussy around my cock made my muscles tense as I fought for control. Jacey was pure perfection. I twisted my hips to give her just the right amount of friction in all the right places, and it didn't take long before she was coming. The warm gush of her release had me groaning and clenching my jaw. The old Ty would have pounded into her, not stopping until he came. But then the old Ty had never been with a woman like Jacey, and I wanted everything to be just right. Making her come once wasn't anywhere near enough, though, not knowing what I did about her. Sweat slicked my skin as I maintained a tenuous grip on my control. I rubbed her clit as I took her slow but deep.

Feeling her inner walls flutter as she came was both heaven and hell. I wanted this moment to be completely different from her times with Beck, but doing the soft and sweet thing was damn near killing me. This wasn't about me, though, it was about Jacey, and I'd give her the world if I could. I made her come twice more before I knew I couldn't hold back another second.

I shifted so that I could grip her ass with one hand, and I drove into her hard and fast, every stroke feeling as if I went deeper than the last. Every thrust banged the headboard into the wall, but I didn't care. I needed her, craved her. Jacey panted and made the sexiest noises I'd ever heard, and when my cock jerked and I started coming, she wasn't far behind me. I didn't stop thrusting, not even after the last drop of cum had been wrung from my balls, wishing I could fuck her for hours.

"I love you," she said, tears gathering in her eyes.

"I love you too, honey."

I kissed her, then rolled to my side so I wouldn't crush her. I pulled her with me so our bodies could stay connected just a little while longer. Venom and Ridley wouldn't keep the kids all day, but maybe they'd hang onto them long enough that I could just enjoy holding Jacey in my arms. She cuddled against me, her leg thrown across my hip.

"It's never been like that before," she said.

"Same for me."

She looked at me and I could see the disbelief in her eyes.

"I'm not saying I've never enjoyed being with a woman, but it's never been that intense or fulfilling. You're not like the others, Jacey. They were one-night stands and short flings, but nothing more. You're the woman I want to hold onto, the one I don't want to let go."

"Ty, I'm not going anywhere."

"You might change your mind. When you see the other side of me…" I pressed my lips together. "I'm not a saint, Jacey, not the gentleman you think I am."

"Stop trying to make yourself out to be some horrible guy. I won't ever believe you. Have you killed someone innocent? Raped or beaten a woman?" she asked.

I hesitated a second, not sure where she was going with this. "No. But I have killed someone before."

"Were they a bad person? Had they hurt others?" she asked.

"Yes." My brow furrowed. "There was a drug deal that went bad. I'd found out the guy was using some bad shit to cut the cocaine he was selling. It was fucking up adults and killing kids. So I took him out in the middle of a drop."

"What happened?" she asked.

"His crew put a price on my head. My club handled it, but I decided it was time for a life change. Back then, no one was married and the only kid was Ridley, but she didn't live here. Things were different."

"Would you want to stay here now?"

"No, I don't think so. They're still my family, and this house is really damn nice and safe, but I'm used to wide open spaces now. I like running the ranch and letting people board their horses at the stable, but at the same time, I don't know that it would ever be safe for you and the kids to go back there, and I don't want to live without you. Unless you decide we can't have a future together. I would never force you to remain with me."

"There's nowhere I'd rather be," she said, then pressed her lips to mine. "Wherever you decide to live, the kids and I will be with you, for however long you want us."

My cock started to get hard again and I rolled her under me. I didn't take her as slowly this time, but I still made sure she gasped my name and trembled beneath me. And as I filled her with my cum again, I claimed her lips in a kiss that I hoped left little doubt about where she stood in my life. Without Jacey, my life meant nothing.

Chapter Five

Jacey

Over a week had passed since we'd arrived at the compound, nine wonderful days filled with family time spent with the kids, and deliciously naughty nights with Ty. I'd been sore and achy, in the best of ways, since our first day here. My kids were happy and carefree, playing with the other children, and I'd finally felt like I could breathe. But this morning was different. There was a heaviness in the air that told me today would not be like the others. No one had said a word to me, but I could tell something was going to happen, possibly already had.

Ty had gotten a text when we'd first woken that had made him grind his teeth and his eyes flash with annoyance, but he'd given me a kiss and a smile, then acted as if nothing was amiss. I wasn't fooled, though. Whatever that message had said, I figured it was something bad. We'd found the kids in the living room, watching cartoons, and Ty had started breakfast. He'd seemed distracted, though, and I was getting more and more curious about what was going on.

Venom and Ridley had picked up the kids after breakfast, and Venom had shared a look with Ty, one that I hadn't missed. After the breakfast dishes were washed and put away, I cornered him, refusing to wait another moment to find out what was going on. If it had to do with Beck, if I was in danger or my kids were, then I needed to know.

"Are you going to keep me in the dark all day?" I asked.

He smiled faintly. "Too smart for your own good, aren't you?"

"Apparently not or we wouldn't be in this mess."

Ty placed his hand at my waist and pulled me against his taller frame. I turned into a puddle of goo whenever he held me close like this, and he damn well knew it. When his lips brushed mine, I knew for sure he was trying to distract me, and it was working a little too well. My body started to warm and I tingled in all the right places.

"Ty, please. If there's trouble, I want to know."

He sighed and pressed a kiss to the top of my head. "Beck's here. In town, not here at the compound. He's claiming that I kidnapped you and the kids, trying to rile up the local police."

"So I can call and tell them I'm here of my own free will," I said. "Does he know that we aren't married anymore? You said Wire hacked into the county and state websites to ensure I was divorced from Beck. He did it, right?"

"Yes, honey. Wire made sure you aren't legally married to Beck anymore. And he went a step farther, but I didn't want to tell you about it."

My body tensed and I braced myself for whatever was about to happen. "What did he do, Ty?"

"Wire made sure Beck's department, as well as the Tennessee Highway Patrol were both notified of Beck raping you, filming it, then selling it. He made sure they had all the information they needed to arrest Beck and throw away the key, which is probably why he's here trying to cause trouble. If his department is as crooked as him, someone would have notified him."

"But we were married, so it wasn't really --"

Ty placed his finger over my lips to silence me. "Yes, baby, that's what it was. You told him no and he didn't stop. It doesn't matter if you're married or not. If you tell a man to stop, then he'd better damn stop."

I whimpered a little as I thought of all those officials seeing me like that, of people knowing who was in those videos and it no longer being some random woman in their eyes. Bile rose in my throat, and I ran for the bathroom and promptly threw up. I heaved until nothing was left in my stomach, then I just cried on the bathroom floor. Ty sank down next to me, rubbing my back, and gave me a moment to collect myself.

"Do you want to know why Wire did that?" Ty asked softly.

I nodded and blew my nose, then dried my tears.

"Because he knew if the police weren't looking for Beck, that when he showed up here, I'd kill him. He didn't want you to see me differently than you do right now."

"Then I'm glad he told someone," I said, my throat feeling raw. "I would have never looked at you differently, but I don't want you to go to jail for murder either. Beck isn't worth it."

"No, but you are. Giving you the peace of mind that you were safe, that he would never bother you again, is worth any price to me."

"What do we do now? If the state police were looking for him, why isn't he locked up already?" I asked.

"Because he's a slick motherfucker and is already working his charm on the locals. Officer Daniels isn't buying it because he already knew about Beck and what to expect, but the others are falling under Beck's spell and believing the shit he's spewing. The problem is that I can't act and have Beck vanish while everyone has a close eye on him, and the fucker knows it."

"Ty, I can't face him. I can't look at him, or take a chance that they'll make me go back with him. I'd never survive it again, not after the last week and a half with you."

He pulled me into his lap and just held me. I could tell he was deep in thought from the shift in his breathing, but I was scared what he might be planning. It wasn't that I cared what happened to Beck, but I did very much care what happened to Ty. He'd very quickly become one of the most important people in my world.

"Ty, you said you trusted Officer Daniels. What if we asked him to come here? I could give him a statement, even let him record it, to show that I'm here because I want to be and not because you kidnapped me. And maybe…" I bit my lip. "Maybe I could talk about the abuse, everything Beck put me through, and explain that it's not safe for me to leave the compound until he's behind bars."

His arms tightened around me. "I'd have to ask Torch for permission for Officer Daniels to be inside the gates, but he might be all right with it. Are you sure you want to do that? You didn't handle it well when I told you what Wire had done. Will you be able to talk about it?"

"I kind of have to, don't I?" I asked softly. "If not for me, then for the kids. I can't let Beck fool everyone into thinking he's this amazing guy, not when there's a monster hidden behind all that charm."

"Officer Daniels might want to speak with the kids too. Are they ready for something like that?" Ty asked.

"Danica might be, but I don't know about Jackson. He's still so small, would anyone really listen to him anyway?"

"You'd be surprised," Ty said. "Men like Beck are put away all the time when a kid has been abused, especially if that child comes forward about what happened to them."

"I've shielded the kids as best I can," I said. "But it's obvious they heard far more than they should have. What if I lose them? What if someone decides I should have left sooner, that I endangered them by staying?"

"Babe, you were scared. I'm sure Beck threatened you if you ever tried to leave. If I hadn't shown up with my brothers at my back, you never would have walked out of there. I think any judge would understand, especially after you tell them what he's done to you." He pressed a kiss to my temple. "You may need to show him some of your scars, let him take pictures. They're obviously too old for me to have done them since you've been here."

"I'll do whatever I have to if it puts him in jail."

"Your stomach okay now? Do you want to go lie down while I talk to Torch?" he asked.

"I don't want you to leave me. Can I stay with you while you talk to him?" I asked.

"Of course you can. Do you want a shower first?" Ty smoothed my hair back and toyed with the ends. "Your stomach feeling okay now?"

I realized I hadn't answered him before.

"Kind of." I took a deep breath and let it out. "I was a little queasy before you gave me that news, but I think I'm all right. Probably just nerves over the Beck situation."

"Go find an outfit that will make you feel confident yet comfortable when you talk to the police, and I'll start the shower." He kissed the side of my neck. "And if you want me to join you, then I will be happy to do so. Or if you need some space, I'm all right with that too."

"Stay with me," I said.

He nodded and patted my hip. I stood up and went to the room we'd been sharing and rummaged through the bag I hadn't completely unpacked. The pills I'd been taking to battle depression had been placed on the dresser, but most of my other things were still in the bag. When I saw the small box of tampons crushed in the bottom, I froze. I tried to do a quick mental calculation, and in a panic, I realized that I should have started my period three days ago. I'd never skipped, not even when I was stressed to the max. The only time I'd ever *not* had a period was when… *oh, God.*

I felt like I was hyperventilating when Ty walked in. He took one look at me and rushed to my side.

"Jacey, what's wrong? Did something happen?"

"I… I…" My throat constricted. How did I tell him that I was late? I frantically tried to figure out how it had happened, and then my stomach bottomed out. I hadn't packed my pills. I'd told him I was on birth control, and I had been back home, but they'd never made it into my bag. I'd left them in the hidden compartment in my purse, which was still back in Mayfair.

"Honey, talk to me. You're scaring the shit out of me."

"I think…"

"You think what?" he asked.

"I may be pregnant," I said in a near whisper.

His hands tightened on my arms. "You said you were on birth control."

"I was." My gaze locked with his. "But I left my purse in Mayfair and they were in my purse. I never even thought about it. It was the furthest thing from my mind until I saw my unused box of tampons in the bottom of the bag."

"You're positive you were taking them up until we came here?" he asked slowly.

I nodded, my heart pounding and the room spinning a little. Would he think I'd done it on purpose? Would Ty hate me? I didn't know what I'd do if he walked away, or made me leave. The thought of losing him after I finally had him nearly made me throw up again. I bit back a sob and looked everywhere but at Ty. I didn't think I could handle it if he hated me now. I wouldn't blame him. I hadn't lied to him exactly. I really had been on the pill. Shouldn't it take a lot longer to get pregnant after being on birth control for so long? What had gone wrong? Well, aside from not taking the pills for nine days, but surely that wasn't enough time for whatever chemicals prevented pregnancy to have left my body. Was it? I was wishing I'd paid closer attention when the doctor had spoken to me about them.

"Babe, look at me," he said, his tone demanding obedience.

I looked up and then couldn't hold back my tears. It wasn't hate or disgust in his eyes. His gaze was soft and I had no doubt that he loved me. He didn't blame me, and it was possible I wasn't pregnant, right?

"What do we do now, Ty?" I asked.

"I'm going to start that shower and you're going to calm down. I'll call one of the old ladies and see if they'll go pick up some pregnancy tests for you. Three should give us a good idea if you're really pregnant. No way all three would be wrong. I don't think." His brow furrowed. "As soon as I have that sorted, I'll come join you if that's what you want."

"I do."

He pressed a kiss to my forehead, then released me and went into the bathroom. I heard the shower start and I finished gathering my clothes. My hands shook a little. When I got into the bathroom, I brushed my teeth and I stripped off my clothes, then got under the spray. Ty gave me one last tender look before closing the shower door and pulling his phone from his pocket. He stepped into the bedroom, but I heard him talking to someone about the pregnancy tests.

I heard him leave the bedroom a few minutes later and I wondered if he was going to come join me like he'd said. I hated feeling so insecure, and knew that Beck had done this to me. I remembered a time I was more confident and outgoing. Those had been my pre-Beck days. Now I was just one big mess, and I knew a pregnancy would just make it worse. My hormones were always way out of control when I was pregnant. Danica and Jackson were the two babies I carried full-term, but I'd lost another when Beck had attacked me. I hadn't known that time I was pregnant until I'd started bleeding and wouldn't stop. The doctor at the hospital said I'd only been two weeks pregnant. The mood swings I'd had during that time should have been a hint.

When Ty came back, he had a few boxes in his hands.

"They already went and got some?" I asked, thinking that was entirely too fast.

"Uh, no. It seems Mara, Darian, and Laken are all trying to get pregnant, so they stockpiled pregnancy tests. They each gave me one from their stashes so you have three different types to take."

Ty set the boxes on the counter and started removing his clothes. When he opened the shower door and stepped inside, I couldn't help but admire the hard lines of his body. Was it any wonder I was knocked-up? I could hardly keep my hands off the man, and we'd had sex more than once a day ever since that first time. If the other guys here had sperm half as potent as Ty seemed to have, then I was sure that the ladies would be pregnant in no time.

He pulled me in closer and placed his hand over my belly, a look of wonder on his face. I let out a little gasp as he sank to his knees and pressed a kiss where his hand had just been, then murmured something to our baby. Assuming there was one.

"Ty, I may not be pregnant. It could be a coincidence."

He smiled up at me. "Well, just in case, I figured the kid should know that they will be loved a great deal."

"You're not mad?" I asked.

Ty stood and pulled me into his arms. "No, baby. I'm not mad, not even a little. The timing could be better, but then I've heard these things usually don't happen at the optimum time. I never thought I'd have kids, not when the only woman I'd ever wanted to keep was so unattainable."

"What happens now?" I asked. "You said you didn't want to stay here, but if we can't go back to Mayfair, then where do we go?"

He glanced at my belly again. "You know, this kid is going to need a lot of aunts and uncles, other kids to play with who will grow up alongside them. I'm not ready to be a full-fledged Dixie Reaper again. I wasn't kidding when I said I needed wide-open spaces. But maybe we could find some land nearby and start a new ranch, build it up together and make our home here. Close enough they could call on me if need be, and vice versa."

"Will they let you do that? Live with one foot in the door? I kind of thought it was an all-in type situation."

"Things have changed since I left, and I think Torch might be agreeable to my proposition. We can still come for any family events, the kids can see their new friends, and if my brothers need an extra pair of hands, then I'll be nearby. But no, I don't want to live this life full-time again. No drug or gun runs, or whatever else they're into these days. I won't let any of that shit touch you and our kids. They seem to have it handled and are keeping it away from their families, but I'm not willing to take that chance. Not after what happened before."

I nodded and cuddled closer to him. I let my hands trail over the hard contours of his body, and I felt his cock harden and press against me. I smiled as I slowly sank to my knees. Ty gripped my hair and tipped my face back.

"What are you doing?" he asked.

"Showing you a little love?"

"Jacey, you don't have to do that."

I could see the concern in his eyes, and I knew he was wondering if this would be a trigger for me. Beck had sorely abused me over the years, but I knew the man in front of me would never cause me harm. He was good, despite anything he may have done in the past. And I trusted him, more than I'd ever trusted anyone.

I wrapped my fingers around his shaft and leaned forward, taking a slow, long lick. Ty groaned and his grip on my hair tightened for a moment, but he didn't force me to do anything. I licked and nibbled, loving the sounds that he made as I teased him. When I finally took him into my mouth, his flavor burst on my tongue and I wanted more. I sucked him, hollowing my cheeks as I tried to give him as much pleasure as he gave me.

"God, Jacey. You're killing me," he said, his voice deeper than before.

I could feel the tension in his body, knew he was holding back, and I wanted to push him over the edge. I wanted Ty completely unhinged and taking what he wanted from me, but even if I asked, I knew he would hesitate, too afraid that he would hurt or scare me.

I gripped his thigh with my other hand and let my nails bite into him. He groaned and starting thrusting into my mouth. He was gentle, until I flicked the underside of his cock with my tongue. It seemed to unleash something inside him, and his eyes burned as he looked down at me, our gazes locked. I hoped he could see that I was extremely turned on and not the least bit afraid. He used the grip on my hair to guide me as he fucked my mouth, his strokes getting harder, deeper.

"Do you like that, baby?" he asked. "You like me fucking your mouth?"

I moaned as my clit tingled from his dirty words.

"Touch yourself, Jacey. I want you to come when I do," he said.

I released his shaft and reached between my legs. I rubbed the bundle of nerves, spreading my legs farther. Ty got a little rougher, but it was just the right amount. As he grunted and growled, telling me how good I was at sucking his cock, I came. Stars burst across my vision. His body tensed, and then the hot splash of his cum started filling my mouth. I swallowed every drop, and his body trembled as his cock twitched in the aftermath.

"Clean me up," he said, not releasing me.

I pulled him from my mouth and licked his shaft, then flicked my tongue across the head, making him hiss. When his grip on my hair slackened, I stood up, my legs barely able to hold me I'd come so hard. Ty gathered me in his arms, kissing me fiercely. I melted against him as he cuddled me, smoothing his hand down my hair. We stood like that, just letting the hot water beat down on us until it started to get chilly, then we quickly washed and got out. I knew taking the tests first thing in the morning would be more accurate, but I was dying to find out now whether or not I was pregnant. Ty stepped out of the room while I peed on the three test sticks, then I set them on the counter and we waited.

When all three showed positive results, Ty let out a loud *whoop* and spun me around, which nearly made me throw up again. I didn't know how the kids would react, but as long as we were all together, then we could work through any little hiccups along the way. But first, we had to handle Beck and get him out of our lives for good. I would do whatever it took to protect my family and make sure Ty didn't feel the need to get his hands bloody on my behalf. I now had three kids and the kindest man I'd ever met who needed me, and I wasn't going to let them down.

Ty made the arrangements for Officer Daniels to come to the house, and Torch and someone named Tank both promised to be present. I hadn't met Tank yet, but Ty assured me the man would help keep me safe. I'd take his word for it. If Ty trusted the men behind these gates, then so would I. I'd learned with

Beck that you couldn't judge a person by their looks, and not even always by their actions.

I never would have thought a group of bikers would be trustworthy. Of course, I'd never met any before now. The men I'd come to know over the last nine days were family-oriented, protective, and would gladly lay down their lives for women and children. The exact opposite of the man I'd married.

Ty was amazing and I wanted to be worthy of him. He needed a strong woman, one who would fight back. I hadn't been that woman in a really long time, but it was time to find my backbone and stand up to Beck. Maybe it made me a chickenshit to do it from behind a locked gate with more than a dozen armed men around me, but it was better late than never. I'd let Beck win for too long, and I needed to do something before he hurt someone else, or came after me and the kids again.

Chapter Six

Ty

I was so damn proud of Jacey. She was scared to death, but she'd calmly talked to Officer Daniels about her life with Beck, how he'd lured her in and then changed after they were married. Hearing firsthand about everything that man had done to her nearly made me lose my shit, but I held it together for her and the kids. Danica had agreed to speak to Officer Daniels, with two Dixie Reaper ladies present. We'd given him a signed statement about everything, including permission for him to film Danica's view on Beck Lane. By the time he left, he said there was no way a judge would let Beck remain free. I hoped like hell he was right.

The kids were both home after playing all day with the kids at the compound, the ones old enough to join them anyway. There were quite a few babies and kids that were still toddlers. It still boggled my mind just how much this place had changed over the years. The guys were still pretty hardcore, but I could see a softer side of them when the ladies and kids were present. I'd never thought to see the day that Torch or Venom turned into teddy bears, much less a guy like Tank, but they were all mush around their families. And fuck me if I wasn't the exact same way.

We'd told Danica and Jackson about the baby, and both were excited once they learned it wasn't Beck's kid but mine.

"Now will you be my daddy?" Jackson asked. "It's not fair you get to be the baby's daddy and not mine."

I glanced at Jacey and there was a soft smile on her face. I knew it wasn't quite that easy, though. Well, not entirely. I could ask Wire to work some magic, but I wanted to do this the right way if at all possible. Getting Jacey free of Beck was one thing, but claiming these kids as my own was another matter.

"Your dad has to agree to terminate his claim to the two of you, or a judge has to make him do it," I said. "But if I'm allowed to adopt the two of you, then yes, I would love to be your dad. Even if I can't be your dad on paper, the two of you are still mine in here," I said, placing my hand over my heart.

Jackson wrapped his arms around my leg and squeezed tight. A lump of emotion grew in my throat as I glanced at Jacey again, and I saw she felt the same. I couldn't believe I was a lucky enough bastard to call this little family my own. I'd never thought I'd have something like this, an amazing woman by my side, and awesome kids, yet here we were. I just needed to make it more official, not just with the kids, but with their mom too.

When I'd told Jacey I was going to run an errand, I hadn't told her exactly what I was doing. I disentangled myself from Jackson and pulled the small box from my jeans pocket. Approaching Jacey, I saw the curiosity in her gaze, and watched her eyes go wide and her lips part as I dropped to one knee in front of her. I snapped open the ring box and presented her with the modest diamond inside. It wasn't small enough to be ignored, but not big enough that people would gawk.

"Jacey. I love you, and I love these kids. I would be honored if the three of you would be my family, if you would be my wife. I want to spend the rest of my life with you and our children, grow old together, and make lots of happy memories over the years. Will you marry me?"

She sniffled and nodded as she fought back tears. "Yes!"

I slipped the ring onto her finger and kissed her softly, then got tackled by both kids. I laughed and rolled on the floor with them, tickling their ribs and making them squeal. All the merriment left my face when I saw the incoming text on my phone, though.

Church.

That one word put dread in my heart. Everything should have been settled. Beck should be behind bars right now, and I couldn't think of another reason for Torch to call Church. I shot a look at Jacey, who was still watching the kids, and I hoped I could slip away without worrying her. This was why I didn't want to come back to this life full-time. She'd been through so much already, I didn't want her to get scared every time I had to go out on club business, not knowing if something would go wrong and I wouldn't return. I wouldn't do that to her and our kids. I just couldn't.

"Torch needs to see me for a second, but I'll be back soon." I smiled at her, hoping she wouldn't see the concern in my eyes. "Why don't the three of you order pizza? The Prospect at the gate can pay for it and have it delivered to the house. Get whatever you want and any extras like breadsticks."

"Will you be back to join us?" she asked.

"Should be. Torch can get a little long-winded at times, but I'm sure it's nothing big. Probably just wants to know how much longer we're staying here."

"All right." She stood up and pressed her lips to mine. "We'll see you when you get back. Love you, Ty."

"Love you too, babe. More than the air I breathe."

I kissed her again, hugged the kids, then left to see what the Pres needed. In my gut, I knew something had gone wrong, but I hoped like hell I wasn't right. My bike was in the driveway and I rode it over to the clubhouse. When I walked into Church, I noticed there was an empty seat. Torch gave a nod for me to claim it. I placed my hand on the back and just took a moment. If I sat down, did it mean he would expect me to be in this chair forever? My allegiance was still to Torch and the Dixie Reapers, but I had my family to think about too.

"Sit down, son. It's a chair, not a bomb," Torch said.

I pulled out the chair and sat, then waited to see what the hell was going on.

"Officer Daniels showed the videos he took of Jacey and Danica to the local judge as well as the Chief of Police. Unfortunately, while he was doing that, Beck was working on disappearing. He's off the grid. Can't track his cell, and no one around town has seen him since this morning," Torch said. "They've put out a B.O.L.O. on him at the police department, but I'm hoping we can find him first. As of right now, we're on lockdown. I'm going to ask that all the women and children be brought to the clubhouse where they'll have round the clock protection while we sort this shit out."

Venom eyed me from down the table. "Cowboy, I know how you feel about getting your hands dirty, especially right now. If we catch Beck Lane, you can take a step back if that's what you want."

My heart hammered in my chest, and I hated that I was fucking right. Beck was like a goddamn cockroach and just wouldn't go the fuck away, like those big ass ones you could spray with half a can of Raid and they kept coming for you. As for catching the fucker… I wanted a piece of him. Even if I didn't end his life, I wanted a chance at payback for all that he'd done to Jacey and those kids. Even if he hadn't laid a hand on them, he'd terrorized them just the same.

"I want some time with him," I said. "Not taking things all the way because I promised Jacey, but it doesn't mean I don't want to make him pay."

Venom gave a nod and I knew he'd make it happen, then make sure Beck Lane never drew another breath. If not him personally, then he'd have someone take care of it. I may have been gone a long-ass time, but these men still had my back. It was humbling, and I knew that staying nearby would be the right thing to do. I wasn't changing my mind about living at the compound, though.

"I'm leaving Tank, Grimm, Saint, and the Prospects here," Torch said. "As soon as I got word about Beck Lane being in the wind, I called in some help. Devil's Boneyard is sending a few men, and there were some Devil's Fury there visiting, so they're coming too."

"What about the Reckless Kings? Don't they have an Alabama chapter not too far from here? With this guy's law enforcement background and connections, the more hands on deck the better," Wraith said. "I know Beck Lane isn't their problem, not like the ongoing issue with The Inferno, but they may lend a hand."

What the fuck? It blew my mind that so many clubs would drop what they were doing to help us out, especially me since none of them knew me. And what the hell was that about The Inferno? I knew I'd missed out on a lot, but was there trouble I needed to know about? Someone who could come for Jacey and the kids?

Back when I'd been an active Dixie Reaper, it had just been us. There was no help to call on, not really. Every now and then other clubs would pitch in for a big deal going down if they got a cut, but this was different. It didn't seem like the men coming here expected any monetary gain from it. It was like they were family, even though they weren't Reapers. I knew that Laken was with a member from Hades Abyss, and Bull's woman was the daughter to the VP of Devil's Boneyard. Our club was growing not just here at the compound, but in ways that connected us with others. It was a lot to take in.

"Reckless Kings don't have anyone in the immediate area, but they have a few men between here and their Tennessee chapter. Their Pres assured me they would keep an eye out for anyone matching the description of Beck Lane, and they were going to put the word out that he's a wanted man by several clubs," Torch said. "They have some reach, so there won't be anywhere Beck can hide. Honestly, I don't expect him to go far. He'll want Jacey."

My hand fisted on the table. The fucker might *want* Jacey, but he wasn't going to get her. I was going to keep her safe, whatever it took. And I needed to let my brothers know they weren't just protecting Jacey and her two kids with Beck. They were also keeping my unborn son or daughter safe.

"There's something I need to tell you," I said. "Jacey's pregnant, and it's mine."

Torch smiled faintly, and Venom gave me a look that said he wasn't the least bit surprised. After a round of congratulations, Torch got everyone back under control. We each had our orders, and as much as I wanted to stay here with Jacey, I knew it was better if I was out looking for Beck. I was the only one who had seen him in person. Wire had made sure everyone had a picture and full description of the asshole.

My first job was to get Jacey and the kids back to the clubhouse. Every brother who had a family would be doing the same. There wasn't a place for them to sleep, which meant Torch planned to end this as soon as possible.

I didn't want to freak Jacey out, or the kids. I couldn't lie to them. The second they got here and saw us preparing to hunt her asshole ex-husband, she would know. Jacey was far from stupid, and same went for her kids. During the ride back to the house, I rehearsed in my mind what I'd say when I got there. There was no way to sugarcoat the situation. I'd just have to tell them straight out what was going on, and why they were going to the clubhouse.

My bike had barely turned off when Jacey threw open the door and rushed toward me. I caught her, holding her tight. Her lips crashed against mine, an almost desperate feel to our kiss. And that's when I knew. Jacey had already figured out that something was up, and that whatever it was would be dangerous. When she pulled back, I ran my fingers across her cheek.

"We need to get the kids. Pack whatever will keep them occupied for a little while."

"Where are we going?" she asked.

"I'm taking you and the kids to the clubhouse."

"Us. But you're not staying, are you?" she asked.

"No, babe. I'm not staying there with you. Beck is still running free, and I can't let that happen. We're going after him, hunting him down like the animal he is, and then my club will make sure he never hurts another person ever again."

She gave me a hesitant nod, and I knew I needed to reassure her.

"Honey, look at me." Her gaze locked on mine. "The club will take Beck out. I won't take his life. I promised you I wouldn't have his blood on my hands, and I'm keeping my word. Mostly. I do want to get my hands on him, but I won't be the one to kill him. One day, if the kids ever ask what happened to him, I don't want you or me carrying the burden that I'm the one who ended him."

"Thank you, Ty. Not just for being an honorable man, but for everything you've done for us. From the beginning, you've tried to make our lives better. I only wish I'd left Beck sooner."

"You're here with me now and that's all that matters, Jacey. Come on. We need to get the kids packed up and get the three of you to the clubhouse. I'll call a Prospect to drive you down there, and I'll follow on my bike. I won't leave until I'm sure you're settled."

She kissed me once more, then we went into the house together, and tried to explain things to the kids in a way that wouldn't terrify them. By the time I left them at the clubhouse, I was more than ready to end things with Beck.

I was tired of that asshole making my woman and kids live in fear. Even if he went to jail, he'd eventually get out, and there was no way to reform a guy like Beck. The second he was free, he'd be after Jacey again. I'd just hoped that if he were locked up, it would buy us some time and give us a chance to plan.

I only hoped we found him before the police did.

Chapter Seven

Jacey

The kids either didn't feel the tension, or they were just resilient. Danica and Jackson played with their new friends. The man called Saint was inside with us, an adorable little girl toddling around after him. He seemed a lot younger than the other patched members. We hadn't had a chance to talk yet, but he looked like he was maybe mid-twenties.

"Better not let Cowboy see you eyeing Saint that way," Ridley said with a grin.

"I wasn't… I'm not…" I blew out a breath. "I was just thinking he looks a lot younger than the others who have club names."

"Saint's been with the club since he was seventeen," Isabella said. "He's twenty-six now, and yes he's the youngest patched member. Aside from the officers, there isn't another man here that my husband trusts as much as Saint."

"And that's his daughter?" I asked, nodding to the little girl.

"Yep, that's Delia," Darian said. "She came as quite the surprise, not just to us but for Saint too. He knocked up the sister of a Hades Abyss member and she never told him. When she died, the brother called and Saint hauled ass up there to meet his daughter. He's really good with her."

"It's sad she lost her mom so young," I said, thinking of my own kids and what would happen to them if I died.

"So, things are good with you and Cowboy?" Darian asked. "He seems completely in love with you."

I smiled a little. I was stupid in love with him too, and I was worried sick something bad would happen today. Either that Beck would hurt Ty, or that my cowboy would do something stupid and end up in jail. He'd promised that wouldn't happen, but I knew Beck. If he felt cornered, he's say some really horrible things, the type of stuff that would set off Ty. My ex-husband was a master of manipulation, as I knew all too well.

"They're going to be fine," Ridley said. "Venom and Torch are with him, and so are the others. Cowboy will come home to you in one piece."

"I just know Beck. He's not going down without a fight. He might not start a physical fight when the odds are stacked that high against him, but he'll know just which barbs to sling to get a rise out of Ty. He'll try to make Ty do something reckless."

"Cowboy has a lot of backup, not just from this club but from two others. He's going to be fine," Mara said. I hadn't had a chance to get to know her before today, but she seemed sweet if a bit quiet. "Rocky will make sure he comes back to you."

I hadn't had friends in such a long time, it was a little overwhelming to have the support of the Dixie Reaper ladies. Well, Ty had been my friend, but Beck had made sure I didn't have anyone else. Anytime someone had tried to get close, he'd found a way to sabotage it. I didn't understand why he hadn't kept me away from Ty, except that he didn't see him as a threat. Ty had been professional and kept his distance when Beck was around, and I'd heard my ex-husband's snide comments about how pathetic and weak Ty was, even though I knew different.

I twisted the engagement ring on my finger. Saying yes to Ty hadn't been a hard decision. I knew that he was nothing like Beck. I might have been fooled once, but Ty was so protective, so tender. There was no way I was making a mistake this time. And he adored my kids, even called them his. I didn't think there were too many guys like him in the world, although the other Dixie Reapers seemed to be cut from that same cloth.

My stomach rumbled and I glanced toward the kitchen. I'd been told to help myself to anything in there, but I still felt like a guest here. So far, I'd only been sick that one time, even though nausea was almost constantly present right now. I didn't know if it was the pregnancy or the stress. Standing up, I went into the kitchen, intent on finding a cold bottle of water and maybe some crackers.

The kitchen was dark and quiet. I flipped on the light and frowned when only one of the four fluorescent lights came on. It seemed strange, but maybe with everything happening they hadn't had a chance to change the others. I made my way to the fridge and found a bottle of water. I'd just taken a sip when I heard a shuffling noise in the dark corner. My heart kicked up a notch as I stared into the inky blackness. The hair on my nape stood up and goose bumps ran down my arms. I waited, nearly holding my breath, but I didn't hear anything else and nothing bad happened. Turning to go back to the others, I gave a yelp when someone gripped my hair and jerked me off my feet.

"Thought you could leave me, you little bitch?" Beck whispered against my ear. "Do you know what happens to whores who don't behave?"

I whimpered and closed my eyes, hoping my kids would stay in the other room. If Beck got his hands on Danica or Jackson, I'd never forgive myself. I thought of the life growing inside me, and I hoped like hell that I could make it out of this in one piece. Ty would be devastated if I lost the baby, but I knew he'd care more about me surviving. I didn't understand how Beck had gotten into the compound, much less into the clubhouse. I'd seen the men they assigned to keep watch outside and the ones in here. I wasn't sure if Beck was just foolish or since he had nothing left to lose if he was being reckless.

"You're going to keep quiet and come with me," Beck said. "If I even think you're trying to alert anyone, I'll snap your fucking neck and light this damn place on fire."

I gave a short nod that I understood and let him pull me through the back of the kitchen, down a short hall, and out into the night. I dragged in the cool night air and wondered how long it would take someone to notice I was missing. If Beck were armed, he hadn't used his weapon yet. Or maybe he just thought I was such an easy target he didn't need one, and it seemed he was right.

"I won't fight you, Beck," I said softly. "Just please, leave Danica and Jackson alone. They're happy here."

"I have to admit, I didn't think that worthless cowboy had it in him. I saw the way he eye-fucked you when he thought I wasn't watching, but he seemed like the spineless type. Never counted on him being a biker." Beck pressed his nose into my hair. "Does he fuck you real good, Jacey? Make you scream?"

I trembled and fought not to throw up. I didn't know what Beck had planned for me, but it couldn't be good. Whatever it was, I'd survived this long married to the man. I could make it through one more night. Eventually, someone would come for me. I only hoped they didn't end up dead in some heroic attempt to rescue me.

"How did you get into the compound, or the clubhouse?" I asked, hoping he would want to brag and boast about how much smarter he was than the others.

"Snipped part of the fencing a few miles down the property line. No one was nearby, and it doesn't look like they have enough manpower to watch that fence twenty-four-seven. As for the clubhouse, it was merely a matter of watching for a pattern. Every twenty minutes, the men outside left that back door unguarded. Or rather, the one stationed there walked off. I don't think that was in the plans, but he's sloppy."

I didn't think Torch would be happy to hear that, and I hoped I lived long enough to tell him. If Beck could get in and get to me, then someone else could get to the other women and kids. This place might not be my home, but it was the first time I'd felt like I belonged somewhere. Those women were my friends now.

"You shouldn't have run, Jacey. I told you that I'd never let you leave."

"I don't love you, Beck. I couldn't help falling in love with Ty."

He cuffed me on the side of the head with his fist and black dots swam across my vision. I fought to remain upright as he dragged me farther into the darkness of the compound. We didn't seem to be heading toward the fence but away from it, and that gave me a little bit of hope. If we stayed inside the gates, then maybe I would be found before it was too late. I only hoped that whoever came for me wouldn't end up dead.

"Couldn't keep your mouth shut about our little games, could you?" he asked, his voice low and silky, like a lover and not the demonic force that he truly was. "You know you liked it, getting my dick and being filmed."

Bile rose in my throat, but I refused to respond or to throw up.

"My little cash cow." I felt him smile as he pressed his face against my neck. "Don't worry. I found a replacement for you the same day you left. She didn't handle it as well as you did, though, so she ended up in a dumpster the next night. There are lots of little Jaceys in the world, my wife. And I will find them all until I have the perfect woman under my control again."

"You're a monster, Beck. No one will ever be under your control again because you're going to prison. Do you know what happens to cops in prison, Beck?" I taunted. "You like raping women? I hope you like getting the favor returned tenfold."

He threw me to the ground and pulled his foot back to kick me, but I heard three rapid gunshots and watched as Beck staggered backward, red blooming across the shoulder and side of his shirt. He snarled, spat at me, then took off into the night.

Grimm knelt at my side, a gun clutched in his hand as he checked me over with his free one. "Please tell me I got here in time."

"He hit me, but that's about it."

"I'm sorry I wasn't here faster. When you didn't return from the kitchen, Ridley alerted me that something was wrong. Didn't take me long to figure out he'd forced you out the back way."

"But how did you find us?" I asked.

"Your husband is so desperate he didn't worry about leaving tracks. Just in case he made it past us, I made sure I hosed down the ground around the clubhouse before you arrived earlier. Should have told someone else about my plan and maybe you'd have been found faster. It was still just wet enough that he left footprints. No one else had come this direction so I knew it had to be him," Grimm said.

He helped me stand just as two more men came running toward us. Grimm gave a nod in the direction Beck had run and they took off after him. He pulled a cell phone from his pocket and sent off a message. With his arm around my waist to keep me steady, we made our way back to the clubhouse. Saint stood on the front porch with his arms folded and a fierce expression on his face.

He glared at me as we made our way to the front door, and I slowed my steps. Why was he angry with me? I hadn't done anything wrong! It wasn't my fault that Beck had found his way inside, or that he'd taken me. I'd kept him from hurting everyone else by going with him quietly, and that included Saint and his little girl. Didn't that count for anything?

"Next time you want something, tell someone," Saint said.

Grimm tightened his hold on me. "Don't be an asshole, Saint. Just because you're worried Cowboy might kick your ass for losing his woman isn't a reason to take it out on her. You want to go after someone? Calder was supposed to watch the back door. Where the fuck was he for so damn long that Beck was able to get into the clubhouse and back out? Maybe that's what you should be asking. Chew Calder's ass out and not her."

He gave a nod and stepped aside so we could enter the building.

"Beck threatened to burn down the clubhouse with everyone inside," I said. "I had no choice but to go with him. I couldn't risk all the kids being hurt."

"Don't be a martyr, Jacey," Grimm said. "Next time, fucking scream or something. That asshole wouldn't have done much when we all converged on him."

I hadn't thought about it like that, but then I'd never had anyone try to help me before. I was used to handling Beck on my own, of being the one responsible for protecting my kids from him. It had only come naturally to me to shield everyone else by sacrificing myself, but I could see that Grimm was right.

He led me to a chair at a table in the corner and made me sit, then he claimed the spot across from me where he could keep an eye on the door. I felt like a kid being scolded, but I knew he was right. I shouldn't have defaulted to the old Jacey and gone with Beck. I should have fought, or done something. Grimm wasn't trying to be mean or blame me for what happened, he was just trying to keep me safe, and that meant I needed to fight back.

"He said he killed a woman," I said. "He used her to replace me for his videos and then put her in a dumpster when he was finished."

Grimm's lips thinned and his eyes darkened. "There's a special place in hell for men like him. I'll make sure Officer Daniels knows. He may contact Beck's old department, or he might go speak to the Tennessee State Troopers. Not sure alerting the Mayfair police will do any good, but it's better than letting that woman rot without anyone knowing what happened to her."

The front door opened and two men came in, neither that I recognized. Grimm gave them a nod, and I waited to see if Ty would come too. I stared at the door, but when it didn't open again, I sighed and looked away. If Ty wasn't here with me, then that meant he was going after Beck. Now that my ex had taken me, I knew Ty wouldn't be thinking rationally. Not only had I been in danger, but so had his child.

I looked at the man sitting across from me and wondered what his story was. I didn't really know anything about any of the Dixie Reapers. Ty had this entire other life I'd never known about, and I was curious about the men he considered his family. I could see the appeal of living here at the compound, but I agreed with Ty that I wanted wide-open spaces. Well, if Beck were ever dealt with. I wouldn't feel safe out in the world if he were still a free man, but I had a feeling the minutes were ticking by before he breathed his last or was locked up for a really long time.

"You're staring," Grimm said.

"What's your story? Why are you here and why the name Grimm?" I asked.

He smiled faintly. "My parents immigrated here from Russia, but not before my father got mixed up with some bad people. I joined the military first chance I had as a way to escape, and when I got out I roamed a bit. Found my home here a year later as a Prospect."

"That doesn't answer the question about your name. The Brothers Grimm weren't Russian. They were German."

"I collect old books. My most prized possession is an 1812 copy of Grimm's Fairy Tales. My mother would read those stories to me when I was younger, not the watered-down version we tell kids today but the original tales. I got drunk one night and told Venom all about it. When it came time to patch in, he named me Grimm."

"You don't strike me as the book collector type."

"Growing up, I didn't have many nice things, but my mother made sure we always had books to read. My parents are gone, and I guess it's a way of keeping my mom with me at all times. She'd have loved some of the books I've been able to buy over the years."

I leaned forward and lowered my voice so I wouldn't offend anyone with my words. "You're not what I expected of a biker. None of you are. I always thought you were scary and dangerous."

"We can be, if provoked," he said, then smiled a little. "But a sweet woman like you has nothing to worry about. Not unless you tangle with the wrong club. There are those out there who are rotten to the core and would make your husband look like an angel."

That made me shiver and I hoped I never met those men.

"Do you think they'll be okay? Everyone who's after Beck?"

Grimm nodded. "They know what they're doing. A lot of the guys here have a military background, or grew up in rough neighborhoods. This isn't the first time they've gone up against someone like Beck."

It made me wonder about Ty. We never really discussed his past, and now I wanted to know why. Was he hiding something from me, just like he'd hidden his past with the Dixie Reapers? And if he was, then why?

The longer I had to wait, the more I started to question everything I knew about Ty. I didn't doubt that he was a good man, that he loved me and would do anything to protect me, but now I really wanted to know about his past. When he came back to me, and he *would* come back, we needed to have a talk. I wasn't going to walk into another marriage completely blind. I didn't think for a second that Tyler Adler would ever hurt me, but my past made me overly cautious.

Come back to me, Ty.

Chapter Eight

Ty

It hadn't taken long for my brothers to track Beck and capture him. His hands were tied and attached to a hook hanging from the ceiling in the old barn at the back of the compound. A few upgrades had been installed since I'd been gone, like the cement floor with a drain and the sink on the wall. At least if I was going to get bloody, I could clean up before I saw Jacey.

Beck hadn't said a word since we tied him up, just gave us a bored look. Either he didn't think I was capable of hurting him, or he just didn't give a shit. Monster like him might even get off on pain, but I figured he was the type that preferred inflicting it. Otherwise, he wouldn't have chosen my sweet, docile Jacey as his target. He'd have picked a spitfire who would fight him at every turn.

Someone had cut Beck's clothes off him and he hung there naked, like a slab of beef waiting to be butchered. The analogy wasn't far off. Before his body was dumped, he wouldn't be recognizable anymore. One of my brothers had already burned off his fingerprints. There were still dental records, but we'd fix that problem soon enough. I remembered every mark on Jacey's body, and I planned to duplicate them on Beck, and add some more. Only seemed fair after everything she'd suffered at his hands.

"On the one hand, I should thank you," I said. "Because of you, Jacey was placed directly in my path. Now I'm engaged to the best woman I've ever met and get to be a dad to three amazing kids."

Beck spat on the ground. "I knew you were a stupid cowboy, but didn't know you couldn't add one plus one and get two."

I grinned. "I was counting the one I already planted in her belly. We're having a baby, Beck. Me and Jacey. And I'm going to raise Danica and Jackson like they're my own, make sure Jackson learns the right way to treat a lady."

"They're all whores," he said.

"Jacey is far from a whore. She was a virgin when she married you, but then you knew that. It's part of what drew you to her. Her innocence, her vulnerability and how easily she trusted those around her. You made sure to destroy that part of her and damn near killed her," I said.

"She loved what I did to her." He grinned. "She's nice and tight when she's screaming and begging. I love it when they thrash around, like squeezing their throats and watching the life start to drain from them."

Tank drove his fist into Beck's ribs and we all heard them crack. The asshole didn't even wince, just kept grinning maniacally. I knew he wasn't right in the head, and I'd known he wasn't redeemable. We were doing the world a favor by ridding it of the likes of Beck Lane.

"Don't worry, Beck. I'll make sure Jacey knows what it's like to live with a real man," I said, then eyed his cock, which was rather pathetic. "I guess if I had a dick the size of a toddler's I'd lash out at the world too."

My brothers laughed and Beck's face turned purple as his lips thinned. Ah, now there was the flash of anger in his eyes that I'd been waiting for. Yeah, I had his number now. I had to wonder if his thoughts about women stemmed from someone teasing him about his dick, or maybe he had a horrible mom. Jacey had never mentioned his parents, so I assumed they weren't in the picture. With a guy like Beck, it was possible he'd killed his mother and she'd been his first. First kill or first fuck was hard to say, but something had warped Beck.

I picked up one of those long lighters used for candles and got to work. I didn't know what he'd used to burn Jacey, but this would do. He eventually started screaming as his flesh sizzled. The smell was horrible, but I'd put up with anything to give Jacey a little justice. Before things got too far, I stripped down to my boxer briefs, not wanting his blood on my clothes. If I had to, I could pull off my underwear before I re-dressed. I wasn't going to taint Jacey with this asshole's blood. She'd been harmed by him long enough.

I took my time, spending the next hour cutting and burning Beck. I'd promised my woman I wouldn't be the one to end his life, and I was going to keep my word. I gave Tank a nod and he set to work, first removing Beck's teeth. His screams were music to my ears as I washed up and got dressed. Before I left the barn and headed back to my family, I stopped and looked at Tank and the others who had my back.

"Make him suffer, and let him bleed the fuck out," I said.

Tank gave a nod and I knew he'd see it handled.

I'd ridden my bike to the barn and I used it to get back to the clubhouse. It felt good, being here surrounded by my family, but there were only three faces I truly wanted to see right now… Jacey and my kids. They fit with these people, and I didn't want to take them away from the support system they'd found here. Now that Beck wouldn't be in the picture, I could start looking for some land. I'd have to sell the ranch in Tennessee and bring the horses here. No task was too much work if meant Jacey and the kids were safe and happy.

When I reached the clubhouse, Saint was on the porch and gave me a nod, but I could tell he had something on his mind. I leaned against the post and waited. Torch said he was a good kid, had been a huge help around here. I hadn't had a chance to get to know him yet, but I hoped that changed.

"I should have watched her closer," he said after a moment.

"It's not your fault, kid. Jacey did what she always does… she protected everyone else. But I would like a word with whoever was supposed to watch that back door."

"Torch is already inside. He ripped into the Prospect and told him he was down to one last chance before he was out on his ass. If you want to lay him out cold, though, I don't think anyone would stop you." Saint smiled. "They may actually clap. That little shit has a tendency to get on a few nerves."

"I'll keep that in mind."

I slapped Saint on the back and went inside. My gaze immediately sought Jacey. Grimm had her in the corner of the room, with his body between her and everyone else, but he'd sat at an angle where he could see a threat coming. I didn't think she'd realized what he was doing, and it warmed my heart that he was willing to protect her like that. I made my way over to them and he stood, then made himself scarce.

Jacey launched herself into my arms and I felt the tremor that ran through her body. She might have looked relatively calm, but she'd been scared as hell. Never again. I wouldn't let anyone hurt her or the kids.

Any fucker who thought about coming after my family would meet a gruesome ending.

"It's over," I told her. "Beck is going to disappear. Even if the body is found, Tank is making sure it won't be recognizable. No dental records or fingerprints."

I clamped my mouth shut realizing that was probably more than she needed or wanted to know. Just because that was my way of life, didn't mean my soft, sweet Jacey needed to know about it. Even after all Beck had done to her, she still had a good heart and thought of everyone else before herself.

"You didn't kill him?" she asked.

"No. I made him pay for what he did to you, but someone else will finish it."

She hugged me tight and rested her head on my chest. "I love you, Ty."

"Love you too, babe."

I heard a throat clear and looked over at Ridley. She gave a little wave and a smile.

"So, Venom and I want to keep Danica and Jackson at our house tonight. The two of you probably have some things to discuss, and could use some alone time for other things."

Jacey blushed from the roots of her hair down her neck.

"Thanks, Ridley. I appreciate it. If they want to come home, don't hesitate to bring them by."

She nodded and then left us alone.

"You ready to go to our temporary home?" I asked.

"What about the ranch, Ty? You've put so much time and money into that place."

"We'll talk about it, honey. But not here."

I led her out to my bike and drove us back to the house where we'd been staying. When we got inside, I went to the kitchen and made some coffee for me and a cup of hot peppermint tea for Jacey. Isabella had given it to her, and I'd noticed it helped calm her nerves when she was upset or anxious. After I fixed our drinks, I set the mugs on the table and sat next to Jacey.

There was a lot we'd need to settle, but I could tell something was bothering her. I sipped my coffee and waited to see if she'd start the conversation. It didn't take her long. She cast a few glances my way, drank half her tea, and then she cleared her throat and fiddled with the hem of her shirt.

"I realized today that we really don't know much about each other," she said. "Until you showed up at my door with your club, I had no idea you'd been part of the Dixie Reapers. Grimm told me a little about his family tonight, and I realized that I know nothing about your past. I trust you, Ty, and I love you, but I don't want to go into another marriage completely blind."

"That's fair enough." I ran a hand through my hair. "My mom got knocked up when she was sixteen by the quarterback at her high school. She'd given him her virginity, and he'd given her a baby. Me. That's all he ever gave her. My grandparents watched me during the day while she finished high school and got her diploma, but college wasn't an option. Back then, it wasn't like you could enroll in online classes and work a job while taking care of a kid. She got a minimum wage job and she did her best. Then my grandparents died when I was three. Overnight, she lost her parents, her home, everything. It took every penny of their life insurance money to pay off the money they owed the bank and bury them."

She reached out and placed her hand over mine. I laced our fingers together, but kept going. If she wanted to know where I came from, then I'd tell her.

"My dad came from a lot of money. Wealthiest family in town. Mom tried to go to him for help when things got bad, but he just laughed in her face. He'd gotten a full ride to a school on a football scholarship, and he wasn't going to let her and a kid he never wanted fuck up his life. His words. We struggled and there were times she went without food just so I could eat. I was sixteen when she finally worked herself to death. I didn't want to go into the system, so I set out on my own. It's when I started hitting the rodeos. I'd learned to ride and discovered I had a knack for being a cowboy."

"You were so young," she said. "You had to be scared."

I shook my head. "Not really. I'd learned early on how to take care of myself. I eventually found a home here with the Dixie Reapers. They became the family I never had. You know already why I left and how I ended up in Mayfair. That ranch was a good investment, but it was never home. I don't mind selling it and starting over here, where we both have a support system and the kids have made friends."

"You've done so much for me and the kids since we met you, Ty. I'll live wherever you want to live. If you want to go back to Mayfair, then we'll make it work."

"No, Jacey. That department is corrupt, and I don't trust Beck's fellow officers not to come after you in some way. Eventually, that town will get cleaned up, but for now we're better off here. I'm going to sell the stable in Mayfair. We'll start looking for a place this week, but right now, I just want to enjoy some time with you and the kids without feeling like we need to look over our shoulders."

She got up and moved over to my lap, curling her arm around my shoulders. "You know, we have the house to ourselves tonight."

"I noticed."

"Then I guess we can be as loud as we want."

I kissed her, tangling my hands in her hair. In a feverish frenzy, we pulled off our clothes, and I set Jacey on the kitchen table, her legs spread as she leaned back on her hands. My hungry gaze devoured every dip and curve of her body. I pushed her thighs wider apart before feasting on her pretty pink pussy. I teased her with my tongue and my fingers, made her squirm and beg for more.

"Ty! Please… feels so good!"

I circled her clit with my tongue before sucking the hard bud into my mouth. I drew on it long and hard until she was bucking and screaming out my name. The gush of her release coated my chin, but I wasn't done with her yet. I fucked her with my tongue, lapping up all her honey before making her come again. Her thighs shook as she panted. The hard points of her nipples pointed up at the ceiling as she leaned back and gave herself to me.

I stood so fast the chair toppled over. As much as I wanted to worship every inch of her body, I needed to feel her, to claim her. I gripped her hips and plunged into her wet heat, hard and fast. Jacey cried out and I watched as her body flushed with pleasure. I drove into her like a man possessed, our bodies slapping together. I could feel her getting hotter, wetter, and knew she wasn't far from coming again.

I stroked her clit with my fingers as I powered into her, so close to my own release but not willing to come before she did.

"That's it, babe. Come on my cock."

She whimpered, then gave a cry as her body shuddered with the force of her release. She came so hard she squirted. I grabbed her ass with both hands and held her in a tight grip as I fucked her harder than I ever had before. Jet after jet of hot cum shot from me, filling her sweet pussy. When I had nothing left to give, I braced my hands on the table and panted for breath.

Her gaze was glassy and unfocused as she stared up at me, and I smiled, loving that I'd pleased her that much. I might be fifteen years older than Jacey, but she was perfect for me in every way. I had to believe that fate had placed her in my path and brought us together. How else would a fucked-up guy like me ever get a shot with an angel like her?

I loved her more than the air I breathed, and would do anything for her. My heart was so full, knowing that she trusted me, loved me. I'd thought I would never find the right woman, never settle down. Then I'd met Jacey. Even knowing she was married, I hadn't been able to keep my distance.

Whatever the future brought, we would face it together, and I would make damn sure that she and our kids had the happiest of lives.

I leaned down and kissed her softly, my lips caressing hers. "Love you."

"Love you too, my sexy cowboy biker."

I carried Jacey to the bathroom and we cleaned up before cuddling in bed. I wasn't twenty anymore and couldn't keep going like the Energizer Bunny, even though Jacey certainly inspired my dick enough that I was able to fuck her several times a day or night. Just needed to catch my breath first.

As she lay in my arms, I stared into her eyes and thanked whatever force had given her to me. She might think that I'd saved her, but really she'd been the one to save me. Without her, my life was meaningless. Jacey was my everything. I only hoped she knew that. No matter how many times I told her, or said that I loved her, I wasn't sure she understood exactly how much she meant to me, but one day she would… even if it took me twenty years to show her.

Epilogue

Jacey
Six Months Later

I breathed in the warm spring air and admired the beauty of the land surrounding me. Ty had found us the perfect place. An old ranch with a two-story farmhouse that boasted five bedrooms and three bathrooms. The day he'd shown the property to me, he'd given me a wink and said we had one more bedroom to fill. I wasn't going to say no. I loved my kids, including the one currently growing inside me. Now that I didn't live with a man so evil that even the devil had probably refused him entrance to hell, I found that I loved my life, nearly as much as the man who was currently riding across the field toward me. Ty had even asked Wire to do his thing so that Ty was officially the father of Danica and Jackson. With Beck having mysteriously vanished, there was no other way for them to be adopted by the caring man who had saved us.

Things had been so chaotic after Beck died that I'd ended up missing pretty much every dose of my depression medication, even though I'd had them out in easy reach. Thankfully, they'd been safe to take while pregnant, but I'd discovered that with Beck out of my life, I no longer needed them. I'd seen a doctor, just to be sure, but I was doing so much better here. It was amazing what the love and support of a good man could do for a woman. Or maybe it just that the monster I'd had in my life was finally gone, and I knew he was never coming back.

I rubbed my belly as baby Langston gave me a kick to the ribs. He was always flopping around in there, and he always got more active when his daddy was nearby, almost like he could sense Ty's presence. Jackson and Danica were in school. Each had been placed with one of Venom's daughters, since Danica was the same age as Farrah and Jackson was the same age as Mariah. They were so much happier than they'd ever been before, and it was nice to always see them smiling. They were thriving here, and not just because of the amazing man they now called Dad, but because of the family they'd found with the Dixie Reapers.

They'd had nightmares and almost constant frightened looks after Beck had taken me that day at the clubhouse, something we'd discovered the following day, but Ty had assured them Beck was never returning. It had taken a few days but they'd eventually begun to relax and act like normal kids. He was so wonderful with them, and they'd even started calling him Daddy long before they were officially his, which I knew thrilled him.

Ty dismounted and came toward me, his cowboy hat casting a shadow across his face. He clomped up the porch steps in his dust-covered boots, then kissed me as if he hadn't seen me in a year. But then, it was always like this with Ty. When he kissed me, I felt it all the way to my toes. He'd leave me breathless and wanting more, but I'd learned that was his mission. To always have me wanting more.

"How's my lovely wife and baby?"

I placed his hand on my huge stomach. "If he keeps growing like this, I'll have to evict him before his time is up."

Ty winked, then knelt and murmured a few words to his son. When he stood, he wrapped his arms around me. We'd gotten married at the Dixie Reapers' clubhouse by one of his brothers, Preacher, barely even a week after Beck had disappeared. Officer Daniels hadn't asked any questions, but the other police officers had. Without a body or any evidence, they couldn't pin anything on the club, even if they were suspicious.

"I'm going to put Sunny up and give Reaper a workout. When I'm done, we're going to shower and get dressed up in something nice."

I glanced at my watch, a present from Ty a few months ago. It was a pretty gold with a little diamond on the face. "The kids are coming home in less than an hour. The bus will…"

I trailed off as I saw the grin on his face.

"Venom and Ridley are getting the kids when they pick up Farrah and Mariah, and they're going to keep them all night. I packed an overnight bag for them and dropped it by the compound earlier when I made a hay run."

"Sneaky," I said.

"I'm taking my woman out for a nice meal."

"Ty, it's only two in the afternoon. Even if you work Reaper for an hour, that's still going to be way too early for dinner."

He wagged his eyebrows up and down. "Who said it was going to be a quick shower? Have to get my fill of this luscious body before it gets too uncomfortable for you to have sex."

I sighed but smiled up at him. He was incorrigible, but I loved him.

"Go finish with the horses," I said, giving him a slight shove. "Then it's my turn to ride."

"Oh really?" he asked, sounding intrigued.

"You know what they say. 'Save a horse, ride a cowboy'." I winked and turned to go back inside, but I could hear his laughter as I shut the door.

God, but I loved that man. Every damn thing about him.

And thankfully, he loved me too, and our kids. My life had been a horrible mess, one nightmare day after another, and now I'd been given an incredible gift. Ty. I would cherish every moment we had together. There was nothing sexier than my cowboy. I loved seeing that Stetson pulled low over his eyes, those tight Wranglers that made his ass look amazing. I sighed and fanned myself. Of course, he was every bit as delicious when he was wearing his cut and riding that old motorcycle of his, off to create mayhem with his brothers. I'd somehow won the lottery when it came to husbands. I had my sweet cowboy with the slow Southern drawl, and a badass biker too. Best of both worlds, and *mine*. So very much mine.

I couldn't wait for him to come inside just so I could remind him exactly how perfect we were together, not that he seemed to ever forget. My life couldn't have turned out more wonderful than if I'd written the last chapter myself, and I eagerly awaited what was in store for us in the future, because I knew it would be every bit as amazing as the last six months.

Harley Wylde

When Harley is writing, her motto is the hotter the better. Off-the-charts sex, commanding men, and the women who can't deny them. If you want men who talk dirty, are sexy as hell, and take what they want, then you've come to the right place!

An international bestselling author, Harley is the "wilder" side of award-winning scifi/fantasy romance author Jessica Coulter Smith, and writes gay fantasy romance as Dulce Dennison.

Harley Wylde at Changeling: changelingpress.com/harley-wylde-a-196

Jessica Coulter Smith at Changeling: changelingpress.com/jessica-coulter-smith-a-144

Dulce Dennison at Changeling: changelingpress.com/dulce-dennison-a-205

Changeling Press E-Books

More Sci-Fi, Fantasy, Paranormal, and BDSM adventures available in e-book format for immediate download at ChangelingPress.com -- Werewolves, Vampires, Dragons, Shapeshifters and more -- Erotic Tales from the edge of your imagination.

What are E-Books?

E-books, or electronic books, are books designed to be read in digital format -- on your desktop or laptop computer, notebook, tablet, Smart Phone, or any electronic e-book reader.

Where can I get Changeling Press E-Books?

Changeling Press e-books are available at ChangelingPress.com, Amazon, Apple Books, Barnes & Noble, and Kobo/Walmart.

Changeling Press, LLC

ChangelingPress.com

Printed in Great Britain
by Amazon

34320868R00144